WHEN VALLEYS
BLOOM AGAIN

ENDORSEMENTS

When Valleys Bloom Again is a charming story of how love is tested by social prejudices, the separation of war, and intrigue. The historical details establish authenticity, and Ms. Davis's talent for writing expressive imagery touched that *ah!* place in my heart

—**Johnnie Alexander,** author of the best-selling novel, *Where Treasure Hides*

Journey to the days of World War II with its myriad challenges for survival. Pat Jeanne Davis weaves a story of young people challenged through difficult times and still finding happiness. An intriguing debut novel of separation and duplicity, love and loss.

—**Terri Wangard**, author of *Promise for Tomorrow* series

In this moving, heartwarming novel set against the backdrop of War World II England and America, author Pat Jeanne Davis paints a tale rich in emotion, drama, and intrigue. Caught between two worlds, protagonist Abby Stapleton must learn to navigate both, despite the many seemingly insurmountable obstacles that stand in her way and stretch her faith to its limits. Will Abby remain strong and steadfast not only amid the trials of an external war, but especially amid the trials of an internal war that threatens to affect her family, her future, and her faith? If you're looking for an inspiring, entertaining read, don't miss *When Valleys Bloom Again*.

—**Dr. MaryAnn Diorio**, Author of the *Italian Chronicles*

When Valleys Bloom Again is a wonderful debut novel by Pat Jeanne Davis. Immediately, you are transported back to the beginning days of fear and anxiety of what became WWII. Pat builds the historical world based on true events of the time. Your senses are engaged and her heroine, Abby Stapleton, is sympathetic as she struggles to make sense of her own life and place in her world. Pat's writing is smooth and lyrical. You'll enjoy this historical romance that overcomes. A clean, sweet Christian romance without being preachy.

—**Donna L.H. Smith**, managing editor of Almost an Author (a website for writers), ACFW Mid-Atlantic Zone Director, and award-winning author of *Meghan's Choice*

Pat Jeanne Davis promises to be a fabulous new author. I thoroughly enjoyed *When Valleys Bloom Again*. She captured my attention from the start, drawing me into a fantastic plotline with wonderful characters. Pat Jeanne Davis has created a wonderful selection of personalities. Some are very likable—others elicit feelings of mistrust as they perform underhanded dealings. A warm and welcoming atmosphere pervades the novel. As homes are opened to family, so the reader feels included as the warmth reaches out from the pages of the novel to encompass us.

—**Julia Wilson**, blogger, *Christian Bookaholic*

WHEN VALLEYS BLOOM AGAIN

To Jane
"Happy Reading"
Pat Davis
11/5/22

PAT JEANNE DAVIS

PUBLISHING THE POSITIVE
ELK LAKE PUBLISHING INC
Plymouth, Massachusetts

Cover and Interior Design: Derinda Babcock

Editor(s): Cristel Phelps, Deb Haggerty

Author Represented by Golden Wheat Literary

PUBLISHED BY: Elk Lake Publishing, Inc., 35 Dogwood Dr., Plymouth, MA 02360, 2019

Library Cataloging Data

Names: Davis, Pat Jeanne (Pat Jeanne Davis)

When Valleys Bloom Again / Pat Jeanne Davis

236p. 23cm × 15cm (9in × 6 in.)

Description: A Novel of World War II—Will Abby Stapleton learn to navigate the two worlds of London and Philadelphia to find happiness?

Identifiers: ISBN-13: 978-1-948888-91-2 (trade) | 978-1-948888-92-9 (POD) | 978-1-948888-93-6 (e-book.)

Key Words: World War II, London, Philadelphia, Romance, Historical, GIs, Spies

LCCN: 2018968303 Fiction

DEDICATION

To John, my loving husband and my hero. Without your encouragement and valuable assistance, this book would not exist. Thank you for the endless times you listened to the countless rewrites of this story. I'm so grateful for the many sacrifices you make to smooth my path. Two are better than one; because they have a good reward for their labour. Eccles. 4:9 (KJV)

ACKNOWLEDGMENTS

First and foremost, I acknowledge the grace of God in my life, meeting all my needs and providing direction as I write to honor Him.

A special thank-you to family and friends who prayed for wisdom and perseverance, championed my writing, and cheered me on as I wrote. You know who you are. To the loving memory of Valerie Armstrong, whose home I stayed in while doing research for this story when in England and whose encouragement helped me stay the course. To the memory of both Jerry and Ernie, veterans of World War II, who answered my questions, shared their stories and permitted me to record our conversations.

My gratitude to gifted writers, some I met in person and others online, who gave generously of their time, steered me in the right direction and showed me where I needed to improve. I'm a much better writer because of your frank critiques of my work.

My appreciation of other authors and their unforgettable stories whose books line my shelves. I desire to be a better storyteller as I consider their works.

Getting a book ready for publication requires the skills of many professionals. Thank you to the team at Elk Lake Publishing, Inc.—Deb Haggerty, Derinda Babcock, and Cristel Phelps—for all your hard work and for publishing my novel.

CHAPTER ONE

London, August 1939

Abby Stapleton slumped back in her seat, convinced any glimmer of hope she'd harbored would soon be extinguished. A crystal chandelier jingled in the draft of an open window. She loved this room with its embossed wallpaper and rich tapestries, vibrant with memories of family. How could she leave all this?

Her father folded the newspaper with its glaring headlines, plopped it on the table and parted his lips to speak.

Abby forestalled him. "I'm nineteen," she said, her nerves rubbed raw by the endless squabbles with her parents. *Speak low and slowly, Abby.* "I don't w-w-want to go." Her voice, thin and strained, echoed back from the high, frescoed ceiling.

"A father can't ignore his responsibilities," he said, clasping her hand. "You know Hitler's taken Austria and Czechoslovakia. Probably he'll take Poland next." He furrowed his brow. "And when that happens, war with Germany will be unavoidable." His hand shook, and he sounded as though he'd aged ten years in the space of a few minutes.

Sunlight shimmered through a bay window, washing the brocaded settee on which she and her mother sat with patches of red and gold. Her mother sidled closer and stroked Abby's arm, her face taut and pale. "Do as your father says, dear. There are sandbags and barrage balloons everywhere, and gas masks are being handed out."

Still determined to speak her mind before it was too late, Abby shut her eyes in a silent prayer. *Lord, help me to keep my temper.* She released her hand from her father's. "I sh-sh-should be able to decide for myself w-w-whether I want to leave." Now of all times when she needed eloquence, this accursed stammer bound her up tight.

Her father leaned forward and ran his fingers through his hair as though engaged in a last-minute tussle with this dilemma. As a senior diplomat in the British Foreign Office, he was privy to the realities behind the rumors of war. If anyone foresaw the hazards facing England, he did. With a pang of regret, Abby noted how weary he looked.

Then, with a quick nod of finality. "It's settled," he said, tapping his finger on the side table. "You will be safer in the States."

Abby bolted upright, blood draining from her face, leaving her cold. She silently acknowledged the signs of impending war that surrounded them. That's why her brother Peter had joined the Royal Air Force. And that's why she wanted to stay—to be useful here, with her family, not marooned thousands of miles away across the sea.

"I'll make arrangements for you to travel to Southampton Dock in a fortnight. You'll go to New York on the *Queen Mary*. Uncle Will and Auntie Val will collect you at the pier and take you to Jolie Fontaine." He rubbed the back of his neck, frowning. "Your mother and I have talked this out and think this is the best solution." His anxiety was palpable. "And when you're settled, perhaps you can resume your voice lessons."

Singing ... that's what set her free. No stutter then. Abby was touched he remembered this. At tomorrow's recital at the Royal Academy, Simon would accompany her on the piano. He alone understood her. When she struggled with her sentences, he never tried to finish them for her, but listened, patient and attentive. She'd be there with Simon, even if her heart wasn't.

Her father crouched before her, casting a sidelong glance at his wife before addressing Abby. "Perhaps you'd like to enroll at university too."

She studied his intent expression. He knew she wanted to be a teacher. But how could she fulfill her dream with this stammer that made conversation unpredictable? She'd stick on a word and instantly be obliged to pluck out another that would then send her narrative in an unwanted direction. Through determination and a few simple tricks, she'd made some progress, but she still lacked confidence when trying to express herself.

As for education, her mother held a contrary opinion. She once told Abby the only aspiration she entertained for her was marriage to the "right sort," and she expected her to continue the trend, as had Abby's older sister, Amelia. She even hinted Simon was not "the right sort," whatever that meant. But as much as she loved her mother, Abby didn't covet her life.

She wanted her own. Besides, she hadn't seen her mother's sister for many years. Whether Aunt Val held the same opinions as her mother was an open question.

Abby sensed that despite her mother's aristocratic demeanor, deep down her roots still clung to American soil. Perhaps she felt homesick. Abby turned to her, brightening. "Then why don't you go back with me, Mother?"

"Your father needs me here. I shan't leave him," she said, her voice trembling. "But you must go. Make new friends." Abby noted the emphasis on "new."

She was being compelled to live with Auntie Val and Uncle Will. *Where's home for me?* Moving here four years ago had been difficult, but she'd made other friends, especially Simon. She must try one more time to convince her father to let her stay.

Abby exchanged a pleading look with her father in a last-minute supplication. "Won't this all blow over?"

He shook his head. "Surely you know there are plans to evacuate all the children, and—"

"But I am n-n-not a child." If only she could make them see that.

After their morning recital at the Academy, Abby strolled with Simon to Round Pond in Kensington Gardens. She wore a favorite short-sleeved green dress flecked with tiny white flowers, a cardigan draped across her shoulders.

She leaned against the gnarled trunk of an ancient willow, arms folded, and studied the slow-moving clouds. "Looks like rain. They're nimbus ... or something like that." Simon squatted at the edge of the pond, flicking crumbs across the water to the swans. Abby swallowed hard. This might be their last time together. She hoped to prepare him for the shock. "I can't imagine not being able to come here with you." She bit her lip in an attempt to hold back tears.

Simon looked over his shoulder at her and smiled. "Nor I with you." He sauntered over to her. "Hello, what's all this? You're crying?"

"Mother and Father are sending me off." Abby dabbed at her eyes. "To America. For the duration. Just in case." She fired out the words in machine-gun fashion, afraid to get stuck halfway through the miserable news.

Simon heaved a ragged sigh. "That's why you're so quiet, then." He took Abby's hand and pointed to an empty bench. "I thought something must be up." He wiped the seat with his handkerchief. "Pesky pigeons," he said, loud enough for Abby to hear. "Wouldn't want that lovely dress to get soiled." He motioned for her to sit. Before them stood a bronze figure of a boy playing a flute, perched on the stump of a tree, with bronze fairies, mice, and squirrels cavorting around him. "And as for you, sir"—Simon addressed the Peter Pan statue—"you could do with a bit of a cleanup too." He clicked his heels together and saluted.

Abby burst out laughing. She couldn't help herself. Though Simon's madcap streak often rubbed against her serious side, he was ever a tonic, cheery in the face of trouble.

Simon moved closer to her on the seat. "War's coming, and London is bound to be bombed. Your folks are right. We have to face facts." He gestured toward a field where a steam excavator rocked to and fro, scooping up and depositing dirt onto a mound. "Bomb shelters. It's all so unreal. My *tate* shut his shop for a few days to build an Anderson shelter in the back garden. And I'm worried for my *bubbe* and *zadie* in Berlin. They're already assaulting people like my grandparents—and me."

Abby touched his arm. She understood his predicament but couldn't bring herself to discuss the topic with him. Bad enough that Jews in Germany were being rounded up and banished, but to know her own mother—no, Abby couldn't tell him her mother didn't trust Jews.

"When ... if you go to America ... I'll miss you." He stared at his shoes and knocked the tips together. "You realize I'll have to join up when the shooting starts?"

She shook her head, loosening her long, red hair. "And your intention to be a concert pianist?" Abby pointed to the music book poking from his satchel. "P-p-playing the piano and fighting don't seem to go together."

He stared into the distance, shoulders slack. "I'll need to put my plans aside. Same as you—it can't be helped. Duty first."

To Abby, the dead weight of this, their last goodbye, and the knowledge Simon might be called up to fight became unbearable. "I'll write as soon and as often as I can," she said, her voice shaking.

He smiled and took her hand. "Same here. Now then, I almost forgot." Simon rummaged inside his satchel. "I wrote this for you a week ago." He pulled out a sheet of music and handed the paper to her. "Think of me whilst you're over there."

She looked into his warm brown eyes and clutched the page to her breast, mindful of the effort he had taken to compose this for her.

Before she could thank him, he reached for his umbrella and popped it open. "Rain's coming on. I'd best get you home before your mother begins to worry."

Worry? She'll be glad I won't see you anymore.

Arms linked, they walked to the gate. Simon stopped, handed her the brolly, and pecked her on the cheek. "On second thought, I should leave you here." The sadness in his eyes didn't match his words. Turning up his collar against the downpour, he spun around and headed along the route they had come. He did not look back. Abby stood motionless until his form vanished in the mist. Had things been different, their beautiful friendship might have grown into something more serious. Now she'd never know.

A wave of regret crashed over her as she stumbled toward the exit closest to home, and her stomach churned. Alongside the gold-topped, spiked railings, an anti-aircraft gun hunched on its concrete plinth, hemmed in by a low wall of sandbags. Two uniformed soldiers crawled over the weapon, making adjustments. The one at the controls swung the long, blue-steel barrel around on its axis, bringing it to rest where Abby stood. She stared into the muzzle, a few feet from her head, and gasped.

Heart pounding, she darted for home as though fleeing a demon. Pushing through the oncoming tide of black umbrellas, she hopped on and off the sidewalk, splashing in the rainwater that bubbled in white torrents along the gutters and gurgled through the cast-iron grids into the abyss below. Double-decker buses and taxis lumbered past—the acrid diesel fumes stinging her eyes and nose, whilst men in flat caps on bicycles flashed by in an endless stream.

Breathless, she reached her front door and leaned against the wet iron railing to steady herself. There was no way out. However hard she ran, Abby couldn't escape the grim prospect that in a few days she would be on a ship to America. She'd submit to her parents' wishes but resolved then and there to come back to the home she loved.

WHEN VALLEYS BLOOM AGAIN

Southampton Dock, August 30

Abby craned her neck and stared wide-eyed and slack-jawed at the colossal liner that stretched full length in its berth, like a tall building lying on its side. Hundreds of portholes ranged along the black-painted hull. From the prow hung the mammoth anchor, frightening in its bulk. She tried to stifle the rising panic in her chest. High above her sat the tidy rows of lifeboats in their goose-necked davits, a mute reminder of the ever-present danger of the sea.

Her mother offered a clumsy embrace and skimmed Abby's cheek with a kiss. "I'm sorry Peter couldn't be here to see you off, dear. The RAF won't give your brother leave, what with the situation the way—" Her mother's lips quivered, and she squeezed Abby's hand tight. "Anyway, let us know when you want your party dresses sent." She stepped back a couple of paces, as though releasing her daughter into the wider world.

Her father held her close. "I might be able to telephone you once in a while through diplomatic privilege, but I'm afraid there's no guarantee on that front."

"But you'll write?" she pleaded, as the last of the passengers boarded the vessel.

"At least once a week." He released her and lifted two fingers to his right temple in a Boy Scout's salute. "I promise," he said, planting a kiss on her forehead.

Clutching her passport, Abby proceeded through the customs barrier and plodded up the gangplank, one ear alert for her parents to call her back and tell her they'd made a terrible mistake. When she reached the deck railing, she gripped it until her knuckles bleached white.

She peered down on the minuscule twosome still waving to her and raised an arm in desultory response. On the pier, stevedores and harbour officials swarmed about, barked commands and eyed the ship, waiting for a signal to loose the beast. Abby clutched the skirt pocket containing the white leather Bible her father'd pressed into her hand on parting with a whispered reminder that God promised to make all things work together for good.

A horn blasted, and a chasm of greasy brown water opened between vessel and dock as a flotilla of tugboats nudged the liner, banging and creaking, from its moorings. As her family blended into an anonymous background, Abby's stomach cramped into an icy knot. There would be no reprieve now. She was really leaving. In a final, gut-wrenching, hallowed farewell, she riveted her eyes on the retreating scene, etching it deep into her memory.

A gust whipped off the water as the ship nosed into the wind. With a muffled bump, the massive engines sprang into life, straining to unleash the ship onto the broad, beckoning ocean. Grimy gray gulls squawked and wheeled overhead, echoing Abby's innermost cry against this cruel and imposed exile. Would the birds, like herself, be carried out to sea, reluctant refugees, unable to find the way back home?

CHAPTER TWO

Aboard the Queen Mary

Abby unlocked the door to her spacious cabin, her father's hand in all the posh arrangements evident. Against one wall stood a plush brown sofa, a small table facing it, and a rack stuffed with newspapers and magazines. Two easy chairs squatted against the opposite wall, and a glossy black dining set occupied the middle of the floor. Abby tossed her hat and gloves onto a table and hurried past her stacked steamer trunks. She kicked off her shoes and sprawled across the bed, her stomach heaving. She lay there, nerves drum tight, listening to the ebb and flow of passing conversation outside her door and the distant *thump* of doors shutting. Vibrations from deep inside the ship hummed through her body. She rolled onto her back and yielded to the sensation.

The next day, she staggered to a porthole, jerked back the curtain and blinked at the bright sun. A clatter of footsteps down the stairwell outside her door announced the meal hour. Abby retched at the thought. She spent that day and the next eating little from a tray and resting in bed, tossing with every movement of the ship.

Finally, free of seasickness, Abby ventured out and strolled with other passengers on the promenade deck lined with steamer chairs. A steward in a crisp white uniform stopped at a chair, removed his cap, and bent toward a well-dressed woman in a wide-brimmed floppy hat. No doubt a rich and famous traveler.

As the daughter of a diplomat, Abby also lived a privileged life and often teased her mother for what she regarded as her social climbing. Her mother's response during one exchange remained with her. "I don't know where you get your wayfaring notions. Perhaps you'd rather be poor?" Then she'd followed up with that expression, "I can give you the kind of life another mother could not." There was an alternative life with someone else? Little things like that nagged at Abby.

On a lower deck, bathers swam in an indoor pool or lounged in wicker chairs. She regretted having never learned to swim. Even if she had, that knowledge wouldn't save her on the ocean. Drowning had to be the worst death possible.

As she wound her way back to her deck, Royal Navy sailors and soldiers in brown serge uniforms passed her. She was reminded of that last day with Simon in the park and the soldiers they'd encountered. The war her father predicted had followed her on board.

In the evening, Abby returned to the promenade deck, a light silk shawl draped over her shoulders against the cool air. The moon hung low, brooding over the black ocean, its reflection angling to where she stood. When she was a child, her father told her the moonbeam was a golden beanpole coming to say hello.

She went back to the cabin and began a letter to her parents but couldn't finish. On her first voyage across the Atlantic, she'd been fifteen and with her parents, leaving America for England. Then, she had wanted to be alone. Now going back alone, she wanted to be with them. She wrote a letter to Simon, enclosing a picture postcard of the ship with technical details printed on the reverse. He would be interested in all that.

One more day on the water and then New York. Abby walked toward the dining room. Creamy white breakers crashed against the ship and fell back, their silver spray carried off in a wild dance by the wind. She averted her eyes from the choppy waves as though they carried a living menace that would grab her legs and pull her down.

She passed two men in a doorway. "As of this morning, Britain's at war," one said to the other. Abby's stomach turned inside out. Mother and Father would be leaving St. Luke's about now. On any other Sunday, she'd have been there with them. Now she couldn't go back.

She entered a grand and spacious lounge and followed the maître d´ through a crowded dining room, abuzz with conversation. A massive mural depicted two unicorns in battle. She sank into a chair and took the breakfast menu from his gloved hand. Across the top was printed "Sunday, September 3, 1939." Mulling over the distressing news and with no thought of food, she selected the first item on the list—poached eggs on toast with Wiltshire ham.

Along the promenade, little girls in white frocks and lads in creased trousers, hands in their pockets, shuffled alongside their parents—a scene so like one from her bedroom window in Kensington—and yet so very different. How had the threat of war affected the lives of these families? War had already turned her own world upside down. Abby pushed her half-finished plate aside, regretting not having told her parents she was sorry for not loving them as she ought. She finished her tepid tea, then headed back up the broad companionway to her cabin.

As she ascended the stairs, the klaxon squawked. A herd of screaming passengers welled over from the deck above and thundered down. The stampede hit her head on, and she tumbled to the bottom, gasping. The block of ice in her stomach grew larger. *Lord, what's happening?* Out of nowhere, a pair of hands grappled her to a standing position and propped her against a bulkhead.

Tingling with fear, she pressed against the hard, unyielding steel and shut her eyes, her hands clapped to her ears to block out the endless babble roaring past. The screech from the horn above her head grated like sandpaper across her raw nerves. She'd lost a shoe and flinched as her bare foot rubbed over the cold, wet deck. Growing vibrations coursed through her body, and she tottered as the ship shifted direction. *Zig-zag. Zig-zag.*

"Are you all right, madam?" Someone tapped her shoulder. Abby opened her eyes. A steward bent toward her, hands cupped around his mouth, shouting. She tried to speak, but nothing came. Then everything blanked out.

A long, white curtain hung around the sides of the bed on which Abby found herself. The strong smell of antiseptic filled her nostrils. She'd fallen. Abby rolled to her side and looked down. Both shoes were on the floor beside the bed. Fragments of conversation came from somewhere beyond the small windowless room. She spun her legs around and sat up, trying to pick out the words.

A tall woman in a white cap and uniform pulled back the curtain, admitting the glare from a ceiling light. "Hello. You must be Miss Stapleton," she said, coming to Abby's side. "Do you feel dizzy or have pain anywhere?"

"No," Abby said, as a cuff was placed around her arm.

"I'm Ruth. The ship's nurse." She gazed into Abby's eyes. "Do you remember falling?"

"Yes, then everything went black."

"The steward carried you here after you fainted." The nurse consulted a chart on the wall. "American?"

"Yes, but I live in London."

Ruth took Abby's wrist and looked at a watch pinned to her blouse. "Good."

"My father's English. He's s-s-sending me to the States," Abby said, cringing at her effort to speak. "He s-s-says I'll be safer there."

"Your father's right, love. I was in London last week. Trenches in the parks, sandbags everywhere, and barrage balloons spread over the sky. Terrible." Ruth ran her eye down the chart. "Nausea? Headache? No?" She smiled. "All good news."

"But w-w-what happened before I fainted?" Abby said, trying to stand. "Why were those people dashing down the st-steps?"

"A submarine fired on us. Lucky for us, Herr Driver was a rotten shot." Ruth laughed. "Some passengers saw the sub surface, panicked, and headed for the lower decks."

"Was anyone hurt? Are we going back?"

"No to both." Ruth helped Abby to her feet. "It's on we go, but we may have a rough ride."

She pointed to Abby's forearm. "You'll have a bruise there and in a few other places. But nothing's broken as far as I can tell. I'm here if you need me."

Abby attempted a smile. "Thank you for everything."

The nurse turned around at the doorway. "Take care, love, and don't be anxious. But remember to wear your life jacket at all times and cover your portholes tonight. Captain doesn't want the Germans to find us again."

Behind, in England, her family and Simon faced a mortal threat. *Please keep everyone safe, Lord.*

Ahead beneath miles of deep water, the enemy prowled.

CHAPTER THREE

New York, September 4, 1939

Finally, after sailing in a zigzag course to evade further U-boats, the *Queen Mary* slipped into the harbor. Abby emerged into the hubbub on deck as they glided under tow into the shadows of the Manhattan skyscrapers. She caught her breath as sirens blared from boats that accompanied them, and water cannon spouted a raucous salute. Abby covered her ears as three thunderous blasts from their liner returned the greeting. Streamers of red and white and blue criss-crossed warehouses and the tall masts of ships moored nearby. American and British flags flapped an exuberant "Welcome" in the salty breeze as music from a brass band floated up from below.

Abby leaned against the ship's railing, letting out a deep breath. She tried to see herself as a brand-new arrival, taking in the scene for the first time. An undercurrent of sadness swept over her, diluting her gratitude and relief at a safe arrival. Reality hit hard. No chance of returning now. Still, merely tolerating her stay here would not be enough. She must take charge of her own affairs and not simply react to circumstances forced on her. And she must put on a brave face for the sake of her family. *Lord, I need your help.*

The swirling mass on the dock below resolved into distinct faces, each searching for an answering look of recognition. Somewhere down there her uncle and aunt waited. Memories came flooding in of visits with her parents to Uncle Will's vast country estate. She hadn't seen Aunt Val in—Abby tallied them on her fingers—four whole years. She had always thought her aunt standoffish and hoped she'd improved in the meantime.

As the *Queen Mary* closed in, men in military garb holding rifles scanned the vessel, their heads in constant motion. *Not here too.* Policemen weaved through the waiting throng below, looking at papers and detaining one here, one there. Abby seized the railing and closed her eyes. *Lord, help me see this is all working to my good.*

Caught in a tidal flow of passengers behind her, unburdened of shipboard courtesies and agitating for solid ground, Abby felt herself shunted toward the gangplank. Clutching at the coarse hand rope, she rode the roiling wave down.

At the bottom, a middle-aged man burst from the crowd and took her hands in his, kissing her on both cheeks. *"Bienvenue, ma chère,* Abby!" He engulfed her in a hug. "Grand to see you again." William Bluette spoke in an accent flavored by long years in America. His thick, dark eyebrows and steady blue eyes drew a smile from her.

"And you, too, Uncle Will." Abby squeezed his hands in return. "It seems ages since you came to see us in London."

"You won't need that coat here," he said, draping it over his arm. He gestured toward an area behind a chain link fence. "Your Aunt Val's over there by that automobile." He plunged into the crowd, Abby trailing.

"'Britain and France Declare War on Germany.' Read it in the Times," hawked the newsboy elbowing past. Abby trembled on hearing anew the troubling announcement that her family faced impending danger. Why hadn't she told Father she was sorry for not being more cooperative?

Uncle Will grabbed the boy's sleeve and pressed a coin into his palm. Glancing at the front page, he shook his head. "Wars and rumors of war. Matthew twenty-four." Jamming the paper under his arm, he guided Abby to a jet-black Pontiac where a chauffeur placed her luggage in the trunk.

Valerie Bluette flashed a tight-lipped smile and extended a gloved hand. "Abigail. Welcome." Stepping back, she gave a foot-to-head review, then peered at Abby over her glasses. "How tall you are. You make me feel like a midget."

Abby smiled. "It's n-n-nice to see you, Aunt." She judged that middle age suited her aunt. Strands of unruly gray hair poked out from under a tight-fitting blue and white topper hat. Aunt Val's complexion was smooth and unblemished, her figure trim and erect. Without a doubt, the image of her very own mother.

"Your uncle and I spent a few days in New York City," Aunt Val said when the car was under way. "We wanted to take you to the World's Fair tomorrow, but this heat is so oppressive." She removed her hat and gloves.

Uncle Will rolled down the rear window. "Besides, it's Labor Day and crowded everywhere, so we decided to go home instead."

Aunt Val waved a fan across her face. "And this talk of war is horrible. To think the King and Queen were here just a few weeks ago."

When they were out of the city, Abby pressed her head against the plush red leather seat and closed her eyes, disoriented. She'd need to get accustomed to riding on the right-hand side of the highway. The drumming of the road beneath the car and the murmur of hushed conversation between her aunt and uncle soothed her troubled mind.

"We're home," a voice said. Abby heard the sound of tires crunching on gravel. She opened her eyes. The sun was low in the sky, the shadows lengthening across the magnificent treelined entrance to Jolie Fontaine. Aunt Val removed her hand from Abby's shoulder. "You had a long nap."

Abby sat up, wide awake. As the car glided along the driveway, a three-story, redbrick mansion—decorated with bright white shutters across its length, many sharp-angled gables jutting up and out—came into focus. She held her breath before a scene even more splendid than her childhood memories. Fluted columns framed a wide porch. A path, bordered by flowers, led to patio steps and French doors beyond. At the farther end of the lawn, a line of silver birch pierced the twilight. She turned to her aunt. "How beautiful."

Abby followed her aunt and uncle into the house. "You two go in," Aunt Val said, pausing in the foyer before turning down a long hallway.

From the balcony above the wide carved staircase, Abby looked down on the great hall by which they had entered. Broad, ax-hewn oak beams spanned the width of the high ceiling. A wrought-iron chandelier fashioned from wagon wheels dangled from a long chain. A colorful fox hunt progressed at a languid pace in the mural covering one wall. Polished pine floorboards glistened in the lamplight. Abby turned to her uncle. "So many changes since I was last here."

"This is where you'll be staying." Uncle Will opened a door into a suite of rooms. "What do you think?" he asked, his eyes sparkling.

A cream plaster cornice ran around a high ceiling and an embossed, floral patterned paper lined the walls. She whistled through her teeth—a trick Simon had taught her. "Thank you," she said, walking across the beige, thick pile carpet to stroke lush maroon drapes that framed a window.

Uncle Will settled on the arm of a chair and took a pouch from his jacket. "I hope to make renovations to the Italian gardens and add more fountains." He tamped tobacco into the bowl of his pipe. "I'll show you the greenhouses soon."

"Greenhouses! I'd love to see them again."

"I cabled your parents while in New York. This came in reply." He produced a yellow envelope from his shirt pocket. "I opened it. Your father says he will telephone tomorrow but must reserve a time with the overseas operator, since it's harder these days with the world in an uproar."

Abby unfolded the paper and read the telegram twice. Her uncle had correctly summarized its block-letter words. A morsel, but a link with home.

They retraced their steps to the landing. In the foyer below, Aunt Val hunched over a slender glass vase, arranging long-stemmed yellow and red roses.

"That looks lovely," Abby called down.

Valerie swung around, knocking her elbow against the container, which toppled off the table and shattered. "Blast! That was one of my best." She looked up. "Why do you sneak up on me like that, Abigail?"

Aunt Val's words hung in the air. Abby had to consider them several times to be sure she heard right. There was no mistaking the angry tone. *What have I done?* A glance at her aunt's dark glower confirmed what she suspected—coming here was a mistake. Abby remained frozen in place on the balcony.

"Valerie, don't take on so," Uncle Will said, frowning. He took Abby's hand, his eyes crinkled in sympathy. Releasing Abby's hand and descending the stairs, he threw his arms around his wife. "I'll get you another one."

Abby turned from the banister and retreated to her room. Her aunt's outburst rekindled a memory of a visit here when she was fourteen. A chill ran through her. She'd surprised her mother and aunt huddled together on the sofa, whispering. When they spotted her, they glanced at each other and quickly scrambled to divert the conversation. "Don't ever sneak around like that, Abigail," her aunt had shrilled then. For days afterward, her mother seemed to go out of the way to be especially nice. Abby thought she'd put the details of that encounter out of her mind. But now, they took on a new, menacing shape.

CHAPTER FOUR

Jolie Fontaine
Main Line Philadelphia

Abby woke up listening for the hum of the ship's engines. Nothing. She hurried to the window. Scraggy pines bent their tips into a wind, and a hawk riding the updrafts circled under a clear blue sky.

Grasping the heavy drapes, she carefully lowered herself to the floor. She sat with her head against a wall, laughing at the absurd situation. Then her silly side gave way to the sober reality of last night's emotional collision. What was her aunt's accusation of "sneaking around" all about? How could things have gone so bad that quickly?

Struggling to her feet, she went to the bathroom and sprinkled icy cold water over her face and neck. The bruise on her arm had progressed to a dark blue. She opened the bedroom door a crack, not wanting to miss the expected telephone call from her father.

The dull chimes of the grandfather clock in the foyer struck the hour. Her broken watch on the dresser still displayed the time of her fall on the ship. If yesterday was Labor Day, today must be Tuesday. But what's the time?

She distributed her personal effects in a large closet with built-in bureau and shelving. On the vanity dressing table, she propped up a framed eight-by-ten tinted photograph of her parents taken on their thirtieth anniversary. Her mother wore a blue silk dress, her father a three-piece suit from his favorite tailor. Abby sat on the bed and studied them. She didn't doubt her parents loved her, but ill-defined uncertainties troubled her. The more she tried to repress the feeling she was merely a welcome visitor in her own home, the more the suspicions asserted themselves.

When the telephone in the hallway rang, she grabbed a robe, eased into her slippers, and careened down the long staircase, her heart thumping.

"Abby! Please descend like a lady."

Abby slowed and exchanged a glance with her aunt before seizing the instrument from her outstretched hand. "Thank you."

"Hello ... Hello?" She pressed the receiver to her ear. "Father, is that you?"

"Yes, dear. I'm glad you arrived safe and sound. Your mother and I heard about your U-boat incident," he said, the concern in his voice unmistakable.

She pushed down the lump in her throat and tried to sound reassuring. "I'm all right, Father, but I worry about you and Mother."

He continued. "You know the *Athenia* went down off the Hebrides? Sunk by a German submarine."

Abby dropped into a chair. *Sunk by a submarine.* Did he catch the irony of it all? That in sending her away from danger at home he'd exposed her to it on the ocean.

"Here, I'll let you speak to your mother."

"Hello, dear. We were worried. I—"

"Hello." The crackling line made conversation difficult. "Are you still there, Mother?" Abby shouted into the mouthpiece.

"I'm here, Abigail. You'll be glad to know Amelia came again yesterday."

Abby sensed she struggled for the right words to say to her.

"But we haven't seen Peter since you left. I do wish he were home."

Abby pressed the earpiece even closer and raised her voice. "I know how important it is that I'm here, Mother, but I w-wish—" A burst of static and the line went dead. "—you wanted me home," she said, the silent telephone still pressed to her ear.

William Bluette embarked on his customary evening stroll around the estate after the rain stopped. Retrieving his battered hat from a nail in the garden shed, he set off, his feet flapping in brown Wellington boots. Across his shoulder, he slung a khaki knapsack into which he threw debris found along the way.

His circuit normally took thirty minutes, but the rising pain in his chest made for slow going. He pressed on until he reached the elm grove, then stopped, panting for breath. Valerie would be watching from the bedroom window. She'd taken to doing that ever since he'd complained to the doctor about feeling tired. Big mistake. But he understood her concerns. After all, he was fifteen years older than she. As they had no children, each concentrated all their affection on the other. Val would be lost without him.

When he saw the light appear in Valerie's window, he smiled. She couldn't see him here under cover of the trees, but she would time his absence by the mantel clock. He decided to abbreviate his circuit this evening—for her sake. And yes, she was right as usual. He should've worn the heavier jacket.

He stooped to add a large pine cone to his bag. Of all his achievements in life, Jolie Fontaine had captured his heart. He'd retired from his business without regret, turned over the day-to-day operation to a handpicked board, and retained a large financial stake in the factory. He and Val were fixed for the rest of their lives.

William had immigrated from France fifty-five years earlier as a youth. And though thoroughly Americanized, his sympathies still lay with his natal land and Britain in the present crisis. Now, on the cusp of another European cataclysm, his business would expand. The tragedy of war repulsed him, even if he would profit.

His thoughts turned to Abby's plight. Uprooting her from her home in London may have been cruel but necessary. He mouthed a prayer. "Dear Lord, please help her to find contentment here." An engineer by training and an architect by instinct, William knew all great plans required patience. God would work out his plan for Abby in due time.

A breeze came up, and newly fallen leaves skittered across his path, their sere edges scratching at the pavement. Will quickened his pace, taking care to lift his feet, aware that his occasional shuffle betrayed his condition. His goal was the lily pond. Grabbing a sturdy branch from under a nearby tree, he used it to tap out the remaining distance. Once there, he collapsed into an Adirondack chair and closed his eyes. *Thank you, Father.*

During her first week, Abby roamed the grounds. A little girl once more, she ferreted out all the nooks and crannies of a carefree childhood when she and Peter and Amelia came here and shinned up trees and bottled fireflies.

The wide meadows, punctuated with sturdy stands of oak, were dressed in the russet and gold of an early fall. Narrow footpaths threaded through deep patches of woodland and disappeared under leafy canopies, luring her on to private niches in which she sat and tried to recapture the old joys. Her uncle's design, executed in lavish style, made Jolie Fontaine a masterwork in progress—four hundred acres of Eden. Could this place ever become home for her?

She'd stayed out too long this afternoon. The rain pelted down, forcing Abby to take refuge inside a bell tower. Soon it would be dark. When the rain eased, she ran toward a grove of trees and clambered over a split-rail fence. Her foot snagged in the bottom rail, sending her down a steep embankment. Brushing at the twigs and dirt clinging to her clothes, she navigated the path in a half-walk, half-run, all the while hearing Aunt Val's critical reaction to the mishap. Why did she seem eager to correct her every move? After all, hadn't her aunt agreed to take her in? Still, she'd be kind to her even if her aunt remained cool. Her own fight for independence might be harder won here than at home.

Abby reached the halfway mark between tower and house when the lanterns surrounding the lily pond appeared through the branches. As she got closer to them, she saw a figure slumped in a chair, one arm draped over the side, head lolled back. *That's Uncle.* She ran, her heart thumping wildly.

"Uncle Will." She dropped down beside him and gently shook his shoulder. He didn't stir. "Can you hear me?" she said, her voice shrill.

After a chill-down-her-spine pause, he opened his eyes and blinked. "Abby."

She searched his face. "Are you all right?"

He struggled to sit up. "*Oui, ma chére.* Just a bit tired. I must have nodded off." He reached for her arm. "We should be getting back, or your aunt will come looking for me. Hand me that branch to lean on."

Abby shouldered his knapsack, and together, they tottered toward the house. After a few steps, he stopped and turned toward her. "When I was at your home, your father and I discussed the political situation and the likely trouble ahead. Your coming here wasn't a whim of your parents, you understand," he said, his voice calm and emphatic. "You can blame me, too, if you like."

She gazed into his eyes and smiled. "I don't blame you or anyone, really."

"I know coming here wasn't your choice, and that it's a big adjustment." He rested a hand on her shoulder. "Know you may come to me anytime you need a friend."

Abby kissed his cheek, her eyes filling. "I'll remember that."

"By the by," he said, as they resumed their walk, "when I was in England last spring, I visited the Royal Botanical Gardens at Kew. You've been there?"

"I went with my fr-fr-friend, Simon, a few times." The scene of that last day with Simon in Kensington Gardens broke full force into her memory. She missed their times together. Had he enlisted in the army? There had been no response to her letter written on the *Queen Mary*.

Uncle Will's soft voice interrupted her thoughts. "In my humble opinion, gardening is the only art form that, if tended to, improves with time."

"I'd like to help in the gardens," she said, shifting her attention back to him.

"Glad you're willing." He paused, catching his breath. "I can arrange something." He chuckled, his blue eyes twinkling. "Anything else I may do for you?"

"I'd like to drive again."

"I was going to suggest that. You'll be more independent then." He grinned. "And that's always a good thing."

Abby squeezed his arm. "Thank you, Uncle."

He pointed to a dim light swaying in the distance and coming closer. "Now who do you suppose that could be?" He grabbed her wrist. "Not a word how you found me."

"I promise."

He furrowed his brow. "Your aunt frets over me too much."

She, too, worried about his health. He'd become considerably older and frailer since last spring. What would become of her if he should die?

After awakening late her first Sunday morning, Abby skipped breakfast. She fashioned a turban from a towel to cover her wet hair and slipped down to the patio for a quiet time with the Bible her father had given her.

The nearby *whump* of a car door was followed by her aunt's voice as she came up the steps. "Hello, Abby." She lifted her veil and removed the long shiny pin from her hat. "Will you at least condescend to join us at worship next week?"

During the past five days, she'd seen little of Aunt Val. She looked up from reading and smiled. "I hope you enjoyed the sermon."

Her uncle came into view around the corner of the house. "The pastor spoke on the importance of putting our trust in God's will."

Abby lowered her head. *That's not so easy.*

"I got a letter from your mother yesterday," her aunt went on, stretching the fingers of each glove as she pulled them off. "She's asked me to arrange more speech therapy for you." Aunt Val smiled. "Your mother tells me you sing well. And incidentally, what about your coming out party?" She frowned. "I'm told you didn't have one this past spring."

Abby cringed. The last thing she wanted was a coming out party. "I'd like to do other things right now, Aunt."

"What, exactly?"

"Attend a teachers' college."

"I shall consult your father about that cockeyed notion."

"Father already gave his approval."

Uncle Will's hand gripped his wife's elbow. "Join us for lunch, Abby," he said, guiding her aunt away.

Abby mustered a smile. "Thank you. I'll be there."

Aunt Val pulled back from him and stepped toward Abby. "You will attend the recital in the ballroom this afternoon? I picked the organist myself."

"Of course," she said, rubbing hard at the strands of her long, wet hair.

"You have such lovely red hair." Aunt Val sighed. "I suggest you wear it up occasionally." Turning, she followed her husband into the house, her heels clicking against the stone floor.

Abby dropped back in the chair and riffled through the pages of her Bible, looking for nothing in particular. She tried to pray but couldn't. The sparring with her aunt left her feeling miserable and more convinced than ever that something was not right with this place. Or could it be her? Her parents had brought her up as a Christian. "Faith will get you through anything," her father would say. That's all well and good, but what did it mean for her now, far from home?

Perhaps she'd left God back in England too.

CHAPTER FIVE

Abby sat on the low stone wall encircling the porch, inhaled the crisp autumn air and ran a finger across the rough surface. Along the brick path by her feet, white and pink begonias fluttered in the breeze that ruffled her hair. She envisioned the tight, soldierly ranks of flowers on parade outside her family's white Georgian house in London. Her watch said eight o'clock. Back home, if things were still normal, her father would be at his office and her mother entertaining her posh friends at a luncheon. But nothing was routine for them either anymore. "The world turned upside down," her father had described the current situation. *Please, Lord, help me be more appreciative and make the best of things.*

Billowing clouds tracked a stately passage across her view. She shaded her eyes against the glare of the sun and scanned the broad meadow covered in long grass as far as she could see. A road ran along the far side of the roughhewn fence. From where she sat, cars appeared like toys floating by, the sound of their motors rising and falling as they passed. A tractor—its bright red paint vying with the golden stacks of hay that dotted the scene—belched its way back and forth, trailing a mower.

Abby traced the path of the noisy combination as it inched toward her. In a few more passes, both tractor and driver came into focus. The stranger waved a gloved hand and flashed a grin, teeth luminescent against a tanned face. Then he lifted his wide-brimmed hat high above his head and slapped it down on the rump of his mechanical steed in perfect pantomime of a bronco rider.

Her heart fluttered. She waved back in appreciation of the prank.

The driver shouted to her, but his words fractured in the noise and surrendered to the wind. Halting his machine, he headed in her direction, his long strides fast closing the gap between them. Waving his Stetson in one hand, he patted down a mass of tangled brown hair with the other. Abby hopped from her perch and started down the steps to meet him.

"Abigail!" The shrill command stopped her short.

The man stopped, too, waiting, spinning his hat around in his fingers.

One foot on the porch, one on the step below, Abby weighed her options. Should she go to him or answer the call of her aunt?

She stiffened her spine and with a shrug in the stranger's direction, turned and walked to where her aunt stood. The tractor's engine sputtered to life, and the contraption resumed its atrocious racket. She didn't turn around.

"Hello, dear," Aunt Val cooed, her tone mellowed. "What are your plans for this morning?"

Heart pounding in her ears, Abby forced a tight smile and compressed her annoyance into one sharp syllable. "None." Was she to be denied the opportunity to make friends of her own choosing?

Aunt Val stroked Abby's arm, as if in appeasement. "I think we should go into Philadelphia to hunt up clothes for your classes. Perhaps something special for your birthday celebration as well."

Abby mustered a smile. "I su-su-suppose I could use more skirts and jackets for college." She squeezed her aunt's hand. "I can drive us there."

"Please. Your uncle tells me you're quite capable behind the wheel." Aunt Val made for the house, addressing Abby over her shoulder. "I'll do some shopping of my own."

At the French doors, she halted. "Our meeting of the League of Women Voters will have a distinguished guest in a few months. Eleanor Roosevelt. I must have something special to wear for the occasion." She swung around and clasped her hands in an onset of ecstasy. "Now that's something to look forward to."

Abby gazed down into her aunt's wide green eyes. "That's so exciting. Mother speaks fondly of the First Lady."

Her mother had told her that years before Aunt Val had been active in the campaign for women's suffrage. Nevertheless, Abby found reconciling the image of a liberal crusader for female freedom with the action of the woman who had just torpedoed an innocent encounter with a farmhand difficult. She knew so very little about her aunt's life.

Abby glanced over her shoulder, only to see tractor and driver wind its way into a hollow and out of sight. Who was the man? Perhaps if she sat on the wall tomorrow, she'd see him again and possibly meet him. But if her aunt could stop her walking twenty-five feet to say hello to this stranger, what other barriers might she put up?

Abby and her aunt entered Wanamaker's and paused before the giant bronze eagle in the court—a favorite meeting spot for shoppers. The rich melodious tones of the great organ with its many gold-covered pipes echoed throughout the store's atrium.

A scene flashed into Abby's memory. She saw herself as a child standing here in this court holding her mother's hand during Christmastime, and colored lights bounced off the fountains while the organist had played the *Nutcracker Suite*. She bit her lip to hold back tears. Those had been happy times with Mother, Father, Amelia, and Peter.

In a fitting room, Abby tried on another jacket. She spun around before a full-length mirror. "I don't like all this padding in the shoulders."

"Most unbecoming." Aunt Val grimaced. "You look like a football player."

Later, after picking out their wardrobes, they entered the Great Crystal Tea Room and waited for a table. Abby found two chairs in the foyer. Aunt Val took the seat beside her. "That teal dress is most becoming with your green eyes and creamy complexion. I'm glad you finally decided to take my advice." Her voice held a sharp edge of impatience and boomed across the short distance between them.

Abby flipped through the pages of the *Ladies' Home Journal*, trying to ignore the stares from those nearby, her face growing hotter by the second. She'd made the selection, not her aunt.

"And will you please do something with all that hair." Her aunt persisted, oblivious to the impact of her remarks.

Abby closed the magazine and plopped it on a table. A knot grew and twisted in her stomach. She chose to wear her hair around her shoulders. *Speak low and slowly, Abby, and don't argue.* Before she could respond, the dining room hostess appeared and led them to a table, foreclosing further discussion.

After a light lunch with little conversation, they got into the automobile for the long drive home. She yanked at the gear stick and made a show of braking hard at the traffic light, setting the car lurching forward on its springs. Who did Aunt Val think she was? Abby was going too fast, but anger suppressed all thoughts of road safety.

"I'm sorry I never learned to drive like you," Aunt Val said, with no hint of irony. "Your uncle wanted to teach me, but I was timid, and he was short-tempered." She gave a wry smile before changing the subject. "What are you doing later?"

Abby jerked to a halt at the next red light, overshooting the boundary line. "I promised I'd help in the greenhouse." She shifted into gear and signaled for a right-hand turn. The instant the light showed green, she gunned the accelerator and shot off.

Aunt Val got as far as "I think you ought not spend time with the hired—" when a panel truck from the left screeched into Abby's path, forcing her to swerve and brake, stalling the engine. Packages rocketed off the back seat, one of them striking her aunt on the head.

Shaking, Abby rolled into the curb. *Please forgive me, Lord.* Her aunt was sitting bolt upright and staring straight ahead, her eyes wide.

Abby reached over and touched her shoulder. "I'm so-so-sorry. It was all my st-st-stupid fault."

Aunt Val adjusted her hat in the rearview mirror. "I'm all right, dear." She sat back, clutching a package. "Let's get going—while we're both still in one piece."

Abby drove on, chastened. She'd behaved like a child.

Valerie enjoyed buying clothes for herself, but this morning's shopping spree with Abby—especially to select a dress for her birthday—left her more confused than ever. They weren't getting off to a very good start. This troubled her more than she dared show. She shook her head. What was wrong with that girl?

She changed into flat shoes, then hung her new suit in the wardrobe. Abby presented her with peculiar difficulties. Headstrong, naïve, and vulnerable too. A bit like herself when she was young. Valerie flinched. Of all women, she should have known better. Campaigning for the right to vote, then getting snookered by a man who assumed he had the right to all of her. It all seemed so long ago.

From the moment Abby arrived, a kaleidoscope of emotions left her in turmoil. She couldn't refuse her sister's request to provide a temporary home for Abby. And then there was her further request to introduce Abby to the "right" people. "The ... *right* people?" Valerie said aloud. Could Ellen be depending on her for something else?

She slid out a bottom bureau drawer and rummaged under a pile of lingerie. Taking out a heart-shaped locket, she snapped it open. The faded photograph of a young child stared back. Her thumb traced the rim of the picture. "What do I know of motherhood?" she muttered. She'd given up that right long ago. "Out of wedlock" and "do what's right for the baby," her parents had told her. The regret she had fought so long to suppress rose up and gripped her heart.

A warm breeze fluttered the curtains and filled the bedroom with the soft, intoxicating scent of an angel's trumpet William had planted below their window. Her husband was the best thing that had ever happened to her. They'd never had children together but not for lack of trying. Private fear robbed her soul and body of peace and vitality, haunting her for years, never letting go. How could she tell William that Abby was her daughter?

And how would Abby feel if she were told she'd been lied to? When Abby was an infant, Valerie had promised her sister she wouldn't say anything. She pressed a clenched fist against trembling lips, her eyes brimming over. Was the decision to keep the truth about Abby's adoption from her the right one? *Lord, I need your guidance.* Surely, the girl deserved to be told. But who should tell Abby—her or her sister? And when?

Abby changed into dungarees and an old plaid shirt and set off for the greenhouse, still shaken by her recklessness at the wheel. She passed the elegant Greek fountain and the numerous shrub-fringed goldfish ponds, their denizens already preparing themselves against winter.

As she got closer, Uncle Will walked in front of her, his shoulders heaving and his head down. "Wait for me, Uncle."

He turned around. "*Ma chère* Abby."

He motioned with his cane. "Let's sit awhile." Even his voice seemed weaker. "Three score years and ten, and all that," he said, as though privy to her thought.

Taking his arm, she escorted him to a nearby bench. "I was told you'd be in the greenhouse."

He chuckled. "I don't know if I'll be able to make it there and back." He removed his hat and blotted his temples with a handkerchief. "So, your aunt's arranging a party for you, and you both went shopping this morning."

"We went clothes sh-sh-shopping for that and for school." She avoided eye contact and fidgeted with her sleeve, remembering her irritation at the way her aunt treated her and her own shameful behavior. Her uncle didn't need to be burdened with her difficulties.

Uncle Will leaned forward on his stick. "How went your visit to the teachers' college?"

"Thankfully, my application was accepted and credits from my st-st-studies at the Academy in London have been applied toward a degree in elementary education."

"*Magnifique!*" He slapped his knee. "We could use more teachers. Even today in this grand country, many schools have four grades in one room and only one instructor."

"Speech exercises have been helpful. But I realize this will be a challenge. Still, I would like to work with children."

"You'll be a fine teacher. Remember that determination is half the battle." He patted her hand. "The other half is jolly hard work."

She managed a smile. "Who was that driving the tractor this morning?"

"Well, either Emil—he's the head gardener—or his assistant, James Wright." Uncle Will smiled. "Young fellah?"

She laughed. "He behaved like one."

"Rather handsome." He winked. "Don't you think so?"

Abby nodded. "He wore a big hat and likes to play the clown."

"That's Jim." Uncle Will chuckled. "But well-grounded and a good worker. He came in today to help Emil with a few overdue jobs. Jim's been with me since he graduated from school. He has two sisters, but Jim's the one his mother looks to." He stared into the distance. "I can't go into details, except to say they've had a difficult time of it."

Abby studied the intent expression on his face. "I thought I might help out this afternoon as I promised." She smiled, then added in haste, "But I'll walk back with you if you'd like."

"*Merci.* No, that's all right." Uncle Will rapped his chest. "I'd go with you and introduce you two, but it's a bit far for me. After today, Jim'll be off awhile. When winter arrives and things go quiet, we won't see much of him."

Abby looked at the sky. "I'm afraid it's getting late."

He pointed with his cane to a path that meandered between the trees. "Jim may still be in the building where he keeps an office. Seize your chance." He jammed on his straw hat and transferred the walking stick to his other hand. "*Au revoir.*"

Abby waved goodbye and set off at a brisk clip. Would Jim still be there? Finally, she reached the building, only to discover he'd already left. How many days before he'd be back?

She strolled to the bell tower, listening to the carillon across the field, then sprinted up steps to a flagstone landing. The horizon blazed with the purples and pinks and reds of an autumn sunset, the glow rolling back across fields and trees and lakes to where she waited, enraptured. Leaning against the parapet, she studied the house, counting the lights that appeared one by one in each window. How long until harsh reality again rose up to disrupt her life?

CHAPTER SIX

Throughout autumn and the long winter that followed, Abby grappled with news of the war. Correspondence and infrequent telephone calls from her parents supplemented newspaper accounts and bulletins on the radio.

Finally, a letter from Simon informed her he'd completed army training and was preparing to leave England, destination not revealed, no forwarding address. From her father, she learned the Royal Navy had waged a successful counteroffensive against German submarines. Perhaps this war would soon be over, and she could go home.

The rhythm of the house was largely undisturbed by the conflagration in Europe. Her aunt and uncle played host and hostess to various civic and church groups most weekends. During the week, Abby attended college. Afternoons, she'd spend studying or reading in her room. In the evenings, she'd listen to serials or music on the radio and play checkers or Monopoly with Uncle Will.

When Abby and her uncle were alone one evening, he turned to her. "Now that spring's here, there'll be plenty to do around the grounds." He picked up a newspaper. "That is, if you're still of a mind to help."

Abby grinned. "Yes, I want to."

He winked at her over the top of his paper. "I thought so. Jim'll be here on Saturday."

When the day arrived, Abby awoke earlier than usual. Dressed in an old, long-sleeved shirt, jeans, and a borrowed pair of Wellington boots a size too big, she galumphed out through the tradesman's entrance and covered the distance to the conservatory in record time.

Inside bloomed different varieties of lilac shrubs—her favorite flower. Huge snow-white oriental lilies vied for her attention. Hyacinths scattered around her—blue, purple, and pink. She drew in their sweet-smelling perfume and caught the sound of chimes swaying in the warm breeze. Her heart surged with the wonder of spring and the prospect of a fresh start. If ever her uncle's art healed and nourished the spirit, it was here.

She emerged into a large greenhouse littered with pots, sticks, bales of wire, and jute bags marked "Fertilizer." She spotted Jim working at one of the tables surrounded by plants and pots, his head bobbing as he labored.

He looked up as she approached. Holding a flowerpot in one hand and a trowel in the other, he called out, "Mr. Stanley, I presume?"

Abby stifled a laugh at Jim's reference to the famous meeting between the journalist and Dr. Livingstone. She quickened her pace, navigating between the rows of wooden troughs to where he stood. "Nice to meet you, Dr. Livingstone."

He gave a low chuckle. "Your uncle warned me you might inflict a visit on my neck of the woods."

Abby's jaw dropped, and heat rushed to her cheeks. "B-but I—"

A sheepish grin spread across his face. "Don't mind me. But you did look much too serious just now." He laughed, revealing straight, white teeth.

Abby laughed along, intrigued by his playfulness and friendly manner. Jim Wright would take some getting used to.

His sapphire-blue eyes regarded her for what felt like minutes. Then he slapped his palms together to dislodge the dirt. "We meet at last."

She took his big hand in hers and smiled. "I hope I'll be of some help. Show me where to start."

He gestured for her to follow him down rows of wooden tables that overflowed with tulips and daffodils. His energetic pace forced her into a half-run, like a schoolgirl on a field trip. "Uncle Will says you're taking care of your mother," Abby called after him. "I hope she's b-b-better."

He raised the back of his hand in acknowledgment. "She's managing. Your uncle told me you're from England," he said over his shoulder. "Funny that you don't have a strong accent."

She tried to keep up with him. "I was born in the States and lived here for fifteen years. Then my family moved ba-ba-back to London five years ago," Abby replied, almost crashing into him when he stopped and turned around.

A ghost of a smile played over his face. "You sound as if you've been uprooted and transplanted like one of these flowers."

She met his gaze and nodded. "Yes. Now that you mention it."

In a swift, fluid movement, he hoisted himself onto a potting table. "I'm sure you miss England." He searched her face. "Things are not going so well there, I hear."

Flustered under his close scrutiny, she grabbed a trowel, tumbling the tool in her hands. "Mother and Father insisted I'd be sa-sa-safe here." Conscious of the sound of her own voice and ever-present stutter, she dropped the tool, compounding her embarrassment.

In a flash, Jim dropped from his perch. "Still, it's a shame to put you through another move and all." He extended the trowel to her.

Their hands touched. Her heart skipped a beat.

He shifted his feet. "No doubt that was hard for them—seeing you leave home."

She diverted her gaze to the ground, her eyes filling. "They did what seemed best."

Jim picked up an armful of trays of flowers with tiny multi-colored faces and beckoned her to follow him outside. "Pansies provide a variety of color that should last for months."

Crouching at the end of a raised bed, Jim set the trays down and divvied up the plants a foot apart along the middle of the row. He gestured toward the far end. "We'll start here and work our way toward that bamboo stake. You stay on this side."

Abby marveled at the speed with which he progressed and the way he seemed to caress each flower as he lowered the plant into the earth. He reached the end of the row before she was a third done. "And when did your interest in horticulture begin?"

For a moment, his hands stilled. Then he looked up, and his grin widened. "When I realized I wasn't college material," he said, plunging his trowel into a fresh hole. "But thanks to the employment scheme at the agricultural school, your uncle—God bless him—agreed to hire me." He dropped a pansy into the ground and patted the soil flat. "I'm lucky to have a job at all with the condition the country is in, and especially when I think about—" He looked out across the grounds. "Well, let's just say that your uncle's been good to me and my family."

Abby shot him a questioning glance. "Oh?"

"I had to stay home and keep things going when Mom fell." He pushed back his hat. "She got some help from President Roosevelt's new welfare system, but your uncle was the one who pulled us through. He kept me on the payroll, even when I couldn't work."

Jim dropped onto one knee. "Someday, I hope to have my own business, if I can earn enough to start one, that is." He rolled back on his haunches and yanked out his empty pockets, shrugged in comic resignation, then promptly fell backwards.

Abby laughed aloud, buoyed by his hilarious antics. "And that muck you're sp-sp-spreading around," she said, flushed from her outburst. "What's it for?"

He reached for a fistful of the dark brown substance. "It's a mixture of shredded leaves and dried grass clippings." He sifted the humus through his fingers. "The mix keeps fungus away, the weeds down, and the soil cool and moist. Cuts down on water too." Reaching into his back pocket, he pulled out a pair of tan leather gloves. "Here, take these."

"Thank you." Abby slipped her hands into the oversized gloves.

Jim pointed at her face. "Would you mind if I wiped that dirt off, or can you manage?"

Abby pulled off a glove and felt around her cheeks. "Oh? Where?"

Jim edged closer, bringing his eyes in line with hers and gently brushed the back of his fingers across her cheek. "Now you tell me. When did your interest in horticulture begin?"

Abby looked into the distance. "Hmm. Probably after I read *The Secret Garden* as a child," she said, her tone masking the excitement inside.

"The book must have left its mark." Jim showed her his hand. "Just like this lucky bit of soil," he said, flicking it onto the ground.

She smiled and lowered her head.

He sat back, legs outstretched. "I used to read a lot once, but I don't remember that one. Now it's mostly seed catalogs." He scratched the side of his nose and laughed. "And about your home. I hear tell England is beautiful, and everyone has a garden. Is that true?"

Grateful for the change of subject, Abby dropped back on her heels and swiped her forehead. "We live across the square from a large park with acres of flower beds. Father has a rose garden, and Mother grows flowers in her window boxes." She furrowed her brow. "But now she writes the lawns have all been turned to allotments for vegetables. And Father says the estates are looking quite unkempt as gardeners are on war work instead."

"That must be painful for your parents to see." Jim stood and stretched. "Still, the ground is being cultivated for food."

Abby raised her hand above her eyes, shielding them from the blazing sun. "Do you suppose America will join the war?"

He cleared his throat. "I certainly hope not. We should mind our own business." He frowned. "We've got enough problems here at home without getting mixed up in some foreign squabble."

"Foreign squabble?" she repeated. He might as well have dumped a pail of icy water on her. Abby sprang to her feet and yanked off the gloves. "I'm s-s-sorry, but I must go now."

She tramped toward the conservatory, boots slapping against her legs. *Foreign? Has the man no idea what's going on in England?* My brother and Simon go off and get shot at while gardener Jim puts plants in pots.

"Will I see you next Saturday?" she heard him call out.

Abby walked down endless rows of tables, searching for the door through which she had entered. "I don't know," she said, looking over her shoulder.

Philadelphia, May 1940

"Don't wander off after the meeting. I'd like you to meet Mrs. Roosevelt." As the car came to a stop, Aunt Val pushed open the door, set one foot on the sidewalk, and turned to face Abby. "This is indeed a rare treat." With a nod of satisfaction, she slid out.

Abby parked across the street and turned off the motor. The gathering of the League of Women Voters wouldn't start for another twenty minutes. Groups of well-dressed women exited chauffeured limousines and filed under an awning and through the plate glass doors of a swanky hotel. She sat behind the steering wheel, waiting until the last minute to go inside.

She squeezed into a seat at the back of the mahogany-paneled room, jam-packed and abuzz with female chatter in a sea of bobbing hats. Aunt

Val approached the lectern to introduce the guest speaker. A wave of excitement rippled through the audience.

To a round of applause, a woman wearing a corsage on a navy-blue suit and a floppy hat stepped forward. "Ladies, I am delighted to be with you once again," Mrs. Roosevelt began, raising her hand in greeting. "Thank you for inviting me."

In a tremulous, high-pitched voice, the First Lady launched into her topic, "The Relationship of the Individual to the Community." She made frequent references to the role of women in politics. Mrs. Roosevelt seemed forthright and genuine.

The ceiling fans struggled to live up to their reputation. *Must be at least eighty degrees.* Abby had never been so uncomfortable. Aunt Val with another attendee raced in and out of the room, juggling hand fans and glasses of iced water. Abby—wedged tightly in the middle of the row—weighed the effort of going to the rescue but salved her conscience with the excuse she shouldn't disturb others.

Sweltering and on the verge of dozing off, she snapped awake when she heard Mrs. Roosevelt say, "We older people must not try to make the younger generation do things the way we did them." Abby whisked a fan across her face, intent on hearing every word.

The First Lady elaborated on the current social and political changes and the expanding role of women in America. With a sweeping, smiling glance, she took in every member of her audience. "It would be necessary to include all women in these changes," she said, rapping on the lectern for emphasis.

Abby recalled her father had said women had taken "men's work" as the war diverted them away from industry and office. The same disruption would occur in America if they joined the fray. Jim's reaction to her question on that topic came to mind, and she bristled. He'd implied she was devoted to an alien cause. He'd let her down.

After the lecture, she joined her aunt at the front of the room where Mrs. Roosevelt waited to greet her admirers. Abby scouted out an escape route. Thankfully, with the help of a therapist, her speech was improving. Still, she dreaded opening her mouth. The stammer was worse when she was anxious—as now. Her aunt prodded her. Abby took several deep, calming breaths.

Aunt Val pulled her forward by the elbow. "I'd like you to meet my niece, Abigail Stapleton."

Face to face with the First Lady, Abby's pulse quickened. She extended a shaky hand and returned what she imagined to be a smile. "I heard a lot about you in England, ma'am."

Mrs. Roosevelt clasped Abby's hand. "The happiest years of my life were spent at Allenswood Academy outside London, and I still have many good friends there." She flashed her famous toothy grin. "You're probably near voting age, my dear," she said, dropping her voice. "I do hope you will use that hard-won privilege." She turned and tapped Aunt Val on the shoulder. "A privilege won by such women as this. Brave suffragists all."

Aunt Val leaned into Mrs. Roosevelt. "Abigail wants to be a teacher."

"I so loved teaching at the Todhunter School. It encouraged me to keep at it." The First Lady smiled. "And opened up my horizons."

As Abby left the reception line, those words struck home. Eager to hear more, Abby joined the queue at the table and bought a copy of *It's Up to the Women*. Perhaps reading Mrs. Roosevelt's book would help to expand her own horizons. Her scalp tingled as she visualized for the first time an independent and useful life in America.

Aunt Val rested a maternal hand on her shoulder. "I'll be a few minutes, dear." Her staid aunt entered a group of chattering, laughing women, magically transformed by their energy. Her aunt had found a pursuit dear to her heart. If only she could have the same passion for a cause.

CHAPTER SEVEN

With Abby's first year at Weston Teachers College over and classes out for the summer, she again offered to help out in the greenhouse. She'd overlook Jim's response to her question on America joining the war and would work alongside him. She found him in the potting area, a large red, white, and blue handkerchief around his neck.

"I'm glad you're here," Jim said, grinning. He gestured toward empty ceramic pots on the ground. "I think we'll tackle those, if that's all right with you?"

Abby flashed a quick smile. Did he remember his curt reply in April and her hasty departure afterwards? She squatted next to a jumble of ornamental containers.

Jim rummaged through them, then thrust his trowel into a bucket of thumb-sized stones. "About two inches of these should do." He tipped the stones into one of the pots. "They provide slow drainage, so the plant won't dry out." He crouched beside her. "Then fill up the container with compost—your 'muck'—and a little top soil."

Abby scooted to one side. He was good at his job. "How much of each?"

"I'm sorry, I forgot this is still new to you." Jim moved in closer. "Half-and-half, see? Put tall daisies in the back, red impatiens in the center, and lastly along the outer edges of each container, the trailing begonias, petunias, and nasturtium, so they cascade down the sides." Suiting action to words, Jim completed one arrangement and set the container beside her. "Use this as your guide, leaving two to three inches between each plant." He smiled. "If you have a question, I'll be nearby."

As she toiled, Abby sensed Jim's eyes on her and tried to catch him in the act. But whenever she'd glance over, he'd look down at his hands and whistle, making a game out of it and beating her every time. Then he set down his trowel and strolled over, giving her one of those captivating smiles. "Off for the summer, are you?"

Abby nodded, focusing on the flowers in her hands. *Please don't come any nearer.*

He removed his hat and twirled it in his hands like the first day she saw him. "Is college all you expected?"

Abby's wall of indifference collapsed, and she gazed up into those intense blue eyes below dark eyebrows. "I'm looking forward to going back." Her throat tightened. "Still, sometimes I feel se-se-selfish. There's so much I could be doing at home for the war effort."

Jim rocked back. "Selfish?" His brow furrowed. "When you complete your training, you'll be teaching kids who'll be future citizens."

Abby—without breaking the lock of his eyes—flinched, taken aback by his response.

"My squirt sister with the big mouth says she wants to quit high school." Jim hunched beside her, lowering his voice. "And the older one who had great dreams—well, she didn't even finish high school, and—" He looked into the distance. "I'm sorry, I shouldn't go on like that."

Surprised by his revelation, her cheeks grew warm.

"I'll probably be one of the first to be called up if we enter this war." He stood and swatted his hat against his thigh. "But until, and if, that happens, my duty lies at home."

In a flash of self-reproach, she understood. She'd misjudged him. His mother and sisters needed him, and he didn't want to leave them. And what had he said about his job and how grateful he was to have this one?

Jim slapped his palms together to dislodge the dirt. "It's none of my business, but you might think about teaching on the estate during summer." He plunged his hands into a watering can. "I know some of your uncle's staff have youngsters who could use help with their schooling."

How clever he is. "That would never have occurred to me."

Jim bent to pick up a toppled container. "I must go. It's trout season," he said, as if to explain the urgency of his mission.

Abby's stomach dropped as he strode off between the long rows of tables. She wished he'd stay longer. When he headed back in her direction, her pulse quickened.

"You're doing fine here." He grinned. "If you like, when I get back, I'll take you to see the new bonsai collection."

She let out a breath. "Let me know when you return." What was it about the young gardener that stirred her senses?

Abby craned her neck to keep him in view as he strode off. He opened the door to his truck and glanced back. Their eyes met.

Jim rolled down the windows and headed for the river. The road wound through the gentle hills and wide fields of Chester County's mushroom country. Passing the cluster of buildings that lined the highway, he inhaled the scent of fresh-mown grass mingled with the pungent odor of manure. He'd spent many summers here picking and cleaning mushrooms for distribution around the nation. It didn't bring in much money, but it helped his mother with household expenses.

He should've forgotten about fishing this morning. Abby was so easy to talk to. And those large, sparkling green eyes and long, curly lashes. He buckled at the knees whenever he gazed into them. She seemed to enjoy the simple things and wasn't afraid to get her hands dirty. Picking up speed, Jim rapped his palm against the outside door panel. He'd get another chance to be with her later today.

His route branched off the main highway and down a narrow gravel track. When he got to the river, he angled the truck under the branches of an ancient hemlock. Getting out, he clambered over a low drystone wall, lugging his gear a hundred yards to a clearing. Here the grass sloped down almost level with the water. His private spot. Jim installed himself at the river's edge and sat motionless, the slack line bobbing in the water. He took pride in his practical outlook on life, but in spite of himself he was infatuated with this young and beautiful woman with the hybrid English accent. She was one of a kind.

The float drifted with the current, and Jim payed out more line. He cursed poverty in general and his own in particular. Early in the Depression, his father deserted the family when Jim was only fourteen, and his two sisters were in elementary school. At the time, Jim thought he might be the cause, though he never revealed this private guilt to anyone—not even to his mother. Today, ten years on, the shame of the abandonment stuck with him. No one knew his father's whereabouts, or if they did, they weren't telling. Jim wasn't sure he'd want to know, anyway. How would Abby judge him if she knew about his father's behavior?

A vivid, bright-blue blur downstream caught his eye. A kingfisher burst out of the water with its prize and flew into the woods. "Well, you've had better luck than I have," he sang out. Jim lost interest in the whole endeavor and packed up his things.

He trudged up the trail to his truck. Did Abby have a sweetheart in England? She hadn't said. But then why would she tell him? *Why did you bring her into my life, Lord?*

One Month Later

Abby sat across from her aunt in the front room. "You take milk and sugar?" Aunt Val said, her hand suspended in the act of pouring.

Abby smiled. "Only milk, please."

"I suppose you'll be going out later?"

Abby reached for the cup. "Jim wants to show me what he's doing in the meadow."

"I do wish you wouldn't spend so much time with that ... that gardener." Aunt Val banged her china cup onto the table, spilling half the contents into the saucer.

Abby flinched. She thought she'd seen the last of these confrontations.

"Many times, I don't even know where you've gone."

"But it's so lovely outdoors," Abby responded, in an attempt to placate her aunt's mood. With smooth irony she added, "And Jim is so easy to get along with."

Her aunt helped herself to another shortbread, holding the piece aloft as if inspecting it. "It's about time you accepted social invitations and met the right people."

"I appreciate all that you've done for me, Aunt. But I sh-sh-should be allowed to choose my own fr-fr-fr—" *Please help me to stay in control, Lord.*

"All the same, I do not approve of this particular friend." Aunt Val paused, as though weighing the blow she was about to inflict. She straightened and pushed back her shoulders. "If you continue to fraternize with this fellow, I'll ask your uncle to discharge him."

"Discharge Jim?" Abby stared into her aunt's face, unwavering. "Do you know how important his job is to him?" she said, a fire raging somewhere behind her eyes.

The clock on the mantelpiece chimed three. Its cheerful sound was a balm to frazzled nerves. Abby pushed the cup away and scraped back her chair. "I must go now."

In her bedroom, she dropped onto the window seat and inched back the curtain. Below, Jim paced across the patio, whistling as he waited for her.

She could defy her aunt and go down to him. But then Jim would be fired, and she'd lose him. Having now discovered him, she couldn't bear that. Still, if she gave in to her aunt's threat, she would be forced to deny her own heart. And she might lose him anyway.

Her hand trembling, Abby let the curtain fall back. Turning away from the window, she bowed her head. *Lord, show me what I should do.*

CHAPTER EIGHT

August 1940

One year since her arrival. Though Abby wanted to return to England, she couldn't exclude the possibility that Jim might be part of God's plan for her life. The roadblock her aunt had thrown up only intensified her longing for him. Chafing under her aunt's prohibition and hating herself for submitting, she took refuge in the belief Jim would keep his job.

She'd botched her attempt to explain things to him. "Something's come up, and I can't work with you for a while," she had told him. *What was that supposed to mean?* No wonder he'd looked confused. But Jim had taken her words with good grace, nodding while she fidgeted and groped for a reason.

Abby scheduled tasks in the greenhouse for Sunday afternoons—the only day Jim was off. Infrequent encounters with him during the summer had been accidental. She gleaned from a remark Jim made that he attributed these absences to anxiety over her family. Abby let the impression stand. Soon, she'd be returning to Weston for her junior year and be away most of the day. Still, she yearned to talk with him as before.

Today, as she went about her work, Abby consoled herself with the realization she moved in the same space Jim had yesterday. She cherished the written instructions he'd left on the potting table, pinned down with a smooth, shiny stone from the garden. He asked her to "snip the blooms from the sweet peas to keep them flowering," and to "pay special attention to watering the container plants." He'd underlined the last task. Abby ticked off each one as she completed it. Boy, Jim was so clever—thorough too. Her uncle had made a good choice with him. As she puttered about, Abby kept up a running dialogue with Jim in her head.

Abby consulted the final item on his list. "For You," Jim wrote. At his suggestion, she cut for herself yellow, orange, and salmon gladioli, taking care not to remove all the leaves from the remaining stems. Jim had said these leaves feed the bulbs for the following year's growth. Cradling her bouquet, Abby left the greenhouse, shutting the door behind her. Regardless of what her head told her, her heart pulled irresistibly to him. Oh yes, and double-yes, she'd fallen in love with Jim. Where would it all lead?

The German occupation of the Channel Islands and France's capitulation demolished the remains of Abby's optimism. A terse note from Simon said he was with the British Expeditionary Forces in France. His next, postmarked England, informed her of his "merciful deliverance" from the Dunkirk beaches in the mass evacuation of British and French forces. He and "the rest of the chaps" were eager to get back into the fight. If she could "manage it," he would be glad to hear from her. She dashed off a reply.

Abby listened to the BBC External Services on the shortwave band—propaganda from both sides in full swing. Vessels departed New York Harbor every day to bring Americans home from Europe. She overheard household staff bickering over whether the country should lend its bulk to the war effort. Opinion was divided between those for intervention and those against it.

In early September, the aerial bombardment of London began. The German pilots had refined their targets and improved their accuracy. Airfields, factories, and ships were hit in one droning wave after another.

Her mother wrote:

> Your father is working long hours in a secret office. Sometimes he's there all night. Even on weekends, he is at his desk. Mr. Churchill is a chain-smoker, and your father's clothes always smell of cigars. Last night on his way home, he took shelter at the Methodist Central Hall. Who would have thought the church basement would become the largest air raid shelter in England! I am so glad you are where you are.
>
> Peter is 'defending the skies around the south coast as part of the RAF Fighter command'—his words. He came to visit while on

leave yesterday. Your brother is under a lot of strain but seems to be holding up all right. He smokes his pipe incessantly and can't sit still. He asked me to send his love to you. By the way, there are American airmen in his squadron—volunteers, he tells me. No time for such things as writing, he says.

Your father says to tell you he misses you and loves you. So do I. You will be hearing from him soon, dear.

Love, Mother

Abby set the letter down. It was affectionate and casual. Her mother didn't want to worry her and was, no doubt, trying hard to appear unruffled.

The same week, a letter from Amelia revealed that large swaths of London lay in ruin and that many mothers and most small children had been packed off to the countryside. Her husband was away on top secret intelligence work, so she and the twins had moved in with his family in North Yorkshire.

Then in another letter her mother wrote:

BBC bulletins have become a daily ritual. The sirens went off while your father and I were on the way home from a rare evening at the theatre. We were forced to spend the night on the platform in the Tube station at Waterloo. We could still hear the booms! There were a lot of people down there with us. It's the mothers and children I feel especially sad for. But, bless them, most made light of their troubles.

In spite of her own fears, Abby could not help smiling at the thought of her very proper mother sleeping on a railway station platform. She knew how much she disliked public transport, especially the Underground. The bombs that pelted the city were cruelly impartial, targeting everyone and no one in particular. She gleaned some relief from the knowledge that her parents could at least hide deep in the tunnels.

"Mother, won't you leave?" Abby asked during one of their treasured phone conversations.

"If the Queen will not leave London, neither will I leave your father," her mother responded. "Anyway, I'm a part-time volunteer civil defense warden. It's my job to maintain blackouts and supervise the shelters and distribute the respirators—gas masks, dear—though civil defense doesn't like us using that term. Anyway, as long as I feel useful, I'll stay."

After their conversation ended, Abby snatched up her parents' picture from the bureau and sat on the bed. Her mother's peevishness and the autocratic manner of her father were no longer so important. In times of crisis, the true mettle of character showed itself. Now her parents beamed out at her with a new heroic aspect, warriors defying the Teutonic Demon, oppressed but proud, carrying on their shoulders the hopes of millions for victory and a free world.

Autumn lengthened into a fading glory of russet, gold, and orange before yielding to falling temperatures and howling gales that ripped the remaining leaves from trees. Weeks ticked over into months, and a watery sunlight bleached the gray-limbed network of trees around the house. A strong wind swept through shutters and rattled window frames, as though trying to enter the house.

Abby burrowed deep into her eiderdown, longing to flee to England and share the risks her parents faced there. But she'd promised to stay until it was safe to return. Listening to the shrill whistle of the wind, she lapsed into a fitful sleep. She stood in the park across from her parent's house. Then a bomb descended from the sky. She tried to run toward it, hands upraised to catch it, but her legs wouldn't move.

Awakening, she bolted upright as tears trickled down her face. A sliver of moonlight cast its glow over the room. She lay wide awake, her body trembling. Why such a nightmare? *Please keep my family safe, Lord.*

Unable to go back to sleep, she went downstairs to the kitchen. A wall clock bathed in spectral light from a standing lamp in the corner showed three o'clock. A warm coffee pot sat on the stove. Who else was up?

Abby didn't remember pouring coffee. It tasted terrible, but she didn't care. She didn't care much about anything. Beautiful though it may be, this place was not home. "Stuck, stuck, stuck," she said, gritting her teeth. She swept her forearm across the table, knocking the cup to the floor and buried her head in her arms. From deep within she cried *Where are You?*

Four a.m. She must've fallen asleep. Abby picked up the fragments of crockery and mopped up the spilt concoction, ashamed of the incident. She'd confess the breakage to her aunt in the morning.

Back in her room, Abby sank to the floor beside her bed. This was more than mere petulance—she was guilty of that often enough—no, this was different. She couldn't return home, and she couldn't be with Jim either. *You know my despair. Help me find my way.*

Later, when Abby opened her eyes, she was propped up against the bed, her legs tucked underneath her body. A sweet calm came over her. She'd been freed from her fear of being lost. She threw the curtains back onto a forget-me-not-blue sky, her mind surged with renewed purpose. "Thank You for hearing my cry, Lord," she said aloud, her heart overflowing with fresh hope.

Abby dressed, then headed downstairs for breakfast. Time to move on.

"*Bonjour,* Abby. Come and sit next to me." Uncle Will rose and pulled out a chair. "You look positively cheery today." He leaned over and kissed her cheek. "I could do with a spot of beauty sleep myself."

"Good morning, Uncle, Aunt."

Aunt Val held out a cup for general inspection. "We seem to be missing one of these. It's one of three," she said, raising her voice a couple of notches. "Your uncle bought them for me in Cape Cod. So, if—"

"I'm sorry, Aunt Val. I dropped one early this morning."

"Oh, I see. And why were you up and breaking my cups?"

Abby lowered her eyes. "I couldn't sleep, and—"

"And she decided to come down for a bracer," Uncle Will broke in. "Sounds logical to me, dear. And then there were two. A real Agatha Christie mystery, eh?" He laughed. "I just finished reading that, by the way. So, one cup for you, Val, and one for me."

Abby watched them from the corner of her eye as her uncle gave a rapid shake of his head toward her aunt and then mouthed something to her.

Uncle Will clapped his hands and tap-danced his feet under the table. "Well, well. Eggs for my legs, and bread for my head. Valerie, I'm as hungry as a whatsit."

With his amiable, crazy chatter, Uncle Will diluted the awkwardness at the table. Her father had often remarked that when in top form, William

Bluette was an antidote for whatever ailed you. This morning he sparkled, rolling out one funny story after another.

Aunt Val laughed, tears rolling down her cheeks. "Will, do stop it. Sometimes I think I married a mad boy."

Abby laughed along and helped herself to scrambled eggs and toast.

Then her aunt excused herself from the table, leaving Abby and her uncle to finish breakfast.

"I think I'm around-the-clock addicted to this stuff," Uncle Will said, nursing his umpteenth cup of coffee.

She moved her chair closer. "I've begun student teacher training." She took several deep breaths before plunging into her proposal. "I'd like to teach during the summer months. Jim thinks there might be a need among your staff's children."

Uncle Will's eyes widened. "What a brilliant idea." He slapped the table in his customary reaction when pleased. "You've heard me complain about our schools not doing an adequate job. Additional help would be welcomed by any parent working for me." He grinned. "Besides, it would be more experience for you."

Not expecting him to accede so readily, she grabbed his arm. "Thank you." She smiled. "Is the vacant gardener's cottage available?"

"Ah, I see you've been thinking on this." He glanced at the ceiling, as though consulting a schedule. "When the weather warms, Jim can help you set up furniture in one of the larger rooms there."

Abby squirmed in her seat, debating whether to tell him about her aunt's threat. "He's much too occupied to help me."

"Nonsense. He and Emil can teach the children about flowers and plants as well."

"But Jim's so busy with the grounds in the spring."

With a stroke of his hand, he waved her protest away. "Jim's our best candidate. And he can start the kids on a vegetable garden." Uncle Will's face beamed as he rubbed his hands together in delight.

The thought of Jim being sent away by her aunt sent a shiver up her spine. "His mother will need him at home," Abby said, in a last attempt to dissuade him.

"Still, I'm sure Jim will be available to help and more than willing."

Yes, but Jim's willingness was the problem.

CHAPTER NINE

Late Spring 1941

Abby's heart leapt as children's laughter rang through the trees outside her classroom. She was doing something useful at last. As promised, Uncle Will had converted a room in the cottage and used his influence on the school board to acquire a miscellany of secondhand textbooks, desks, and chairs. She opened the door as Jim pulled up towing a trailer piled high with more furniture. Did he think of her as often as she did of him?

Throughout the winter, there'd been less need of Jim's services. She'd chanced upon him intermittently when he was shinnying up a tree to lop off ice-covered "widow makers," as he called them, or laying mulch in early spring. Only a few words here and there passed between them in all that time.

While Jim carried desks and chairs in various styles and conditions into the room, Abby barked instructions. "Put that desk over there, please. Place a chair beside my desk. No. The other side. A stool in this corner. And the bookcase against that wall," she said, her hands on her hips.

Jim removed his hat and ran the sleeve of his shirt across his forehead. "A slave driver, you are."

She laughed, relishing the excitement of being with him. No more concealment.

Later in the afternoon when the children had gone, Jim came up to where Abby stood in the doorway and propped himself against the porch handrail, one foot on the bottom step. "Is that all, boss?"

She turned around to survey the room. "Looks like it. Thank you."

Jim twisted his hat in his hand. "Perhaps Sis could help out."

"That's a wonderful suggestion. Ask her to come around in a week."

Jim pushed back his hair and angled his hat on his head. "Carol might be a bit sassy and a flibbertigibbet but try to ignore that. She's really a nifty kid."

As Jim whirled around to leave, Abby called after him. "Thanks again for your suggestion about my tutoring and for everything you've done today."

He headed back, kicking a stone in his path.

Her heart raced at breakneck speed. "You've been very helpful." Her cheeks grew warm. "It's changed things for me."

"Glad to hear it." A sheepish grin spread across his face. "See you later."

Jim walked to the red tractor, his stride confident but not swaggering. He mounted and coaxed the machine into life. As the gear bit, the tractor jerked forward with a tinny rattle, its jagged outline silhouetted against the blue of the cloudless sky, vapor billowing from the tall exhaust pipe. Abby lingered in the doorway, gazing at the blank smoky space left behind.

Aunt Val stood at the French doors, neck craned in an attempt to see what was happening. Had Uncle taken care of her aunt's objections to Jim? Or was she waiting for the right time to pounce? Abby checked her suspicion and lifted her face to the clear blue sky. *Thank you, Lord.*

Hearing a loud crash from behind, she jumped. The heavy slate blackboard had fallen and shards littered the polished wood floor. She made a mental note to tell Jim. Another reason to see him again tomorrow. The school project had forced them together. What might this lead to?

"So why would you wanna spend your whole summer with these kids?" Carol shot the question out like an accusation.

Abby wiped the replaced blackboard and set the cloth down in the tray. She turned to face Jim's sister who stood in the doorway, hands on her hips. "I want to help them learn to read and write."

"Huh." Carol shrugged, her mouth full of chewing gum. "I'm only here because my fuddy-duddy brother ordered me." She blew a raspberry. "Jimmy says I've got to stay away from trouble while school's out and our mom's at work."

"He's right."

"But when I'm sixteen, I'll decide for myself." Carol marched between the rows of desks to where Abby stood. "I'm quitting school like my sister Sally did."

Abby winced. Snapping off a length of chalk, she turned to the blackboard. "What Is Wrong With School?" she scraped out in large letters, underlining them with a flourish. Then replacing the chalk in the tray, she dusted her hands together and swung around to face the girl.

Carol rammed her hands into the pockets of her dungarees. "Huh. My brother talks about you all the time." She heaved gum from one cheek to the other and rolled her eyes. "He told me you were rather bossy."

"I asked about the school," Abby persisted, gesturing to the blackboard.

Carol flopped down in a seat. She placed her elbow on the desk and propped her head against one arm, doodling with her finger across the damaged top. "I don't like to be called on in class, that's why. I get scared and then I can't speak." Baring her teeth, she removed the chewing gum and pressed it under the rim of the desk.

Abby raised her eyebrows. Jim's prediction was right. But despite the girl's bluster, she liked her.

"But Mom says I'm good at keeping house." Carol leaned forward. "She taught me to sew. I can make a few things myself, but they ain't as nice as the other girls' clothes."

"I know how you feel." Abby squeezed herself into one of the desks opposite. "When my family moved to England, I was only fourteen. I didn't want to go to a new school. In fact, I got a stammer, and the other kids made fun of me. I decided to run off." Seeing she had Carol's attention, Abby paused for effect. "But I didn't know my way around the country, so that was that."

Carol laughed.

"Anyway, my parents got help for me, and I stuck at my books. But that isn't all. I want to be a good teacher, so I need to go further with my studies."

"That's all right for you," Carol said, the harsh edge returning. "My family's poor. And if it wasn't for my big brother living at home and helping Mom with expenses, we probably wouldn't have a house." She leaned back in the seat and sighed. "But I suppose all that'll change when he gets married."

Jim's getting married. Carol's announcement hung in the air as Abby fought to quiet the turmoil inside, her heart pounding. The last bit of hope she'd been nurturing had been snuffed out.

Carol rambled on. "I couldn't go to college even if I wanted to, and you talk better than me." She sighed. "My Engulish is sooo bad." Then she laughed at her own wit.

Still struggling to remain calm while working through her muddled thoughts, Abby took refuge in the flow of Carol's words, only half listening. *Why, Lord, did you bring Jim into my life only to take him out of it?*

Scrambling for an excuse to end their meeting, she placed a trembling hand on Carol's arm. "Come over Saturday morning when we can spend more time together."

Sitting alone at the cramped little desk, her eyes darted around the room. Had she deluded herself in thinking Jim cared for her? Or had he become discouraged waiting for her to come around?

Sitting in her uncle's study—its ranks of books and blueprints towering to the ceiling like a fortress—Abby found a haven to flee to when disappointments arose. Her uncle was a godsend. He, too, stood as a fortress when her confidence disappeared.

Uncle Will swiveled around in his chair and faced her. "The parents have expressed appreciation for the added help we are providing. Your suggestion to supply a hot meal and get part-time help was brilliant. None of this would've happened without your willingness."

"Thank you for telling me." She sorely needed to hear those encouraging words today. She smiled. "But first and foremost, credit goes to you. And I can't forget all of Jim's work."

He chuckled. "Jim's sister and your friend Ginny seem to get along well."

"Ginny's a capable teacher. Carol's learning fast and a big help to her and in the kitchen as well."

"Speaking of Jim, he tells me he's putting together a baseball team. Why don't you join up with him?" Uncle Will said, puffing on his pipe. "It'll do you good to get out."

She half laughed at his suggestion that she might "join up" with Jim. Two strikes against that now—her aunt's assault on their friendship and Carol's announcement that Jim was getting married.

"I don't think Aunt Val would want—"

"Your aunt isn't always the easiest to get on with, but she wants only what's best for you. Sometimes worry gets the best of her and brings out the worst of her."

"But she—"

"I know." The smile on his face faded, and he leaned forward in his seat. "There were her threats to let Jim go."

Startled, Abby shot him a surprised look.

"Yes, I do know about that. It slipped out when your aunt and I were having a heated discussion." He gave a soft chuckle. "A bit of a barney, as your father would say. Anyway, I gave her my opinion on that score." Moving closer, he touched her arm. "Are you troubled about something else today?"

Abby caught the concern in her uncle's voice. He seemed to be reading her mind.

"Out with it," he prompted.

She swallowed hard, uncertain how to answer.

He cocked his head. "Have you lost your voice?"

"Carol told me that Jim's getting married," she blurted.

"Is that so?"

"She sa-sa-said when he gets married things would be different for them at home."

"And you thought .... But that doesn't necessarily imply Jim has a *chérie*, does it? To the best of my knowledge, he hasn't. Anyway, not yet," he said, humor lurking behind his blue eyes. "But I expect someone will snatch him up soon."

She straightened and fixed her gaze on his face. His words hung in the air, the hopeful tone in his voice unmistakable. His cleverness was matched by his wisdom. Could he be right? But how was she to know?

CHAPTER TEN

Jim resumed clearing brush during the early morning hours to avoid the sun. By eleven, the air crackled with heat, and he quit. He did a tour of inspection around the swimming pool, then dived in to cool off. He covered several steady laps, oblivious to everything but the rhythm of his stroke.

He wanted to give his work the time and attention it deserved. God knows, he didn't merit all the blessings that had come to him since he started working here. But no matter how hard he tried to concentrate on other things, the compass needle of his mind swung round to Abby. She was the dream he fell asleep to each night. And she'd turned Carol around. Perhaps she was also instrumental in his helping to set up the school. Was this feeling for Abby merely an infatuation, or was he in love with her?

What would it be like to be married? His parents' relationship offered him no guide. He cringed when he recalled their constant bickering and his father's dalliances with the local women. After his dad left, his mother put her heart and soul into raising him and his sisters. In time she began to flourish. He couldn't tell Abby all this. But suppose she found out from somebody else? He pushed the notion from his mind.

Jim saw something to aim for in the marriage of the Bluettes. They loved each other. Of course, he wasn't blind. He guessed that Valerie Bluette could be difficult. Abby had hinted as much on occasion, though she offered him no details. If only he could have a marriage like that. Still, he wouldn't get his hopes up—yet.

Jim corkscrewed to the side of the pool, rested his elbows on the ledge, and looked out. His breath caught in his throat. Abby reclined in a chaise lounge under the shade of a tree. Beside her stood a card table, teetering with books stacked at crazy angles. How had he missed seeing her there?

She removed her trademark floppy hat with the wide brim and shook her hair free, framing her heart-shaped face in an angelic portrait.

What a beauty. He followed up his observation with a low through-the-teeth whistle, then grabbed a towel from a nearby chair.

He ambled over, affecting his best casual manner. "Been here long?" he called out.

Abby dipped her sunglasses and waved in his direction. "Long enough to see you jump into the pool."

Jim came within ten feet of her—so close he caught the scent of the fragrance she wore—his heart hammering against his ribs. "Do you swim? It's a good way to cool off on days like these," he said, resisting the urge to come closer.

"I never learned, but I've wanted to."

He folded his arms across his chest. "I can show you. One never knows, it might come in handy."

"Just as long as you don't let me drown."

Jim threw back his head and laughed. "Of course not. Besides, I'm a lifeguard."

"Then I accept your offer."

Under the spell of her beguiling smile, he diverted his thoughts in time to maintain control. "Let me know when I can start giving you lessons," he said, focusing on the dimples in her cheeks. He mustn't rush her and risk scotching everything.

Abby pointed over his shoulder toward the rows of flowers that ringed the pool. "You planted those?"

"A few weeks ago. And I've a mind to plant poppies, snapdragons, pinks, and a few other varieties." His arm described a wide arc. "Over that way, I'm clearing the meadow. That will give a balance of hues across the area."

Abby shifted in her seat. "Perhaps we could work on it together?"

He locked eyes with her and grinned. "As before, in the greenhouse?"

A book tumbled off Abby's lap onto the grass. Jim knelt, picked up and handed the runaway book to her, his fingers brushing against hers. He remained on his knees, his chest thumping.

Abby held his gaze. "As before."

He took a deep breath. Was this just another one of those beautiful dreams? "Let's start with the swimming lessons."

To escape the stifling afternoon heat, Abby retreated to the screened porch. A drizzle changed to a steady downpour, clattering against the corrugated tin roof above. Reaching into her pocket, she took out an envelope with her brother's return address. She unfolded the letter, leaning into the feeble light to read.

Her gaze fell on the second paragraph, the words leaping out. "Simon. North Africa. Missing in action." The blood drained from her face as the paper slipped through her fingers, glided under the table, and landed face up on the soggy planks. Rivulets of ink trickled across the page and converged in a black smudge. Trees whipped into a crazy dance by the howling wind as if they too were angry at this terrible news. Tears slithered down her cheeks.

She loved Simon for the nobility of his character that made him want to do the right thing. She loved him for his cleverness with music. And she loved him for his zany sense of humor, how he made her laugh in spite of herself. She loved Simon for all these things. But not as a woman loves a man.

The heavy rain pelted against the screen mesh, lashing her face. Slumping back against the wet cedar bench, she pressed her eyes tight and conjured up the image of their last water-soaked rendezvous in Kensington Gardens. The hurt on Simon's face when she told him she must go away. She had other memories too. She had the piece of music he wrote for her. Would he be found? Would she ever be able to tell him how much their friendship meant?

Convinced the war would catch up with her wherever she might be—like some malign pursuer—she raged at the disruption and the sheer cruelty of it all. "How many men will go missing or die before this war is over?" Abby wrote to Amelia. Only after she'd mailed the letter did she regret writing this. Hardly what her sister wanted to hear, considering that her husband and their own brother were in the thick of the fight and facing death daily.

When Abby returned to college in September as a senior, the mood on campus was tense. A voluntary military program was in place where men drilled with a professor who was an Army reserve officer. Two seniors had left to enter the University of the Air to receive their degree from one of the Navy's advanced colleges and become flying officers. Other classmates had enlisted in anticipation of being drafted.

She signed up for noncredit defense courses. Saturday mornings, Abby tutored elementary pupils as a volunteer in the campus defense council's Education for Democracy Program.

Through late autumn, Indian summer weather prevailed. On a day when the heat was palpable, Abby sat studying on the porch. She looked up to find Jim standing in front of her, hands thrust into the back pockets of his jeans.

He plonked down beside her. "You were so engrossed in that book." He snatched it from her and glanced at the title. "You're on the same one, slowpoke."

Abby reached out her hand, wiggling her fingers. "The other one was called *Principles of Secondary Education*. Give it back."

He looked at the book's spine again. "I don't suppose you could tear yourself away from *Principles of Curriculum Construction* to go over to the conservatory?" Jim handed it over. "You've not been there for two weeks. The mums are out, and"—he opened and closed his mouth and goggled his eyes—"I've added more goldfish."

She sprang to her feet and slapped him on the shoulder, laughing. "All right. Lead on."

Jim set off down the steps, Abby falling in beside him. She pointed to the harmonica that poked from his shirt pocket. "Can you play that thing?"

"I'm a real Larry Adler." Jim chuckled. "What would you like to hear?"

"'The White Cliffs of Dover.' Do you know it?" she said, surprised by her own enthusiasm.

He ran up and down the scales of the instrument to set the key, then launched into the tune. Unable to resist, she picked up on the lyrics, but when she got to "the valley," her voice snagged, and she went quiet. Jim stopped, smiled, then continued playing.

He eased open the tall glass door of the conservatory and stepped back. The *swoosh* of mingled scents caught her by surprise, transporting her to scenes of Kensington and leisurely walks on a Sunday afternoon.

Jim's hand folded over hers, as if it belonged there. Now and then she'd pass a plant of interest and pull Jim back to admire it with her. A thousand butterflies flitted in her stomach. Her affections for this man went far deeper than she had expected. With her feelings past the point of no return, she harbored no intention of questioning the magic of this hour here with him. But did he feel the same way?

Their circuit along the paths seemed to be endless. He was retracing their steps to draw out the visit, but she was glad. She wanted this thrill to last forever. He stopped before a large, elaborate copper fountain, ancient and weathered with the patina of years. Water bubbled up from the mouth of a fish poised at the top of a waterfall and trickled over happy nymphs cavorting among the intricate hammered-out foliage. The cascade foamed and sparkled in the sunlight shafting down from the skylights high above.

Nickels, dimes, and pennies blanketed the floor of the shallow bowl. From his pocket Jim produced a coin and pressed it into her palm, closing her fingers over it. "Make a wish," he whispered.

When his shoulder pressed against hers, a sweet electric sensation ran through her body.

"Go on."

She closed her eyes, then opened them before flicking the coin toward the basin. The nickel hit the rim, spun, and bounced in with a satisfactory *plop.*

Jim raised her hand to his lips and kissed it. "Tell me your wish."

"Some other time." No chance she would risk her wish not coming true.

December 7, 1941

After attending church with her aunt and uncle, Abby parked the car, ran into the house and raced upstairs. She would meet Jim on the river bridge for a walk, then they'd attend the concert in the park. Perfect weather for a perfect Sunday.

She switched on the radio and sat at the vanity dressing table, half listening. Even before that mad dash a few minutes ago, she was breathless. Tugging at the snags in her long hair, she replayed that enchanted scene in the conservatory, unable to take in fully the rapid turn of events. First, she was friendly with Jim, then forced to be aloof, then more than friends, and—who knew what next? She still couldn't believe it.

At the full-length mirror on the door, she turned sideways. "Best I can do," she said out loud, before glancing at the clock. It would take ten minutes to reach the bridge.

Dropping on all fours, she rummaged beneath the bed for her walking shoes.

The symphonic music stopped, followed by a burst of staccato speech. Cocking her ear, she caught one sentence. "The Empire of Japan has attacked the US naval base at Pearl Harbor." One was enough. Her spine stiffened and she sucked in her breath. *War is here.*

In her stocking feet, she ran down the hall to her uncle's office.

He sat at his desk, head resting in his hands.

She tapped on the door, trembling.

He looked up. "You heard, then?" He sighed. "I suppose we shouldn't be surprised. All the signs were there. Still—"

She dropped into the chair beside him. "Does this mean America will go to war?"

He stared out the window. "Nothing short of it."

"Where is Pearl Harbor?"

He eased himself out of his seat, shuffled to a large world map mounted on the wall and peered at it through a magnifying glass. "Right here."

Abby went over to where he stood.

"See? Hawaii," he said, stepping aside for her. "A big naval facility."

Abby turned away. "Do you think Aunt heard?"

"I'll go and break the news to her myself." Uncle Will put his arm around Abby's shoulder, and they walked across the room.

At the door he stopped and half-turned, his voice quivering. "I'm sorry for all you young people. I think our generation has let you down." He shook his head. "The sins of the fathers are visited upon the children once more."

Taken aback and unable to think of anything to say, she watched him disappear down the hallway.

She whirled around and caught sight of her parents in the photograph her uncle kept on his desk. It was an old one, early 1920s, taken when their own bitter memories of the Great War were probably still fresh. Now she would be a comrade with them in their present suffering. But even this meager consolation yielded to a fear closer at hand. What would all this mean for Jim?

CHAPTER ELEVEN

"I have in past years spoken about the blessings of this season and how we may count on God's grace for the coming year," William said, addressing the staff assembled in the great hall five days before Christmas. "That's still true, but it's evident that this Christmas is different."

A log fire roared up into the wide stone chimney. Abby turned to Jim and whispered, "I'm worried for Uncle. He looks so tired."

Jim leaned into her shoulder and squeezed her hand.

William knocked out his pipe against the mantelpiece. "Things will go on being different for some time to come." He reached out to Valerie, drawing her to him. "We've entered an historic phase in the course of our beloved country with far-reaching effects. I expect some form of rationing will be brought in." Will cleared his throat before continuing. "Things may get tight around here. Jolie Fontaine has the resources to keep going, but we may have to trim our cloth." He raised his hand, as if to forestall comments. "But I don't intend to let anyone go. Some of you may be called up or choose to enlist. However things turn out, I want you to know my wife and I appreciate your loyal service." He paused then chuckled. "Speech over. Let's eat and get on with the celebration."

After the festivities in the house were over, Jim and Abby drove to a nearby lake. He arranged wood over a bed of stones and started a fire.

"Thankfully, the surface is solid for skating," Abby said, inhaling the scent of smoke that hung on the breeze.

Dressed in a red skating outfit and white fur hat, she propped herself against an oak tree, while he helped her on with a pair of white skates. They glided across the ice, taking the occasional tumble.

Returning to the fire to warm up, Abby studied Jim's profile in the flickering light as he stared into the distance. *Something's on his mind.*

He turned toward her, then looked away. "I've been called up," he said before clearing his throat. "If I pass the examination, I'll leave soon after."

She struggled for some intelligent response. "I ... I guess we knew it was bound to happen," she said, preparing herself for an adjustment in the mood of the evening.

The fire flared up and sparks shot into the night air. "I need to be at the induction center early in January."

"Early January, but that's only a few weeks away." she said, tears stinging her eyelids.

Jim jumped to his feet, snapped a branch in two and crouched by the fire.

"You will wait for me?" he said, poised for her response.

Large fluffy snowflakes drifted down as Christmas lights from nearby houses flickered through swaying branches. She had tried to picture what form his proposal might take—though she'd expected something less oblique. But this was so natural, so like Jim.

"Maybe I shouldn't ask." He came and sat beside her, eyes lowered. "What right have I to suppose you would want to marry me," he said, his voice soft and pleading.

It was all she could do to maintain her composure as her heart thudded away and her mind whirled. She didn't doubt that she loved him ... but. Again, she tried to say something, but her throat swelled with questions. The snow fell faster. Putting her arm around his shoulder, she traced a gloved finger down the side of his face. "I can't give you my answer now. Give me a little time?"

He looked up and gazed into her eyes. "As much as you need," he said, taking her hand.

Jim yanked the truck around the corner and down the narrow road toward home, elated one minute and the next feeling sorry for himself. The few hours with Abby this afternoon had been unsatisfactory. How vulnerable she looked when he broke the wretched news to her. The present uncertainty became unbearable. He was off to war and might never come back. Perhaps she was afraid of getting too close to him.

The snow fell in clods, and weak headlamps and arthritic wipers offered little assistance. The eerie light ahead of him yielded to blackness within a few yards, and he lowered his speed. Caught in a slow-motion ballet—the muffled drumming of tires on stone and the tinkling of pebbles thrown up against the fender—he drove on. Suspended in this unreality, he lost track of time. Was he awake or dreaming?

The distance was less than two miles. Tonight, the journey seemed interminable, a cramped and endless conduit that began and ended at nothing, with misery in between. Dull thumps on the roof and hood accompanied his progress, as clumps of snow descended from the tall pine trees along the route. Who was he that she should want him anyway? His missed opportunities and reflections on his incompetence haunted him down the road. Old fears gave birth to new ones, casting shadows over an unsteady future, so close he could almost touch them. On more than one occasion, his distractions threatened to send him careening into the deep gully that ran alongside.

Jim scouted the space in front of the vehicle. The dark outline of his house lumbered into view. Extinguishing the headlights and the motor, he coasted up to the side and pulled on the handbrake. He burrowed deep into his thick jacket, his gloved fingers wrapped tight around the steering wheel. If only he and Abby had more time.

The United States was at war with Japan, and the possibility existed the enemy might strike the mainland. He had to do something. Employment at Jolie Fontaine was not classed as essential war work. That would've been his first choice so to be near Abby.

Although he didn't consider himself a dyed-in-the-wool patriot, he never questioned he'd be ready to serve his country should the time come. That is, until he got the yellow telegram this morning with its "invitation" which he promptly stuffed into his shirt pocket to hide the missive from his mother. Jim tore off his gloves and flattened the notice against the dashboard. He struck a match and squinted at the words. The officious tone of the summons hadn't improved in the interim, and in this sulfurous glow, seemed even more menacing. The match burnt down and out, leaving him in the dark. *The timing is all wrong.* He punched the dashboard, recoiling as his knuckles made contact with hard steel. If the army could only know what sending him away meant. Should he just ignore the telegram? How would anyone know? They can't follow up on millions of men. He would marry Abby—*if she wants me*—and they would run away together. Mexico or South America.

Jim heaved open the cab door and clambered out. "No, that's not good," he muttered, trudging through the snow. He knew that as much as Abby did not want him to go, she wouldn't want him to stay on dishonorable terms. He tugged his collar up around his neck then touched the small box in his jacket pocket. That's what he loved about her. He was eager to please a woman with integrity, to be esteemed worthy by such a one steeped in reality. So, he would do his duty and go anywhere, any distance, ten times over, if it meant when he returned, she'd be waiting for him.

Abby watched the falling snow outside her bedroom window. The radio forecast a blizzard. Would Jim get home safely? She tried to conjure up an image of what being his wife would be like, to feel Jim's arms around her, to give herself to him, to bear his children. She pictured their romantic interludes as if on a screen, remembering how in the cinema Jim would reach out his hand and squeeze hers three times, in an "I-love-you" pledge to the future. But even in films, the future was occasionally bleak.

She returned to the timing of Jim's proposal. He'd be leaving in a few short weeks, and she wouldn't see him for months. She could easily pretend he'd be safe. The loss of Simon tore at her every day. To wait for Jim was one thing. But did she love him enough to marry him before he went away and then lose him? She'd already given him so much of her heart. *You know that, Lord.* She couldn't bear it if she gave him this last piece, and he never came back to her. Or if he survived, he might be injured or crippled. Did she possess the fortitude to face that possibility? She dropped to her knees beside the bed.

The next morning Abby tried to telephone Jim, but the line was down. By mid-morning the temperature hit the thirties, and the air buzzed with the noise of chain saws and shouts of cable riggers engaged in repairs. Thanks to her uncle's foresight in fitting two large generators at the back of the house, the electricity functioned without interruption. And so long as supplies of heating oil were adequate, the place would stay warm. She shuddered to think of Uncle Will suffering in the cold. His health had improved a little over the past few months. Still, he appeared noticeably weaker than when she arrived.

By the third day, she got through to Jim. When he drove up, she ran to meet him before he got out of the truck and jumped in. "I've missed you so much."

He drove a few miles down the road before pulling off into a clearing. Snow covered the landscape with its thick, icy down that sparkled in the mid-morning sun. Squirrels hopped from one barren branch to another. Jim sat staring straight ahead, his fingers gripping the wheel.

Hearing the low call from a flock of snow geese, Abby looked up to see them glide under a clear blue sky. How foolish she'd been to think she could keep herself from falling too deeply in love because of fear of the unknown. She turned to him. "So, which is it? Are you asking me to wait and marry you later … or to marry you first and then wait?" she said, touching his shoulder.

He sucked in his breath. His eyes darted to hers, and a smile flickered across his lips. "Well, I—"

Without hesitation, she removed a glove and ran her fingers down the back of his hand. "The only future I want is the one with you in it. I love you."

Releasing his grip on the wheel, he leaned over to kiss her, catching the horn with his elbow. Then he hit the horn again, three times, in celebration. She joined in his laughter. Jim swept off her hat and drew her to his chest. "I don't know what to say," he murmured, stroking her hair. "I dared to hope, but—"

Abby threw her arms around Jim's neck and looked deep into his eyes. "Then stop talking." Jim tilted her chin up. Abby closed her eyes.

Jim flipped open the lid of a small blue box. "I never want to take you for granted but cherish you always, darling." He took her hand, slipped a white gold band with beaded edges on her finger and kissed her again. "I love you," he said, a gleam in his eyes.

Abby held out her hand to admire his ring. "It's perfect."

"Has your wish come true?" Jim said, drawing her close.

Abby laughed, happy tears flowed down her cheeks. This was a moment to cherish all her life.

His lips grazed her forehead. "I think it's only right we tell your parents."

"I don't hold out much hope they will give their approval." She sank back in the seat and sketched her mother's attitude about marriage. "It makes sense to try and first win my aunt and uncle," she said, attempting to forge a plan and still apply a steady hand. "Perhaps if we can win them over, we can win my parents." If only she could herald their news from the house tops.

As though struck by inspiration, Jim raised his forefinger in the air. "Wouldn't it be swell to get married in England?" He tucked a stray curl behind her ear. "When this is all over."

Abby touched his face, unable to contain her joy. "Oh, yes. And in the same church as Amelia. But wherever it is, just as long as I have you," she said, confident that since a raging war brought them together, nothing could ever keep them apart for long.

"*Bon.* Splendid," Uncle Will said when Abby broke the news to him on Christmas Eve. "I would have been disappointed in that lad, mind you, if he let you get away. And the converse, I might add."

"Jim and I wanted you to know before anyone else," she said, her heart surging with joy.

He placed his arms around her. "I'm so happy for both of you. Such a wonderful Christmas gift." He chuckled. "Where's the ring?"

"We agreed not to make an announcement yet."

"And your aunt?"

Abby fidgeted. "I wasn't going to tell Aunt. At least, not yet."

"It's up to you and Jim, but your aunt does love you." He furrowed his brow. "You'd be asking me to keep a secret from my own wife. I know I wouldn't like it very much if she kept a secret from me." A faint smile crossed his lips. "You'll understand that when you're married."

She lowered her head. She hoped she and Jim could duplicate their strong, loving marriage. "I don't think—"

Uncle Will put up his hand to stop her. "You and she got off to a bad start. Put that behind you and forget it. Your aunt had some hard experiences when she was young, and she's learned to be rather defensive. And suspicious."

His revelation took her aback. "Suspicious?"

Uncle Will dropped his voice. "We don't need to explore that. Just take it from me that things aren't as dark as they might appear. They never are. Be patient. Give her time."

"I will," Abby said, counting herself blessed to have Uncle Will in her life. She hoped such insight and compassion would rub off on her.

"So, Jim is going away soon?"

"He will be leaving in two weeks for training," she said, her newfound joy slipping away.

Uncle Will patted her hand. "It'll be easier for Jim if he knows you stand behind him and are waiting for him when he returns."

CHAPTER TWELVE

Weston State Teachers College
January 1942

Abby inched forward in the snow toward a gray stone building. An icy-cold wind lashed her face, and she drew the collar of her heavy coat around her neck. The first day back to classes in five weeks. Four months to go before she'd be a state-qualified teacher.

She could pinch herself this morning. So much had happened during the Christmas recess—war had been declared, she'd become engaged to Jim, and then he'd left for boot camp.

She shielded her eyes from the large falling flakes. Her friend Ginny trudged toward her in black rubber boots. Together they climbed the steps to the main entrance and went through a heavy oak door with beveled glass at its center.

A broad grin erupted across Ginny's face. "Good morning, newly engaged woman," she said, poking Abby with her elbow.

"Shush. Not so loud." Ginny was the only one, other than Uncle Will, she'd told when last week they went to see Frances Langford in *All-American Co-Ed*. Her engagement still seemed unreal.

In the main hall, Ginny removed her coat and fur hat, then shook out her long, brown hair. "You got the letter from the Dean saying we're to assemble first thing for an address?" She rubbed her hands before a fire burning brightly in the corner fireplace.

Abby shook the snow off her scarf. "Starting in a few minutes."

At the bottom of a winding staircase stood a long table marked "Civil Defense," stacked high with pamphlets and booklets with such titles as "Handbook for Air Raid Wardens," "What to Do in an Air Raid," and others. Abby removed her woolen gloves, recalling the course on civilian defense she'd taken last autumn and what she'd learned about incendiary bombs, air raid drills, and shelters.

Ginny sauntered over, pointing to Abby's hand. "Why don't you put your ring on that bare finger instead of around your neck, all covered up? What's the harm, anyway?"

Abby rummaged through the literature. "Hmm. I've read most of these. But not this one," she said, picking up "What Can I Do: The Citizens' Handbook for War" from the Aircraft Warning Service.

"If I were engaged, everyone would hear about it." Ginny laughed out loud and gave her a playful punch to the shoulder. "Lucky duck."

"It's a good thing we had a civil defense council here before war was declared," Abby said, attempting to divert her friend's attention.

Ginny smiled. "The Youth Division Corps." She tapped a pencil against her front teeth. "And I was on the committee that helped set it up." She grabbed a copy of "Handbook for First Aid." "Here's one I want."

They sat in the front row of the auditorium, the place humming with female conversation. Ginny leaned over and addressed Abby. "There are even fewer men in our graduating class than there were last semester."

Dean Sheridan came to the front and looked out over the audience. Everyone fell quiet. "Ladies and gentlemen. I trust everyone had a good Christmas holiday." He then delved into the reason for the assembly. Abby leaned forward and listened intently. "This war will have an impact on every aspect of student life. Many who were students last semester are serving in the Armed Forces. A question that's being debated is whether college students should be permitted to complete their education before being drafted. The remaining instructors on campus who are not serving their country will be putting in long hours of extra teaching duties. So, remember to let each one know that you appreciate this."

He looked down to where she and Ginny sat. "You are ending your college years in a world very different from that of any previous graduating class. You are beginning your careers when our nation requires your intelligence and your energies during a time of global war." His words directed at her class were a sharp reminder that her life had long ago changed dramatically, and life on campus and elsewhere would continue to change in ways yet unseen.

The dean cleared his throat before continuing. "Your studies come first, but in your free time more of you will have opportunity to take first aid courses, do civilian defense work, and volunteer for many kinds of activities directly related to our war effort here at the school." He walked across the stage floor, reached down, and held up a pamphlet. "This informational bulletin outlines these activities.

"The college has converted one of its buildings on campus into civil defense headquarters to protect students and property in the event of an emergency. Since this school is so close to Philadelphia and the Navy Yard, there's increased fear of an air raid. We want to provide a service to people living in our community. An air raid spotter station has been established on campus under the auspices of the Army. All students who are interested in this aspect of defense work can see Dr. Andrews for more information. So you see, the college and faculty have been very much employed during your recess." He raised his hands. "Thank you, ladies and gentlemen. You're dismissed to your first class of the day." The sound of hushed voices filled the room.

Ginny tugged on Abby's arm. "Will you be volunteering?"

Abby wondered what she could do and still have time to study during the next four busy months. She glanced at the booklet in her hand. "I'll read this from the Aircraft Warning Service before I make up my mind." Her brother daily sacrificed his life protecting the British coastline and flying on raids into France. She needed desperately to feel she was being useful somewhere.

"Plane spotting interests me too," Ginny said. "I've always been fascinated with airplanes and my brother's models. He's going to join the Navy's V-7 Program for Sea and Air. Who knows? Perhaps in time, there'll be a place for women aviators. I'll be one of the first to apply for training."

Abby laughed out loud. "I wouldn't doubt it. My brother said that women pilots are delivering a full range of aircraft from factory to airfields all over Britain. Thanks to them, the Air Transport Auxiliary is keeping the front-line airfields equipped."

Ginny punched her fist in the air. "God bless them one and all."

They walked to the student lounge. Ginny poured a cup of coffee. "About this Friday, have you decided if you're going to the homecoming dance?"

"I wouldn't enjoy myself. Only missing Jim all the more."

"What. No more fun?" Ginny rolled her eyes. "Are you gonna put yourself into a deeper freeze this winter?"

"Good question." Abby finished her tea and left for the first class.

Dr. Andrews taught her class in US History II and Civic Education. Within a week of Abby's signing up as a plane spotter, he approached her. "Miss Stapleton, can you be in Room 107 tomorrow at 3:30? I'll be holding an information session for those who've shown interest in becoming a ground observer."

"Yes, sir. I'll be there." Perhaps now she'd be able to aid in the war effort.

"Be prepared to spend Saturday morning here as well."

"It's encouraging to see volunteers for this important service," Dr. Andrews said, looking around the room the following afternoon. "Now for the logistics. In case you don't already know, our school has set up an observation post in Grey Tower on the far side of Kenny Hall, behind the women's dormitory." He turned to the man seated next to him. "This is Lieutenant Brisco, a staff officer from the local army base. He's here to explain your mission."

A tall man dressed in uniform, a peaked cap under his arm, stepped forward to address them. "First, thank you for your willingness to assist our great nation as a part of the Ground Observer Corps. Each of you will watch the skies for penetration by enemy aircraft. You will be an essential part of air defense, saving our country millions of dollars and freeing up manpower for use on the battlefront.

"As observers, you will be under the authority of Fighter Command of the Army Air Force. Any questions? No?" He shrugged. "Your mission is to track all aircraft within a predetermined area so that the US Army Air Force can have notice of enemy aircraft before substantial damage can be inflicted by bombing or strafing. Be aware that just spotting your aircraft is not enough. Each sighting must be identified as to number and type, single or multiple engine, bomber, fighter, or transport, friendly or enemy, and include direction of travel and approximate altitude, if possible. Questions?"

Ginny looked at Abby as if to say "what did we get ourselves into?"

"When do we start?" someone shouted.

The room erupted in laughter.

"That's the spirit," Lieutenant Brisco said, breaking into a grin. "Good. This post will go on twelve-hour duty, manning the binoculars, starting in two weeks. You're being recruited in pairs and each pair takes a two-hour duty shift."

He held up a book for all to see. "This has photographs and drawings of all known warplanes around the world. Take a copy with you and study every plane in detail over the next few weeks. Commit them to memory. Report to Grey Tower, Room 412, on the top floor, Saturday at 0900 for further instructions."

When Abby, Ginny, and ten other recruits arrived at the Tower, a man introduced himself merely as a "government official." Inside the room was a table on which sat a black telephone, two sets of binoculars, a pad of "flash" message forms, and a book with illustrations to identify different types of aircraft. "Sorry, there are only two chairs." He cupped his hands, blew into them and rubbed them together. "Cold in here, isn't it? Someone should be designated to see you have heat up here."

"I'll see to that," Ginny said.

"Good. I'll get started with the procedures you will follow. You have everything you'll need right here," he said, tapping on the table. "When you, as an observer, hear or see an airplane—*any* airplane—record as much information as can be ascertained about the craft on this flash message form. This includes the number of planes, the model—if it can be determined, number of engines, altitude, whether actually seen or just heard, Observer Post code name, direction, and approximate distance from the OP, and direction the plane is headed. A typical message might read: 3 B-17s, high, seen, Code N, SW, 1, E. That information is immediately telephoned to the tracking center." He picked up the receiver to demonstrate, holding it to his ear, and spinning the dial. "They will answer with 'Army, go ahead please,' and you, the observer, will say, 'flash' and read the message out to them. Then your job's done."

Abby listened and watched his every move. Would she be able to remember everything? "What happens at the other end?" she said.

"At the Army Filter Center, your information is plotted on a big board containing a map of the area. This information is compared with other reports, and the plotted flight path is checked against known Army, Navy, and civilian flights. The officer in charge determines if the flight is friendly or enemy and if the latter, orders a response in fighter planes or anti-aircraft fire." He paused and looked around the small room. "Any questions? None?" He smiled and opened a case. "Each of you gets one of these," he said, handing out blue armbands with embroidered gold wings and a round white Aircraft Warning Service insignia.

Abby linked her arm in Ginny's as they walked away from Grey Tower. "It looks like we've been paired." Hearing the roar of engines overhead, she looked into the clear blue winter sky as a squadron of Curtiss P-40 Warhawks headed out over the Atlantic.

Ginny raised a hand in salute. "I feel nervous. Don't you?"

"And this from a girl who wants to be a flyer."

Abby ran her finger over her armband. She wasn't heroic as Simon or her brother or her parents and sister, under daily threat of invasion. She could do little to help secure peace for the world. But she'd do her best with this chance to serve.

May 1942

Since January, Abby had served as a plane spotter on campus, but that would come to an end when she graduated in two weeks. She needed to weigh her future and make the best of things while Jim was away.

She tracked her uncle to the porch, where he was sitting with papers spread across his lap. "Have you a minute for me?"

He pushed his pages aside and pulled out a chair, motioning her to sit. "What's on your mind?"

"I'll graduate this month, but what then?" She sat back. "Girls in my class have accepted teaching posts, others will be going to Washington to work, and others are getting married and living on base with their husbands." She shrugged her shoulders. "I'm not sure what I ought to be doing. But I want to be useful in the war effort."

"There appears to be no quick end to the conflict, and I've been thinking the same as you." He lit his pipe. "Recently your aunt read to me the First Lady's column in the New York Times."

"'My Day'. I read it sometimes," Abby said, leaning forward.

"Well, the gist of Mrs. Roosevelt's piece was that men have either enlisted or been drafted, and their places in industry have been taken by women. A lot of these women have children who need looking after during long working hours." He puffed on his pipe. "The First Lady sees a tremendous need for properly organized day nurseries." He tapped on the table beside his chair. "This need exists here in our community within many families." He smiled. "I've this idea that I think you may appreciate."

Abby drew her chair closer, her interest piqued.

"My old plant has a government contract to produce steel for army vehicles, tanks, and so on. Demand is up. A lot of the women workers are on three eight-hour shifts and much overtime. I've been thinking about what we can do to help those mothers that are working at defense jobs."

His words struck a chord. "Jim's mother and his older sister work long hours at the shipyard, and Carol takes care of her niece when she gets home from school."

"Do you see what I'm leading up to?"

Abby tilted her head to one side, perplexed.

He chuckled. "Well, this is where I think you come in."

"Me?"

"My point is, would you be willing to organize the staff here to provide care for those youngsters who don't attend school and have no one to look out for them during the day?"

Abby's mouth fell open.

"We could reopen the cottage, but this time as a nursery. And we've lots of room elsewhere too." His eagerness for the project was infectious.

"Go on," she said, aware that if she took this on, she'd have to abandon an earlier plan to teach full time.

"For those children in school during the day and whose mothers work until eight o'clock at night, we'll provide meals and help with their schoolwork. We could convert part of the main house into bedrooms for any children with mothers working the night shift. My nephew, Henri, who's also a lawyer, thinks it's not such a good idea because of liability and all that. But I can bring him around." Her uncle waved his hand, as though brushing off Henri. He sat back, beaming. "Well, what do you think?"

"I don't know what to say. Teaching here during the summer was one thing, but I've never had such responsibility."

"You don't have to give me an answer now." He got up. "Hand me my cane, and let's take a walk." He chuckled. "A picture's worth a thousand words and all that."

At the margin of a big field, he stopped and swept his stick over the scene. "In addition to the nursery, each family will be given their own plot of ground. As soon as the soil can be worked, we'll put in vegetables for our use. I'll have to speak to the local committee about all this first."

Abby smiled. Jim would like this idea. But another concern crossed her mind. "Everyone must be instructed in emergency preparedness, and we will need our own designated air raid shelter."

He turned to face her and grinned. "I was coming to that. And as soon as possible, I expect to do all those things. Also, your aunt is keen to raise funds for war bonds since reading Mrs. R's article." He laughed. "And she's come up with the bright idea of using the ballroom for entertaining the servicemen stationed nearby. Dances, and so on. She'll arrange this with the army base through her own committee contacts."

Uncle Will plunked down on a low wall and looked across the field. "All our intentions may coincide. Singularity of purpose." He eased her down beside him. "I'll see to it that you're compensated for all the work this entails. In short, you'll get everything you need. He reached forward and placed a hand on her shoulder. "You're an answer to my prayers. Mull it over."

"Uncle, thank you for your confidence in me." *Was this the solution to her dilemma?*

CHAPTER THIRTEEN

This had been the longest four months of Abby's life since Jim left for boot camp. In two hours, he'd be returning on furlough to see her graduate and spend ten days with her—just the two of them.

Abby turned up the music on the radio before sitting at her vanity dresser. Butterflies flitted in her stomach as she listened to the latest Frank Sinatra recording while combing her shoulder-length hair. She got into a blue silk dress with a white bow at the neck—his favorite—and completed the outfit with a blue doughnut-shaped hat, letting her hair gather around her shoulders. Lastly, she transferred her engagement ring from a chain around her neck to her finger. She hadn't felt this ecstatic since Christmas when he'd asked her to marry him.

Mid-morning, she got into the Chevy sedan Jim had left for her to use. She picked a shortcut to the railroad station. By the time she parked, his train stood at the platform.

Taking several deep calming breaths, she hurried up the narrow metal steps in her white high heels, almost tripping, and stood there, winded. People crowded the platform and porters wearing crimson caps helped with luggage. They all melted from view when she saw Jim, one foot on his duffel bag, and cap in hand, craning his neck to catch sight of her.

When he did, he bolted across the platform as she rushed to meet him. Running with abandon, she barreled into his outstretched arms, nearly bowling him over. He swung her round and round before drawing her to his chest. She buried herself in his embrace, oblivious to everyone and at a loss for words. She'd been imagining herself once again in his arms. And now here she was. "It's been such a long time," she said, withdrawing her arms from around his neck.

Jim tilted her chin up. She closed her eyes as he leaned down to kiss her. Then he stroked her cheek. "You're gorgeous. I almost forgot how much."

Under his close scrutiny, Abby blushed. She stepped back to inspect his uniform. "Turn around." The insignia on his right shoulder was embossed with a big red numeral 1.

"Dress uniform, I'm afraid." He chuckled. "They never let you forget you're a soldier."

Weeks of Florida sun showed in his heavy tan, emphasizing his white teeth and blue eyes. "More handsome than ever." She ran her fingers through his trimmed hair and grunted. "Must your hair be so short?"

She latched on to his arm. When they reached the parking lot, she stretched up on her toes and kissed him again. "Welcome back, darling. This is the best graduation present I could have had."

The next morning, Jim and Abby strolled the grounds, hand in hand. Jim stopped before a hedge. "I like the way your uncle's had these shrubs carved." He whistled. "Liberty bells and *V*'s. Aha, that one's an eagle—very clever."

Abby laughed. "He wanted to show his patriotism."

Jim gazed into her eyes. "So, you're decided on this new project?"

"I'm looking forward to the challenge. With God's help, of course."

With his little finger, he pushed back a tendril of her hair. "If anyone can do it, you can."

She squeezed his hand. "Uncle keeps reminding me of my tutoring last summer."

Jim hopped up onto the deck of the swimming pool. "You should have a fence installed for the kids' safety," he said, casting a practiced eye over the area.

Abby winced. "I'll warn Uncle about the danger."

They made their way to the lake, arms locked and swinging.

"Mom's making twice as much working on Victory Ships and won't accept money from me. She insists on putting my service pay in an account for our use later."

"That is so generous of her. Please let your mother know I appreciate this."

"I hope you both can get together when I'm away. She's grown very fond of you."

Abby smiled. "I promise to keep in touch with her."

He scooped up a pebble and skimmed it across the water. "Mom's on 'A' rations for gasoline but getting fuel for my old truck's a problem. She's restricted to three gallons a week. I hope they switch her to the 'B' coupon soon. Besides, the truck needs new tires—that might present another problem, with rubber rationed."

Jim plopped onto the grass and pulled Abby down beside him. "My sister complains because she can't get clips and bobby pins, and she'll have to use leg paint instead of stockings, while Mom is concerned about food, gas, and tires."

"Don't be too hard on Carol. She's matured since last summer and graduates soon."

"Sis has come a long way, thanks to you."

Abby tickled his nose with a blade of grass. "She's been an eager beaver working with Ginny, and the kids love her."

In the evening, Abby's aunt and uncle held a dinner dance in her honor. She and Jim danced cheek-to-cheek to the music of a swing band with a vocalist hired for the occasion.

Later, Aunt Val took a seat next to Abby. "You and Jim are getting married, then?" she said, pointing to the ring on Abby's finger.

Abby nodded assent. "We were going to tell you tonight."

"And your parents. Do they know?" Her emphasis on "they" was not lost on Abby, but she let it go.

"Not yet. I would like to be the first to tell them, Aunt. But that might not be for a while."

Valerie looked first at the floor, then into Abby's eyes and smiled. "Well then, two celebrations in one day. Good."

Abby placed an arm around her shoulder and returned her aunt's smile.

The marquee at The Warner movie house announced *Mrs. Miniver*, starring Greer Garson and Walter Pidgeon. Jim pointed to a work crew fitting a trumpet-shaped contraption above a traffic signal. "What are those men doing?" he asked, taking his place at the end of a long line waiting to go inside.

Abby looked up. "They're replacing the air raid siren and possibly the control box."

A woman behind them spoke up. "We were treated to a false alarm when the siren short-circuited last night."

Jim turned to Abby. "How frequent are these air raid drills?"

"I've been in a few. At college, senior air wardens carried flashlights and first-aid kits and directed us all to shelter spots during the exercise."

Jim shook his head. "It's unlikely the Japs will get this far, what with the Civil Air Patrol." He winked. "And your plane spotters."

Abby smiled. "Did I tell you I earned my merit badge?"

Jim drew her close. "Not surprising."

Once inside the movie house, Jim and Abby stood at the back. The house lights dimmed, red curtains swept apart, and the screen lit up with the words "Movietone News." Jim removed his cap and laid his hand over his heart, as a choral group on the screen sang "The Star-Spangled Banner," sing-along lyrics rolling across the bottom of the screen.

An usherette escorted them by flashlight to seats on the aisle. A young lad and his dog appeared on screen, followed by an appeal for patriotic citizens to donate their animals to the defense effort. Then came the usual exhortation to buy war bonds.

When the film began, Jim leaned back in his seat and reached for Abby's hand. She snuggled into the soft velveteen material and rested her head on his shoulder, laughing and crying with the Miniver family as they coped during the Blitz. During one scene, the stationmaster showed Mrs. Miniver the rose he'd cultivated and asked her permission to name it after her. Jim had Abby's promise to let him change her name to his. He turned the ring on her finger and smiled. Someday he'd cultivate a rose, too, and name it after Abby. Maybe enter the bloom into a flower show.

Out on the street, Jim replaced his cap, straightened his tie and gestured toward a passing car. "When did you start blacking out the headlights?"

"Last month. And blackout drills are held frequently in cities as far inland as fifteen miles. We had one at Weston. All the lights were turned off, and we each had an assigned place."

As they walked back to their car, Jim picked up his stride, slowed down, then again speeded up.

"Stop that," she said, pulling on his arm.

"Maybe next time you won't wear those high heels."

She looked up into the starry sky. "The news bulletins say Americans are losing in the Philippines, and the Allies are in retreat in Africa. Suppose the enemy wins?"

"I think we've got the clout to win." He kissed her cheek. "Don't worry, sweetheart. We've not yet seen the full weight of our power combined with the British and their allies, and our heavy industry—like your uncle's, for instance."

From a secluded table nestled inside a pine grove, Abby looked out across the shore to the water. Wispy white clouds scurried across an azure sky. Four more days to spend with her soldier. She spread out a red-and-white checkered cloth.

Jim ambled down to the ocean, where a line of masts and turrets stood out in diminutive relief against the horizon. He turned back to Abby, cupping his hands around his mouth. "Those are ours," he called out.

She went to where he stood, shielding her eyes from the sun. "They must be some sort of defense. Residents along this coast have reported rumbles and thuds in the distance and say they've seen an orange glow on the horizon from explosions."

They headed back to their table, arm in arm. "That explains the precautions along the eastern seaboard," Jim said.

She cast another glance over her shoulder at the convoy. "Rules are strictly enforced here. During a dim-out, drivers have to turn off their headlights when traveling seaward."

"It seems a small price to pay for safety."

Abby nodded. "I remember coming here with my parents as a child," she said, determined with God's help to be cheerful in spite of the looming uncertainties and her nagging fears.

She unfastened the wicker basket and set out their picnic. Sitting astride the bench, Jim twisted the cap off a Coke bottle and took a swig, then ran the back of his hand across his mouth.

Abby slid a glass in front of him.

"Uh-oh." He laughed. "I'm sorry. It's just that living with a bunch of men day in, day out, I forget my manners."

"You're excused, soldier."

He handed her a Coke. "Still, what's to stop German subs from coming closer to our coast, landing, and letting out spies to do their dirty work?" He banged his fist on the table. "I'll bet they've recruited spies here already. Probably right under our noses."

"Do you really think anyone here would work to help our enemy? I couldn't imagine it."

"If I knew anyone like that, I'd—"

"Fried chicken, potato salad, deviled eggs. Would you like mayonnaise on your bread?" she said, in an attempt to change the subject.

After the meal, they waded in the water and strolled barefoot on the beach under a blazing sun. Hearing the roar of aircraft, Abby looked up. "Those are P-47 Thunderbolts."

"I'm impressed, sweetheart." He bent down and kissed her cheek. "We need to leave if we want to get to the Goodman concert."

Abby gathered up the picnic things and stuffed them into the hamper, aware of an even longer separation that would soon come. But for now, she'd make these remaining days memorable for them both.

The train station teemed with soldiers and their sweethearts by the time Jim and Abby arrived. Her heart sank like lead under the weight of all the other goodbyes on the platform.

Jim drew her near. "I can see your aunt's ballroom full of soldiers for one of her events. I'm jealous already."

Abby tightened her grip around his waist. "Can't foresee any competition."

He stroked her cheek. "Just don't let them hear you sing and don't smile too much."

They went over the footbridge to the quieter side of the platform, keeping an ear out for the announcement of departure. She reached into her purse and handed him a small tinted photograph of them on graduation day.

Jim broke the silence. "This is more painful than in January when I left for training."

She nodded, the specter of separation hovering over them threatened to drain away the joy of the past ten days.

The train whistle blew, and she jumped, legs trembling. She'd hoped to be prepared for their parting. But she wasn't. She hated the Japanese for taking Jim away from her.

He snatched up his duffel bag and with his free arm, grasped her hand. As they clattered up the metal steps and along the steel-walled gangway over the tracks, their footsteps echoed. Abby shrank from the cold, hard noise. A cloud of steam rose up and engulfed Jim. She tried to drag him back. He pressed on, pulling her behind him, his head turned away, as if heedless of the silent shriek inside her—*please don't go!*

They stood together beside the train. "I wish you didn't ha-ha-have to go," she said, clasping his hand to the side of her face. Setting his cap straight, she stepped back and flashed a mock salute, determined to be strong for the sake of others here, all brought together by the sorrow of parting—but especially for Jim.

A tight, desperate embrace and a last kiss before Jim hopped onto the bottom rung. The conductor made an inspection of the platform before giving the "All aboard." Abby gripped Jim's arm. Clutching his hand, she ran alongside the rolling train—taking him hundreds of miles away—until she fell behind and had to let go.

The train wiggled out and away from the platform. Long after it had shrunk to a pale silver dot on the blank horizon, Abby stared down the track, hollow inside and unable to will herself away. The crowd dissolved into its melancholy components, and she flowed out with them to the exit.

On her return home, she pulled the drapes across the window before dusk set in, then curled up in a chair, arms wrapped tight around the cushion. Had they made the right decision to wait until after the war to get married? Many of her former classmates were making wedding plans even now. Long after the first owl announced its presence and the chill of night settled in her body, Abby sat there. Not until the egg-yellow light of a new dawn filtered through the window shutters did she fall asleep.

CHAPTER FOURTEEN

Summer 1942

"I've brought something to cool us down." Abby walked into her uncle's study, ice cubes rattling in the glasses she carried as she set a tumbler of lemonade on his desk. Then she collapsed into a chair, fanning her face, as hot as if she'd put her head inside a chimney.

Uncle Will wiped the sweat from his brow. "Oh, for the fair zephyrs of England." He took a long drink then smacked his lips. "That hits the spot. Now then, down to business. We've had a good response to our piece in the *Local*." He handed her a legal-sized notepad. "We'll need to interview the families of these children who have no arrangements for care while mother is working."

Abby scanned the list of names and addresses. "They're well spread out. Should I telephone them or talk with the mothers here or in their homes?"

"Not all have telephones. I suggest you arrange to visit them. It's a bit of a chore but the most effective approach."

"What do you want me to ask them?"

"I'll give you a list of questions."

She looked up. "And about meals?"

"We can handle two meals a day. The household staff has agreed to work two hours more each day and to alternate working Saturdays with Sundays off. If needed, I'll hire more staff."

Abby took a long cold drink. The rattling metal fan perched on a bookcase provided little relief. "Jim's sister wants to work here, at least until the end of the year."

"Splendid." Uncle Will reached across the desk and picked up "Wartime Suggestions." "There's handy advice in here on how to use and maintain refrigerators," he said, passing the booklet to her. He scratched his head. "But I must look into getting another one before their manufacture stops. Our cook says she'll require more refrigerator space. Jot that down."

"I will," she said, scribbling faster to keep up with the flow.

He leaned back in the chair and stoked his pipe. "I'll talk to the ration board about extra food supplies. Fuel oil will probably be rationed this winter. The house must be kept warm for the youngsters." He smiled. "Here's another booklet that provides some guidance," he said, holding up "How to Keep Warm and Save Fuel in Wartime." "Still, it will be necessary to put in for an extra quota of oil from our local board. But these are not your concerns, my dear." He cleared his throat. "And the next time I have an appointment, I'll ask Dr. Ferguson if he is willing to be on call for the children."

"When can we start taking children?"

Uncle Will yanked his tie loose. "By mid-July we should be up and running. The decorators did a good job. Furniture is being delivered soon." He tapped his pencil against the desktop. "I'll have someone come in and put up gates at the top of the stairs. Don't want any accidents."

"There's the pool." Abby said. "Jim says there ought to be a fence around it."

"Ah, Henri did mention that. Glad you reminded me. Jot that down."

"I already have."

"And again, naysayer Henri tells me I should reconsider the whole thing." Uncle Will sighed. "He handles some personal legal matters for me in addition to the estate's. He's telephoned me a few times since he got wind of our plans. Says we need to be licensed and pass inspection for fire safety and food safety and all that. Says the whole thing will be more trouble than it's worth. Henri thinks you're too young and inexperienced to assume the responsibility." He slapped the desk. "What malarkey. I don't put any stock in his views in that regard."

Abby frowned. "But he knows nothing about me."

"I've opened a bank account in your name, along with a line of credit to cover repeat supplies. Now as to the legal rigmarole, Henri may have a point, but I'd like it better if he were looking for a way to make a go of this and not forever throwing up obstacles. Anyway, he'll be over this afternoon for a rare visit." Uncle Will leaned back in his chair. "It's odd, but lately he seems to be off gallivanting in foreign parts."

"Probably why we've never met."

He looked up at the ceiling. "Well, if you had, you would remember him." He laughed. "You would not forget Henri." He stood. "*Excusez-moi.* I'm off for forty winks before nephew Henri gets here. Val's orders." He yanked out a pocket watch then held it up to his ear, giving it a thorough shaking. "Thing's stopped. Must go," he said, a shadow of a smile flitting across his face.

Abby smiled, recalling Aunt Val telling her that she'd bought the antique watch as an anniversary token, that Uncle Will was sentimental about it and carried the timepiece with him everywhere even though the mainspring was broken, and the watch hadn't run for six years.

At the door he turned around. "Nearly forgot. Your aunt said she'd like to see you."

Abby stepped out onto the porch, hot air hitting her face. No rainfall in weeks and oppressive heat cast a pall, making living difficult even during the best of times. And these were not ideal times. Her gaze swept across the grounds, thankful Jim couldn't see the estate in such a sorry condition— the lawn brown and plants and flowers dead.

Her aunt sat under a big yellow umbrella, batting at mosquitoes and licking envelopes. Abby went over to her. "You wanted to see me?"

"I'm sending invitations for a benefit to raise money for defense bonds." She grimaced, waving a hand across her face. "And hoping to get an orchestra to play here, though I think perhaps Tommy Dorsey and Frank Sinatra are too big to aim for." She laughed.

Abby pulled out a chair and sat next to her. "Do you want me to help with those?"

"No, thank you." Aunt Val set her pen down. "But there is something you can do in the musical department." She smiled. "I've been listening to the songs from that new show by Gershwin, *Porgy and Bess.* You know it?"

"I bought some of the sheet music."

Aunt Val leaned back and removed her spectacles. "How about your singing a few selections at the benefit ball next month?"

"I don't know that I'll have the time. Uncle asked me to help organize the school." What had she let herself in for when she volunteered? Her aunt's expression dropped. "But I think I can fit it in," Abby added in haste, not wanting to disappoint her.

Aunt Val brightened. "Good. Who knows, perhaps we can get that English actor fellow, Claude Rains, to come." She laughed. "You know he's moved in, practically next door."

"I must tell Father. Rains is his favorite."

Aunt Val sealed the last envelope. "I've seen many good changes here since you arrived." She fiddled with the stack of invitations. "I admire your courage and the many decisions you've made for yourself," she said, her voice quivering. "I do hope you won't take offense, but I'm as proud of you as if"—Aunt Val reached out and took Abby's hand—"as if you were my own daughter." She held Abby's gaze, her eyes overflowing with tears.

Abby's mouth fell open, and her breath caught in her throat. She bent over and kissed her cheek. "Offended?" Her shoulders fell back, and she let out a deep sigh. "Oh, Aunt. I've been so afraid you were not pleased with me."

"I'm sorry if I made you feel that way." She rubbed Abby's back. "And your Jim. I can see he's a good man."

Abby wiped a hand across her eyes, touched by the warmth in her aunt's voice. "Thank you for your acceptance of Jim. This means so much to me." Placing a hand on her aunt's shoulder, she gestured toward the envelopes. "If you like, I'll take those to the post office after my swim."

On such a hot day, Abby didn't need any persuading to jump into the pool. Jim had made good on his promise to give her lessons. She wasn't a skilled swimmer, but she'd picked up the rudiments and could go from one end of the pool to the other in a semi-respectable fashion.

After a few laps, she dried off and walked to a covered table where she kept a box of stationery and a pen. She couldn't get her aunt's words out of her head nor the sadness in her voice. What could've been the hard experiences Uncle Will spoke of? He'd also told her to be patient and that her aunt loved her. This afternoon she'd seen that love in Aunt Val's face and actions. She'd try to do more to reciprocate.

Abby dashed off a letter to her mother, then lingered over one to Jim. She scooped up the envelopes. If she hurried, she could get them and her aunt's invitations to the post office before five o'clock. Throwing a robe over her swimsuit, she set off for her bedroom.

She reached the house as an expensive-looking convertible squeaked to a stop in the driveway. The driver's door burst open. A tall, broad-shouldered man in a suit and wearing a gray Homburg with briefcase in hand bolted toward the entrance, oblivious to her twenty feet away.

The scene unfolded with such brusque efficiency that Abby was sure the stranger was Henri. And why should she care what he thought about her qualifications? He may have his doubts about the viability of the school, but she had none. Besides, this meant so much to her uncle. Given the state of his health, it might be his last magnanimous gesture. She couldn't let him down.

CHAPTER FIFTEEN

Abby sat in the middle of a group of children, reading aloud a favorite story. She looked up to see Carol at her side. "Jim's on the telephone. I'll fill in here," she said, taking the storybook out of Abby's hands. "He says it's important."

She rose from a stool, her heart beating faster. Jim wrote whenever possible and only called occasionally—but never in the middle of the day. It must be urgent.

When out of sight, she sprinted down the hall, dropping breathless into a wooden chair beside the telephone. "Hello, Jim," she said, pressing the receiver tight to her ear, as if to draw him closer.

"Hello, darling. I had to call. But I haven't got long to talk."

Silence.

"Jim ... Jim?" Leaning forward, she rapped the cradle switch. "Are you there?"

"I'm here. Sorry to call like this," he said, his voice cracking. "They're shipping me out."

She slumped back in the seat. "When?"

"I board a train for New York next week. Then a troopship."

Abby attempted to speak, but a lump rose in her throat.

"Sweetheart, I'm sorry I won't see you before I leave," he said in a subdued voice.

She swallowed hard. "Can't I meet your train s-s-somewhere?"

"I looked into that. There's nowhere." The hopeless tone in his voice was unmistakable.

"Then I'll come to New York."

"No time for that."

Her eyes filled. "No time for us?"

"Besides, there's no more furloughs or passes. Look. It's not all bad. I'll probably get to London. Maybe even see your parents when I get a pass."

Abby sensed he was struggling for words.

"So, that's at least a cheerful bit of news, isn't it?"

"S-S-Some," she said, trying to conceal disappointment in her voice.

"Darling, there's a line of men waiting to use this phone. I'll have to go."

She was losing the battle to stay calm and accepting. "Must you hang up so soon?"

He cleared his throat before speaking again. "I'm not so good at always saying what I feel. Still, you know how much I love you." His voice carried a wealth of emotion. "I'll be back."

"I'll be waiting for you," she said, then mumbled a muted, "goodbye." With a click, their connection was severed.

She replaced the receiver and closed her eyes, her lower lip trembling. She hadn't reacted the right way to his disappointing news. After all, Jim was being sent off. He was the one at risk, not her.

When she got back to the room, Carol and the children were gone. She cleaned the blackboard and tidied up before leaving. Then she strolled to the tower and sat there until the light faded. How much longer would this war go on? Scenes from the latest Pathé newsreel—devoted to the progress of the war—flashed before her eyes. *Please, Lord, keep Jim safe.*

Returning to the house, she found her uncle listening to the president's weekly fireside chat. He pressed a finger to his lips and motioned for her to take a seat. "Nearly done," he mouthed. On occasion, she would join him and her aunt for these broadcasts. Uncle Will proclaimed his liking for Mr. Roosevelt out of patriotism and Aunt Val by way of a fondness for Eleanor.

When the president finished, Uncle Will turned off the radio. "I see that Eisenhower's in England and has command of US Forces in the European theater."

Abby went straight to her complaint. "Jim's being sent to England."

"Oh, dear," he said, leaning back and folding his arms. "This afternoon, his sister hinted something was up." He furrowed his brow. "I know how disappointed you must feel. But look on the bright side," he said, grinning. "Perhaps he'll get to meet your parents."

"Yes, that's what Jim thought." She forced a smile. "It's something to hang on to."

"Let me show you this." Uncle Will went over to the map on the wall that bristled with tacks of different colors. He pointed to one section, motioning for Abby to join him. "Mr. Roosevelt says that because of our navy's victory over the Japanese here at Midway Island, there's been a decisive turn in this phase of the war. This affects everything else to come."

"Surely, this war can't go on much longer," she said, her voice quivering.

He rubbed the back of his neck. "I wouldn't go so far as to say that, yet. Your Jim is off to fight to ensure our freedom. Pray God may help him to do what needs to be done for however long it takes." He placed a hand on her shoulder. "Jim must do what he needs to do, and you must have faith that he will come back to you."

"You always say what I need to hear, Uncle."

Ten days later a letter came from Jim, written on board the *Queen Mary*. Abby dropped into a chair in her room, savoring the thought of opening it. She turned the envelope over, re-read her name, then ripped it open.

Aug. 3, '42

Dearest Abby,

My thinking of you is now a reflex action, and writing is a most pleasant way to put some of those thoughts in tangible form. First, please accept my apology for the abrupt way in which I told you of my deployment.

Must keep this brief but will try to write soon with a forwarding address. The same ocean liner that brought you to America three summers ago is now a troopship taking me back to England. Isn't life strange? This is the first time out of the States for most of us on board. We're trying to see it as an adventure as well. Spirits are high. To pass the time we play poker (with matchsticks).

You have filled my life in a most wonderful way. I cannot properly express my joy. I want to share my thoughts, my life, my being with you. That you accept my love is wonderful. Thank you for letting me love you.

Always yours, Jim

"Always yours, Jim." Abby repeated.

She reached for the engraved wooden box on the dresser in which she stored a miscellany of souvenirs with memories to be cherished a lifetime—a ticket stub from a movie, a concert program, a menu from the restaurant on their first date—all mementos of experiences that had not yet merged into a real life together. She removed the lid and fingered a shell from the seashore where they'd strolled at sunset.

Then she kissed his letter and numbered the envelope before adding it to the other dull gray ones bound with red hair ribbon—all sent when Jim was stationed at boot camp. "Until your next one," she said out loud, slipping the stack back into the drawer. This communication with him was only one end of a slender thread that must tether them across the miles if their love was to stay alive. Letters by themselves weren't much, but she would have to settle for them.

CHAPTER SIXTEEN

Abby's schedule for the nursery fell into shape, transforming Jolie Fontaine into a place filled with squeals and laughter. By mid-summer, she had children from early morning to mid-afternoon. After three o'clock, those of school age arrived and stayed until evening, when their mothers returned from shifts at her uncle's plant or nearby factories. With Carol's help, she devised a routine to care for the youngest ones while assisting older children with homework. She spent hours collating files and cramming notebooks with suggestions for the curriculum. Abby threw her heart into the enterprise, blunting the sharp edge of loneliness that threatened to rush in and fill the vacuum created by Jim's absence.

One morning on her way to the office at the rear of the house, she rounded a corner and collided with someone heading full throttle in her direction. She fell backwards against the wall, winded. He lurched forward. His briefcase skidded across the shiny wood floor, hit a table leg and tumbled open, disgorging its contents.

Abby stared open-mouthed at the comic figure in a dark suit resting on one knee and shaking his head. He looked up and gave the hint of a smile.

She threw back her head, laughing. "You must be Henri."

Her cue seemed to soften his gaffe. "And you must be Abby," he said, clearing his throat. He stood and knocked the dust off his jacket and trousers. "Not an auspicious beginning to our acquaintance, I'm afraid."

Abby advanced toward him, hand outstretched. "It's the most exciting introduction I've ever had."

"If you say so, but—"

She got down on her hands and knees and rummaged under the table for his loose papers.

He bent down beside her. "I'd like to make up for this." He eased himself to his feet. "How about coming with me to the county fête?" he said, helping her up.

"You don't think I'm too young?" She laughed.

"I don't understand."

Abby shrugged her shoulders. "Oh, just something I heard."

"I'll have my daughter, Edythe, with me. She'll make a threesome. Do let me make amends," he pleaded.

"Well—" She handed him his hat. "All right, but it's not necessary."

"Then I'll telephone you about the time." He busied himself arranging documents in his case. "Now, I must see Uncle." He spun around and vaulted up the stairs two at a time and disappeared down the landing.

Abby grinned on recalling their clumsy encounter. Henri was certainly no Gene Kelly, but he was charming in a way. From the chatter among the household staff, she gathered Henri was self-defining and few had a neutral opinion of him. Still, she'd wait and form her own judgment.

Abby stood waiting outside when Henri pulled up in his two-door Cadillac convertible, the top down. Bounding up the steps, he took her arm, pressed a proprietary hand into the small of her back, and led her to the car.

"And this is my Edythe," Henri said, a cigarette dangling from his mouth. "Seven years old last month."

Edythe—dressed in a blue ribbed-cotton pinafore—held a doll and bounced up and down in the back seat.

Henri gunned the engine, raced down the long driveway, and shot out onto the main road.

Edythe squealed. "That was fun, Daddy."

Abby stroked the lacquered dashboard. "A lovely automobile. With a built-in radio too."

"She's no flivver, that's for sure." Henri beamed. "A Sixty-Special. Some say it's not as good as the '40 model, but I don't agree with that assessment." He propped his elbow on the door ledge. "True, it's not quite as sharp-looking, especially with the chrome grayed out. But that's what Washington in its infinite wisdom has decreed."

Abby shot him a quizzical glance, but Henri kept his eyes on the road.

The field that served as the car park for the fair was full. Henri drove through the crowd traipsing over the grass. Halting before a roped-off area—a "Reserved" notice tacked to one of the posts—he honked his horn three times. An attendant scampered from a nearby tent, removed the rope and waved him into the space. Switching off the engine, Henri put up the top and handed the keys to the man. He turned to Abby and whispered, "That's the beauty of knowing the right people at every level."

Abby forced a smile.

He squashed his cigarette in the ashtray. "I hope you and I can become good friends."

Before Henri had time to come around to her side, she was already getting Edythe from the back seat.

Abby on one arm and Edythe on the other, Henri bypassed the queue that snaked endlessly toward the ticket counter and hurried them through a side gate. The knot of attendants lollygagging on the other side stood erect and smiled in his direction.

"How about popcorn, Miss Whatsyourname?"

"Oh, thank you, Daddy."

He reached into his pocket and pressed coins into her palm. "And get one for Auntie Abby too." He turned to Abby. "May I refer to you that way?" he said in a well-oiled voice.

"If you wish—but no popcorn for me."

After Edythe finished her treat, Henri led his daughter straight to the merry-go-round, paying enough to keep her on for a long time.

"Perhaps we can meander and chat as we go?" Without waiting for a response, he linked Abby's arm in his and started off at a brisk pace. In their march around the fairground, Henri regaled her with his own success story. If he didn't stop talking about himself, she'd forget her resolve to not rush into an unfavorable opinion of him. Maybe she shouldn't have come.

Finally, they returned to the rides. Edythe came running toward them, arms flailing. "You were gone so long." Henri crouched, and she ran into his embrace.

"Can we go on that?" Edythe asked, pointing to the Ferris wheel towering above them.

"You too, Abby," Henri said, laughing.

"I'll look around over there instead," she said, gesturing toward the colorful exhibitors' tables, overflowing with quilts, preserves, and baked goods.

Shortly, Henri with Edythe on his shoulders returned to where she waited. "Edythe would like you to take her on a bumper car."

"Let's go," she said, taking the girl's hand. "My favorite."

Edythe skipped along, a red balloon tied to her wrist and a black and white stuffed panda under her arm. "I like you, Auntie Abby."

Abby smiled and squeezed her hand.

Throughout the afternoon, she and Edythe sampled homemade dishes and desserts and they all had a chicken dinner under a large, white tent as a glorious sunset of pink and purple appeared in the west. In the evening, a brass band played John Phillip Sousa favorites. Abby stamped her feet and clapped her hands with the music. Edythe watched, squirming and giggling. When the national anthem started, Henri snatched up his daughter, swung her onto his shoulders, and set off for the parking lot. Abby struggled to keep up with him.

Henri set Edythe down on the rear seat. Abby slipped into the front seat, leaned over, and covered the girl with her jacket. Edythe was fast asleep by the time Henri slipped out of gear and coasted to a stop in front of the house. He eased open the car door for Abby and placed a finger to his lips, motioning toward the sleeping form.

She reached out a hand to shake his. "Thank you for today."

"The pleasure's all mine," he said, lifting her hand to his lips.

She drew in a breath, surprised and flattered at the same time.

"Perhaps we can go out again."

She pulled back and turned to leave.

He got in his car and raised one arm in casual farewell. "Until next time, then. *Adieu.*"

Inside the house, Abby glanced at the letter holder. Empty.

"Did you have a nice time?" Abby followed the sound of the voice to the landing, where her aunt stood, peering over the banister.

"Yes, thank you, especially the concert band. And Edythe seemed to enjoy herself."

"Well, that's good, I suppose. Goodnight." Aunt Val's door clicked shut.

In the bedroom, Abby sat at a vanity table and brushed out her hair. Even if she hadn't had such a good time, Henri's daughter had. And that's more important.

Then her eyes lighted on Jim's photograph. *Oh, Jim, please come back.*

Was she being self absorbed? No doubt about it. Women all over the world were daily in agonies over their men, praying for them to come home. Of course, they couldn't come home. If they did, where would everyone be? And like those millions of others, she wanted peace in the world. "This fight is necessary if oppressed people are to be free," her uncle had said many times.

What would Jim think of her, blubbering like a juvenile with all the work to be done and her uncle depending on her? She wiped her eyes. With God's help she'd stop whining and get on with it.

Henri's Office, later that week

"I'll have your divorce petition filed at the courthouse on Monday, first thing," Henri told the attractive woman in the mink stole and expensive jewelry sitting across from him. Anxious to end this last appointment, he telegraphed his impatience with a rapid drumming of his fingers on the desktop. That failing, Henri rose from his seat and ushered his client to the door.

He returned to his desk and rested his head on his arms. Early on, Henri realized his own decade-long marriage had been a mistake. The last few months had been filled with bitterness and his wife's tantrums. She made her decision—filed for divorce, alleging rigid and controlling behavior including mental and physical abuse.

Claudia had never made a satisfactory adjustment to life in America and an even poorer one to their union. Moaning incessantly about "vulgar" American culture, she maintained her life had been much better in France. "And you have no sense of fashion here," she lamented. Was she aware, Henri had argued without much inner conviction, that vulgar, unfashionable American men risked their lives to free her beloved France? If not for his 4-F deferment he, too, might be engaged in that enterprise. He smiled at the irony of that ridiculous possibility.

He loved his daughter. His marriage to Claudia had been a temporary distraction as far as he was concerned. But Edythe was the result. In the terminology of his legal mind, she was a proxy for his better nature. In loving her, he loved himself. If not for that stupid Frenchwoman, he could have refined his work on Edythe. Claudia would handle the feminine side of things, and he would cultivate the rational, philosophical side of the child's mind, qualities he had always admired in the race from which he was descended. He even taught Edythe to speak and read German. Claudia scuttled the whole thing with her chaotic temperament.

Not the sort to wallow in self-pity, his dark mood passed as quickly as it came on. He adjusted his glasses and surveyed the well-appointed office. Rich mahogany furniture floated on an ocean of polished pine. An elaborate crystal chandelier hung from the ceiling and a large quarry-built fireplace occupied one long wall. Floor-to-ceiling bookshelves towered over the scene. The practice thrived, and his fees reflected that singular fact.

Freed from Claudia, Henri's weekday had become pleasantly routine. Each morning, he departed his house at 6:40, bought a newspaper from the corner stand, boarded the city train, and walked two blocks from the terminus to his office on a redbrick tree-lined avenue. At day's end, Henri would pick up a cold supper at the delicatessen. His solitary repast over, he'd study the legal briefs and read those parts of the *New York Times* he'd missed on the train. But tonight would be different. He would pick up Edythe and take her to see *Bambi*. He smiled. In her, the family resemblance asserted itself. She had his thick, dark hair and eyebrows and Claudia's pale blue eyes. But Edythe had seen far too much unhappiness between them. She'd always been sickly, and Claudia had delegated her care to a nanny. Edythe needed a real mother. Someone like Abby.

CHAPTER SEVENTEEN

This morning, after Uncle Will's examination, the doctor emphasized to Abby and Aunt Val the seriousness of the situation. Then he followed with a litany of instructions on what must be done to aid his recovery.

The unfavorable report only added to her uncle's distress. When they returned home, he went straight to the indoor conservatory without taking off his coat. Abby had noticed when her uncle received upsetting news, he'd spend more time there.

Abby removed her jacket. Three envelopes from Jim awaited her. Cheered by the prospect of reading each one, she dashed up the stairs and curled up in the window seat. Organizing the envelopes by date of dispatch, she slit open the first one.

Sept. 15, '42, England

Dearest Abby,

My buddies tell me their folks complain it's feast or famine regarding the arrival of letters. I have yet to receive mail from you or anyone. I miss you so much. The training is long and hard. It looks like a [censored] by our troops [censored]

Much of the time I get around on a bike, which I've borrowed from one of the villagers. They're very nice to us. It's hard to remember to ride on the left side, but I'm getting better at it. On a pass last weekend, I hopped a train with a few buddies, and we went to the [censored] for the day. Most shops and restaurants are closed from [censored], so it's a good time to spend the day in the country or at the seaside. We traveled through tidy cultivated countryside with green fields dotted with cozy stone houses. I love the way it looks. The trains still run, but many tracks have been destroyed by bombs and lines are closed, with long delays at both ends. The sun and sea felt wonderful after a week of gray, cold, and wet days. I've taken to beer at the local pub, where we can play darts. Some Tommies invited us to a village cricket match next week at [censored].

We went to a Glenn Miller concert at another base. What a show! He played all the favorites, including "Moonlight Serenade"— remember? That's the one you and I danced to on our last night together. (Seems so long ago!!) We had some trouble getting there as street lights are blacked out all night. [censored] are down so if [censored] do land, [censored] will be [censored]. We sometimes are as well.

I've written some poetry (ha, ha) and started a diary. I'll let you see it sometime. Do you know "You'd Be So Nice to Come Home To"?

Your Jim XXX

Abby smiled. She'd bought that record by Frank Sinatra when shopping in town two weeks before. She dropped the disk on the way back to the car, spent several minutes on her hands and knees collecting the broken pieces from the pavement, then dashed back to the shop in time to replace it. She'd decided to make the song one of their "special" ones. She sat at the open window and let the breeze play in her hair, imagining Jim's fingers there.

Abby folded the letter and slipped it back into its sleeve. She opened the next one.

Oct. 25, '42, England

Dear heart, as my thoughts are full of you, I should let some of them spill onto paper. Finally, your letter of 8/2 arrived today. We got a visit from Mrs. Roosevelt. It was a great honor to meet her and shake her hand. What a morale booster! She's wildly popular with the troops over here.

Abby ran a pencil under this section. She'd read this to her aunt later, since Mrs. Roosevelt's concern for the soldiers was of interest to them both.

I had to sit during her visit because of blisters on my feet due to socks being cotton and too tight. Wool ones have been promised to us. Can't wait.

I like the Brits' sense of humor. I saw a sign next to a store window that had been blown out and someone had written "more open than usual." And the people are very clever at getting the most out of the supplies available. Food, clothing, and fuel are strictly rationed. Soap is hard to get. I often hear them say "we're all in it together." Many working sixty hours a week. The food in the pubs is flat and tasteless, but I am getting to like English tea. I have gotten into the habit of asking for a "spot of tea" off base. They put little knitted covers over the pot while the tea "brews." But why am I telling you this? You already know. I suppose it's the observer in me and my need to put it in black and white.

The absence of children playing in the streets seems odd. But I wouldn't want our children here, either. By the way, last month our camp held a party for some of the city kids left behind. We gave them candy and let them climb on the tanks.

All my love, darling, J XXX

Abby re-read the last paragraph. She toyed with the expression he had used, "our children." She got pleasure from reading his thoughts but would rather have him here and the two of them married. Would he remain in the relative safety of England? She longed to believe there was a purpose in everything. Was God testing her?

She picked up the next letter.

Oct. 28, '42, England

Dearest Abby, tell your uncle I went to the Royal Botanical Gardens at Kew and saw what they're up to with the exotic plants. Seeing is believing for me. A section of the gardens is used to grow food, and most of the gardeners are women who've replaced the men called up. Unfortunately, the Germans decided to drop a few explosives on the place, and the water lily house is all shot up.

We listen to Armed Forces broadcasts every day. Continue to send letters to this address until you hear otherwise. I won't be able to write for a while after [censored]. So I'm writing to Mom and my sisters to let them know this. I miss you so much, sweetheart. "Cheerio!"

Until soon, forever, and always, Jim XXXX

In his correspondence Abby saw a different Jim, adaptable to new experiences. A man of the soil, not the warrior type, yet he appeared to have fitted in well with army life and its peculiar demands.

She kissed his letters and filed them in the usual place, comforted by performing this ritual.

That night while listening to Sinatra singing "Night and Day" she wrote Jim a long, cheerful reply, letting him know he was always in her thoughts and she'd give anything to see him and hear his voice again. "May our hearts grow and be knit together in a love that is unbreakable," she wrote, underlining each word and adding, "Love always," in bold red ink. She carefully blotted each page and kissed the sheet. A breeze scattered her flimsy airmail pages across the floor. Dropping onto her elbows and knees, she hunted for them in the lamplight. "Near distance, middle distance, far distance." Jim told her he learned that at basic training. That's how the army taught you to look for something. And she'd seen Pathé newsreels of soldiers advancing on all fours, wriggling under barbed wire. Being shot at like animals. She drew in a sharp breath. That could be Jim.

CHAPTER EIGHTEEN

Destination Unknown, November 1942

Wherever they were going, it would be a long voyage. Jim shouldered his way through the crush as his unit joined hundreds of others at dawn on a troop train bound for Scotland. The scuttlebutt said North Africa. Everyone knew about the fighting there, the victory at El Alamein. Perhaps this operation had to do with Montgomery's campaign.

Two days later, he filed onto a dingy merchant ship. All but the essentials had been removed from the hold, converting it into a gaping chasm. Hammocks strung end-to-end dangled above straw mattresses set on tables beneath. They wouldn't do much sleeping here. He made a mental note of the latrines and calculated how long it would take to reach them and the difficulty of clambering over all those sleeping forms.

Most of the time he spent on the crowded deck, catching the salt spray. The ship would zigzag for hours at a time. The constant booming of depth charges on the starboard side was a potent reminder of the threat from U-boats that had already sent Allied ships to the bottom.

Eight days in and Gibraltar bulked into view. Their convoy passed Tangiers, heading for the broad expanse of the Mediterranean. Jim—dazzled by the bright lights on shore—watched English soldiers weep at the sight. Such illumination hadn't been seen in Britain for years. The line steamed by Oran and the half-submerged hulls of the French fleet.

Another two days brought them up against the tantalizing landscape of Algiers, shimmering in the heat. A small force dispatched across the bay soon overcame resistance from Vichy French forces. Over forty-eight hours, the ships were emptied of their cargo by tugboats and small vessels.

After his group disembarked, the platoon billeted in a large manse overlooking the bay. Robin's-egg-blue shutters adorned the front of the house, and a verandah trimmed with white wrought-iron railings ran the full width of the second floor. Jim shared this space with six men. How could anyone work in such unremitting heat replete with flies and mosquitoes? They kept the balcony doors open—the stench from below at times unbearable.

From this vantage point, he watched the unloading of heavy equipment, marveling at the organization required to manage such a feat. The harbor was chock-a-block with vessels and tugs scurrying back and forth with troops and supplies. Seagulls made their own noisy transit between ship and shore, swooping for scraps of food offered to them by men on board.

Jim's unit was assigned to firing practice, but in the evenings, there was time to relax. That's when he discovered a large garden, overgrown and long untended, at the rear of the chateau. If only he had the time and tools to rescue it from a sure fate. He reconnoitered the area. The garden was enclosed by a thick wall about seven feet high and surmounted by the corrugated red pantiles common to the architecture of this town. Foot-worn brick paths trailed out of sight behind compact groves of cypress and palm. At strategic spots, stone benches were fixed. Into this way station he retreated, when duties allowed, to read and write letters and poetry.

The vulgar fact of total war blighted everything and sucked all enthusiasm from him. Odd, to be sitting in this exotic place—in the middle of a war—writing love notes. Was he shirking his duty now? Jim slammed his eyes shut. His duty—as he saw it—was to shoot at people he didn't know before they shot at him. The only rifle he'd ever fired in anger had been directed at the rabbits that preyed on his mother's vegetable patch, an essential source of food in those Depression days.

He'd soon be on the move, but the sprockets of his mind went only backwards. He dreaded the future, an ever-narrowing ribbon of time which ran down to a gloomy horizon, swallowing him and all his bright hopes for a long life with Abby. Funny how every train of thought carried him back to her. It seemed like only yesterday that he'd never heard of Abby Stapleton, and now he couldn't get her from his mind. He smiled.

It was no laughing matter now. He wanted to get back home to her, but the grim task intervened. Was he prepared to die? He couldn't bear to think of his mother or Abby getting that dreaded telegram, "sorry to inform," or whatever it said. He conjured up the searing image. At the same time, he had a job to do. He would do it for Abby, for his mother, for his family, and he would attempt to trust God for the rest.

Unable to sleep, Abby listened to the ticking of the alarm clock. Almost midnight.

Early tomorrow morning in England. Jim would be getting up soon. The memory of fresh English dawns and the cooing of doves above her window warmed her heart. She hoped he would have such an invigorating morning. In her mind's eye, she saw his handsome face and heard his melodious voice. She pictured herself running to him across the park, surprising him, and being swept up in his embrace.

But even as she fought to maintain the scene, it began to mutate. "I won't be able to write for a while after"—that's what his letter said.

Switching on the bedside lamp, she hurried over to the dresser and untied the ribbon around the cache of envelopes. She took out the latest one and scrutinized every word. "Oct. 28 … 'for a while after' …" The censor's thick black line obliterated the rest of the sentence.

Abby set the letter down. *After what?* She stared at the clock, as if it held the answer. Its luminous face stared back. Till now she had contained him within scenes familiar to her. As long as Jim remained there—where she could see him—he still belonged to her, and she could nurture the hope he was safe and would come back to her. By the time midnight came and went, he'd gone from the orbit of her mind's eye.

Sitting on the edge of the bed, she trembled. She had to abandon him to—who knows where? No matter where, it was no longer England, and it completely excluded her.

Abby looked up from measuring sugar to see Carol and Phyllis working side by side. In spite of Carol's many complaints, Abby sensed she and her mother were close.

Abby wiped her hands on a red polka dot apron. "I never baked with my mother." She heaved a loud sigh. "I missed out on all this." Startled by a *clang*, she swung around. Aunt Val stooped to pick up a dropped baking pan.

"I'll get it, Auntie." Abby knelt beside her, noting a confused look in her eyes.

"I can manage, dear. Don't fuss."

Abby returned to her counter. "We're much better off than they are in London. Jim wrote that brides have to make do with cardboard wedding cakes because sugar's rationed."

"Then why bother at all?" Carol said, turning on the electric mixer to blend the ingredients for cookies.

"We must have our situation reviewed again by the ration board," Aunt Val said from across the room. She added chopped walnuts to her batter. "I do hope this war's over before next autumn."

"Then maybe we'll have butter again," Carol said, lining a cookie sheet with parchment paper. She worked dough into large balls. "And not this awful oleo."

Valerie poured the contents of her mixing bowl into baking pans. "I don't see much choice about that since butter costs eight points a pound, while oleo only costs five," she said, scraping the bowl. "Still, William likes butter, so we'll have it occasionally."

"By pooling all our ration points, we got everything we needed. Even enough sugar." Abby shaped dough into crescents. "My sister tells me even toilet paper and quality soap are rationed."

Carol put an arm around Abby's waist. "Thanks to you, I'll have a new dress and coat for Christmas with your unredeemed clothing coupons."

"I look at the consumer report each month to see how I can best use my points." Phyllis stood at the sink, washing the utensils. "But I shouldn't complain. There's much to be grateful for."

Valerie opened the double oven range door, sliding her pans inside. A miscellany of copper-bottom pans hung from brass hooks above the range. "Our cook complains she's finding it hard to stock the pantry for the children and needs stamps for almost everything and that meat is scarce." She shook her head. "She says those instructions on how to use stamps are too complicated."

Soft laughter filled the room, while the delicious smell of baked goods filled the air. Abby bit into a scone. She pictured Jim opening the box with their treats. He'd written saying the men in his division held a party for the children near the base. She set aside some for Edythe. Jim would want her to. It was her habit to mentally submit her decisions to Jim for approval. How did she manage before without this reference point?

Carol transferred the cookies to a rack, taking one. "Do we need to send all these?"

Phyllis grabbed a dish towel and whacked her across the shoulder. "They're for your brother, not you. And our package must go out tomorrow so as to be there in time for Christmas."

Carol loosened her mother's apron strings. "Don't snap your cap, Mom."

While mother and daughter bantered back and forth, Aunt Val watched the playful scene in silence. Then she turned toward Abby and their eyes locked. Abby smiled. Why did her aunt look so unhappy?

CHAPTER NINETEEN

Jolie Fontaine
Autumn/Winter 1942-43

Abby poked at the logs in the fireplace, then switched on the light near her uncle's chair and adjusted the brightly colored afghan over his knees.

Uncle Will picked up the newspaper and skimmed its pages. "That's not so good."

She sat on the settee, kicked off her slippers, and picked up a book. "What's that, Uncle?"

"There's an item here by that young reporter, Walter Cronkite. Let's see ... 'the invasion of French North Africa by our soldiers and the British under General Eisenhower has not been going so smoothly, and there is much confusion there. Skirmishes between Allied and Axis Forces. The battle for Tunisia has begun.'"

She winced at the images those words conjured, confirming her suspicion that Jim was in a new and dangerous theater of war.

Her uncle rustled through the pages of his paper, grumbling. "Doesn't look like this war will end any time soon." He tossed his paper aside. "You need to go out more. To the pictures or something. I've not seen your friend Ginny here for months."

"Ginny joined the Women's Flying Training Detachment as a civilian volunteer at Camp Davis, and she now has her pilot's license," Abby said, sensing he was oblivious to the turmoil this latest news had set off inside her.

"That's one adventurous girl. I'm happy to hear she's been accepted."

"Anyway, it wouldn't be the same without Jim." Her voice caught, and she kept her head down.

"I don't know if we'll be able to hold the New Year's ball and fundraiser your Aunt's working on. My nephew insists we comply with these complicated regulations. More malarkey! This time about exit signs, fire drills, and this and that—"

"Aunt Val certainly won't want to hear that," she said, marveling at Henri's facility for upsetting his uncle. He must know Uncle Will was not in good health. She'd told him on several occasions. She tempered her irritation with the excuse that Henri was merely doing his job.

"I agree. Sure, the event needs to be safe, but we're in unusual circumstances. There's a war going on. Just how safe is that?" He sighed. "I only hope the work can be done before the end of December."

The doorbell chimed. Abby looked at her watch. "That's probably Carol."

Uncle Will got up. "I'll leave you two alone, then." He pecked her cheek. "See you in the morning."

"I've put in for a class in the Women's Army Auxiliary Corps," Carol blurted, throwing her coat over the back of the sofa and dropping into the seat next to Abby.

Abby's heart sank. Two employees had already left for the War Office. Now Carol was off. "I will miss you."

"My recruiter said if us women step forward, more soldiers can go fight and come home sooner." She took a deep breath of finality. "So, I decided this is what I'm gonna do."

"When do you leave?" Abby said, unwilling to throw a damper on Carol's excitement.

"Next month."

Abby smiled. "You've made a decision that took a lot of courage." *Didn't the First Lady say more would be required of women?*

Carol threw her arms around her. "Whew! I knew you'd understand. Look out Herr Hitler, here I come." She furrowed her brow. "But I do hate to leave you on one leg."

"Don't worry. We'll get by," Abby said, proud of Carol for having risen to the occasion.

"Oh, and my big sister is getting married after Christmas. Mom's glad about the marriage but not about the groom's duty overseas."

Still struggling to control her own fears, Abby decided not to mention her suspicion where Jim might be. Carol would be informed soon enough.

The envelope that arrived was smaller than usual. The lettering, "V ...—MAIL" in red, ran along the bottom. Abby uncreased the letter to reveal a photographic image of Jim's cramped handwriting.

Nov. 15, '42

Dearest One, can't write much or tell you where I am or where I'm going, but you'll probably figure it out from the newspapers. It's hot as the dickens here, so definitely no snow this Christmas. I got your letter of Sept. 20. Keep them coming!! They'll catch up sooner or later. Sarge says it takes about two weeks for our letters to reach home. A lot will be cut out, so I must be careful what I say.

Along with camp duties, I'm on guard watch this week. I went to church services yesterday. We're doing a lot of marching. I use my helmet to hold water and for cooking. Field rations are Spam or cheese, crackers and cookies, a few cigarettes (which I trade for more Spam), and powdered coffee. The wind blows the sand into my hair and attaches itself to the sweat on my face and gets in between my teeth. Man! The flies here are real bad, always dive bombing us when we bring out the food, so I eat with a coat over my head.

You probably think I'm complaining too much. All right, here we go, a change of subject. I had hoped for ye olde English Christmas as we got an invitation to dinner from a family living near our base in Dorset, but Uncle S. had other ideas. Was looking forward to pulling those Christmas crackers you talked about last year. Remember our time together then, darling? A real white one. Seems ages ago. Picked up a present for you before I left. You should have it by now.

Jim's package lay on the dressing table. Until now, she'd resisted the temptation to tear it open. Her current mood stifled further curiosity.

From the bureau, she took down the picture taken of them during that glorious week of his furlough. Was it really seven months ago? She placed it on the pillow and sat on the bed, studying their faces in the picture. Had they done the right thing in postponing marriage until he returned? Suppose he didn't come back? Abby pushed the thought aside and returned to Jim's letter.

> The guys and I listen to AFO Radio for the Stateside news and the new dance tunes. Sometimes we pick up the German broadcasts by "Lord Haw-Haw," telling us we're gonna lose. I see a lot of Brits here. They're teaching me how to play soccer and tell me I'm pretty good at it.
>
> I remember last year how things looked after Pearl H. Your uncle's party was such a lift and we had such a happy week, didn't we? Please send any food you can—cookies, nuts (no sand!).
>
> Wish I could be with you, darling. Gotta go.
>
> My love always, J XXX & XXX

Two months passed before Abby received another V-form letter from Jim.

> Feb. 10, '43
>
> Dearest Abby, at last a letter from you dated Jan. 5. I've received only one other dated Dec. 31. I'm told eventually the mail will catch up with me. It's been so busy and there is little privacy here. I'm sorry for the long delay since you last heard from me. You should have by now received my letters sent while in [censored].

While in ... where? She'd not received any mail from him since the end of last year. She noticed his handwriting was becoming more illegible.

> In case you haven't received that letter, know the box of Christmas goodies finally arrived. Please thank everyone who baked them. They were a big hit here. And I got the toothbrush (not much water here for hygiene), socks, books, and Bible. When I can

snatch a little time, I'm reading *The Robe*. Thanks, sweetheart, for sending this book.

Abby smiled. She'd only just finished it herself.

I got Carol's letter saying she'll be stationed [censored] as a [censored]. My sister Sally wrote telling me about her and Mike. Sad they only had a few days together with the baby before he left for boot camp. I love the picture you sent of us. Looking at your picture lifts my spirits. I'm sending a photo of myself and the boys in front of a half-track that carries infantrymen, supplies, [censored]. Notice how dark my skin is now. My field equipment has a [censored], [censored] supplies and [censored].

The picture she'd sent was one Jim had taken of her when he was teaching her to swim. He especially liked this one with her in a light green bathing suit with a pleated skirt. He said the color was great with her auburn hair but kidded her about being too pale.

Our camp is set up near an [censored]. We expect to remain in this temporary location for a few more days and then move on. We get our meals from a kitchen train. The days are very hot, but the nights can be cold. Most of the times I'm black, dirty, unshaven, and tired. Water is rationed. I wash my socks in my helmet. It serves as many things. There's been a lot of rain and mud everywhere, not so good for marching on foot. Not even a blade of grass here. Mosquito nets and gas masks have been issued.

I spend much of my time caring for and cleaning our equipment, along with other camp duties. It seems like such a long time ago since basic training this time last year. I'd give almost anything to be with you in a lovely, cool garden right now. I memorized the poem by Kipling called *The Glory of the Garden*. It's the one on the wall in your uncle's study. Do you remember that poem? I dream of Jolie Fontaine and the fountains and our swims in the pool.

I've discovered the Scripture in Isaiah that says the desert shall rejoice and blossom as the rose. And in the same book it says, "nation shall not lift up sword against nation, neither shall they learn war any more." Reading these verses in this place gives them all the more meaning for me.

I'll close here. You fill my thoughts and hopes for the future. Longing to see you. Forever, Jim

Abby tried to conjure up images of Jim in North Africa. Her knowledge of geography had never been very good. But she'd tussled with that place before. Simon went missing there.

North Africa
March 1943

Jim tipped his helmet back and buried his face in the dirt, as shells from the destroyers off shore exploded above. The smell of the ground in this foreign field reminded him of home.

He lay still, tense and expectant. Was there a giant hand moving lives around on a master chessboard, some winning, some losing? Anyway, why should he be one of the winners? Besides, this same God-given ground that had nourished generations was now blotched with the blood of his own countrymen. And he might be one of them today. How fragile the human body.

Today, forward movement was sporadic. They'd gained and held large swaths of ground, only to fall back. Blistering fire from German and Italian artillery kept Jim's platoon pinned down. He ran the back of his hand across his brow, never imagining such carnage. Men dying around him and others on the verge. He'd seen their bodies blasted to bits, their ghastly injuries—once men, now half men. The sights and sounds around him dented his straight edged view of a world that operated under the rule of law. He'd witnessed men change from quiet, decent farm boys to hardened killers who derived an unhealthy pleasure in the assassination of the enemy. The wholesale loss of faith in God was, perhaps, a tragedy greater than the net loss of life.

He pushed the fear of his own destruction deep down inside and made a good show of courage and faith in God. Still, he knew his love for Abby and his overwhelming desire to see her again kept him going. Incoming and outgoing letters had been stalled for several weeks. Though he wrote to her every day now, his heart was not in it. He churned out bland epistles laced with clichés, a pablum that in conveying nothing, said everything. He didn't want to frighten her. Besides, he knew he could not adequately describe the horrors he'd witnessed.

He didn't doubt her love for him, but she loved someone different than the man he had become.

As the shells whistled overhead, he hated what warfare was doing to him. His cynical attitude could not last long in the glare of Abby's honest and open gaze. He longed for her reproof, her candor, her warm assurances that everything would be all right. He shuddered at the thought that he might be returned to her whole on the outside but broken on the inside, alienated from her heart by inexpressible agonies of his own.

Then a breach opened in the enemies' line of defense. He gripped the stock of his rifle and secured his helmet with its strap. As if trapped in a vise, his throat tightened, and breathing became laborious. Each grinding minute wore away his certainty that he would see Abby again.

Surging forward with his men, he prayed for an easy death in this foreign field.

CHAPTER TWENTY

Jolie Fontaine, Spring 1943

Abby tucked in the corner of the bedsheet. "I'm fixing this room for Uncle. He will need to stay downstairs for a while."

Henri pushed the door back. "That serious, eh?"

"Aunt Val's worried. So am I."

He stepped into the room. "I've been looking all over for you. How about lunch? With me."

Abby punched the pillows with one fist and then another. She'd been out with Henri once since the county fair. Edythe made a threesome both times. These occasions were harmless. But the girl was spending this month with her mother.

"I'm rather busy."

"Nonsense. All work and no play."

The asperity in his tone didn't surprise her. She'd encountered it before. "Another time perhaps."

"We'll go to Taylor's. They have a good lunch menu. You remember Taylor's?"

As if she could forget. During the meal, she'd asked why he hadn't been called up. Perhaps his legal occupation was protected? His peevish, rambling response made her wish she'd kept her mouth shut.

Abby fussed with the corners of the bedspread, playing for time. Hadn't Uncle Will told her to get out of the house more often? Besides, she and Henri were ersatz cousins. If Jim knew the circumstances, he'd understand and raise no objection.

Henri persisted. "He will be taking a nap shortly, and Aunt's on the verge of falling asleep." He winked. "All right, then. I'll see you in the foyer."

Abby called after him, "Give me fifteen minutes. *Why did Henri say* "*he—he will be taking a nap*"? *That's Uncle Will.* It hadn't escaped her notice that Henri took a condescending view of this wonderful man. Was he really looking after his uncle's interests—or his own?

And he'd done it again. She'd hesitated, and he'd seized the opportunity to make up her mind. Still, if striking out on her own meant spending time with Henri, she'd have to do it.

In her own bedroom, she threw herself together. Although Henri could be annoyingly insistent, she borrowed some resolution of spirit from his. She'd always admired people who knew their own mind. The independent sort.

Henri lolled on the bench below—trimming his fingernails—with his legs outstretched, one well-polished shoe resting atop the other. He sprang to his feet when she started down the stairs. "Excellent," he said, grinning.

As he looked her up and down, the roots of her hair burned.

Inside the restaurant, diners congregated, waiting for a table. But the waters parted for Henri. A gesture and a subtle nod and within a few minutes, the manager led them to a quiet booth in the corner. Abby fell in behind, marveling at the ease with which he always got his way. Even with her.

The waiter came around with the menu. Abby picked the least expensive meal—a private concession to the rigors her parents were enduring on the home front. This little act of self-denial also maintained the gap between Henri and herself. She didn't mind being with him, but she didn't want to live his life.

"Heard from your soldier?" Henri said, reaching into his inside pocket for a cigarette.

Henri never asked about Jim. Whenever she'd brought Jim into the conversation, he'd always change the subject.

"He can't say too much about his location because of security."

Clenching the cigarette in his teeth, Henri leaned into the padded upholstery. "It seems to me that you've taken on quite a bit with this school business." He draped his arm along the backrest, rippling his fingers on the smooth Naugahyde. "Well-intentioned, but perhaps impractical, don't you think?"

"Impractical. And s-s-still too young, am I?" she said, fixing her gaze on him.

Henri smirked. "I admire Uncle Will. He's got a sound business sense." He let out a petulant breath.

Abby awaited his favorite word hovering in the gap that followed his sigh, resisting the temptation to mouth it for him.

"*But*, let's face it—he's failing." He tipped his head back and puffed smoke rings toward the ceiling. "You've said as much yourself. And Aunt Val can't possibly take over." He rapped his knuckles on the table. "That shifts everything onto your shoulders."

Her fingers tightened around the water glass. "I've coordinated everything for the past year with help. Uncle knows I can handle it."

"Perhaps." Henri prodded his steak with a fork. "But there are other complications."

Abby set down her corned beef sandwich and frowned. "Such as?" she said, her uncle's complaints that Henri was obstreperous, constantly raising objections, came to mind.

"The three R's"—Henri trilled the *R*—"Regulations ... Renovations ... the swimming pool, for one."

"We passed fire and food inspection. And we're licensed," she said, twisting the napkin in her lap.

"The swimming pool needs a fence around it."

"As a trained lifeguard, Jim said the same."

"I wouldn't want anything to happen to my Edythe or the other children," Henri said with some heat. "Then—"

She leaned toward him in a countermove. "But in the event of an accident, Jim has demonstrated to the staff and me how to revive someone."

"Then," Henri repeated, as though she were invisible, "there is insurance for novel use of the buildings. School furnishings. Various and sundry precautions. Legal things."

Abby threw up her hands, exasperated. *Such a wet blanket.*

"You'll need help with all that," he cooed, evading her glare. "I'm your man. I am a lawyer, after all. Perhaps we can work together on the problem?" He pointed at her plate. "You're not eating?"

Abby sat back, her stomach doing somersaults.

"And of course, there's the third 'R'," Henri droned on, looking up at the ceiling as if his script were written on it. "*Re* ... imbursements. An enduring Power of Attorney, *POA*," Henri said, punctuating each letter with his fork. "That's what's needed."

In spite of herself, the remark sparked Abby's curiosity, and she looked at him. "What is a POA?"

Henri sat back and smiled. "Basically, the right to spend money on behalf of someone else. But only as necessary, of course." He poked a toothpick in his mouth and rolled it from side to side with his lips. "You see, we can't possibly proceed with any alterations until we have that," he said, his eyes wide.

"But surely, as Uncle's lawyer, you already have that?"

Henri pursed his lips and shook his head. "Perhaps you could have a word with him. He trusts you."

Jolie Fontaine

"I want to put house and land under a perpetual trust with my stated intention that it be run for public benefit some day." While his uncle spoke, Henri kept his eyes glued to files on his lap. As executor of the estate, he was here at his uncle's urgent request to discuss alterations to the will. Henri yanked his tie loose, snapping off a collar button. He swore inwardly.

"We'll set up a three-member panel to operate the estate as a garden and learning center." Uncle Will opened his desk drawer and pulled out a sheaf of papers. "I'd like you to be on the panel." He dropped the stack on the desk. "Also, your Aunt Val and Jim Wright. He will be a good choice." Uncle Will grinned. "I expect he and Abby will get married, anyway, so it will be in the family."

The mention of Jim Wright sickened Henri, but he dared not show it. The idea of someone like Abby in the arms of someone like the farm boy .... He remained poker-faced, feeling the walls closing in on him.

"Valerie can continue to live here for the remainder of her life. The staff, too, if she needs them." Uncle Will leaned back in his chair and stared at Henri. "When I'm gone, I want Abby appointed as day-to-day administrator of my estate. Most decisions would rest with her." He nodded to himself. "She has what it takes to do the job. She would have a home on the premises and a decent income—drawn from the trust." He tapped his pen on the desk, as if in afterthought. "Of course, Abby might decide to move back to England, so we should make contingency provisions for a successor to the post." In an offhand manner he added, "You might want to suggest someone."

Henri bristled. His uncle was generous to a fault, but these fresh arrangements astonished him. Still, he knew better than to try and talk the old man out of it, as he wasn't easily moved once his mind was made up. Henri shifted in his seat, heart pounding.

Uncle Will leaned back in his chair. "Now all this means that a sizable chunk of the assets will have to be fenced off for this new trust, say a quarter-million. Your aunt is to receive a lump sum of around twenty-five thousand dollars, to invest as she likes, drawing on the interest. She might need your help on that, Henri. And there'll be a further ten thousand dollars set aside in escrow as a cushion. In any event, your aunt won't lose out in this new arrangement." Uncle Will removed his glasses and rubbed his eyes. "I haven't told Valerie all this yet, so keep mum until I do."

Henri scribbled in his notepad, but his mind raced ahead of his pen, his throat thick.

"I think I've covered the essentials. Still, I will probably think of something else after you've gone." His uncle pinched the bridge of his nose. "I'm not so sharp as I used to be. Heart is not what it was." He leaned forward and slapped the desk, bringing an end to the discussion. "But you get the gist. Work up a draft and let me see it in the next fortnight or so." He chuckled. "I think I'll last that long."

Henri emitted a hollow laugh. He knew the estate held possibilities, but his own assessment of them was not quite what his uncle may have had in mind. He'd spent his childhood years roaming around the grounds of Jolie Fontaine. He knew every crack and crevice, all the climbable trees and the best swimming holes. In his ideal moments, he had considered it a sanctuary for the soul. His ideals these days were of a different temper, cold-forged in the service of Mammon.

"Here you are, Henri." His uncle's words snatched him from his wandering. "I've written my instructions down. If you have trouble with my handwriting, just call me and we'll go over it."

"I'll ring you when the drafts are ready." Henri rose and shook his hand.

"Thank you. Now, if you don't mind, I must lie down for a while."

After his uncle left, he bundled the documents into his briefcase. These new developments complicated things a bit, but they weren't fatal to his own plans. He'd have to speed things up.

Henri did his best thinking when driving. The fluid ride of his glossy black two-door Cadillac and the purr of its eight-cylinder motor supplied the background music to his thoughts. He took pride in being a man of action, a cut-the-chatter-and-get-on-with-it type of individual. That's what he admired about Adolf Hitler. The man had turned Germany around in less than a decade and built a huge fighting force right under the noses of the French and the washed-up British. Hitler had the right idea—put the most capable, the most intelligent, the purest in charge. Henri nurtured a strong dislike of Roosevelt, a quasi-aristocrat. Dear old Franklin was damaged goods.

He rolled down the window and let his arm dangle over the side. He congratulated himself on his choice of work, on his choice of automobile, and now on his choice of Abby. Beautiful, no doubt about that. Intelligent, too. But suitably uninformed and malleable. And a bit too eager to please. That aspect of things suited him. Too bad she's besotted with that soldier. He considered his uncle's prediction that she might marry the doughboy, a farmhand with no profession, no money, no property. He stood to gain a lot, that yokel. He spit out of the window. "But I'll change that," he muttered. That GI was so far away, but he had—he searched for the expression—proximate advantage. *Oh, what a lovely war.*

He slapped his fleshy palm against the door and rammed the accelerator, then swerved to avoid the deer that loomed in his windshield. The animal bounced off the grille into the ditch and lay writhing in pain. He walked to the front of his vehicle, inspected the damage and drove off.

CHAPTER TWENTY-ONE

Valerie peered through the shafts of light slanting through the branches of trees that flanked the driveway. A mirage of heat rose from the tarmac and shimmered in a crazy dance. When would the dog days of summer come to an end?

Ensconced at the window of her bedroom, like the captain of a great ship, she watched the daily currents of life ebb and flow. A stream of vehicles and pedestrians rippled along at all hours. A cavalcade of mothers and children, hand in hand, traipsed to and from the house. Gardeners, electricians, and carpenters followed in quick succession. She waved to the letter carrier. His sack looked heavier than usual. And there went Anna, their young housemaid, sneaking off with her soldier-boy.

"Ah, there he comes, right on cue," she grumbled, spotting Henri's automobile. He honked his horn to shoo pedestrians aside and drove over the stones to his favorite spot.

Previously absent for long periods at a time on his mysterious jaunts to South America, Henri was now a fixture. She could set the clock by his daily arrival and departure. She knew his routine by heart. Car door, *slam*. Front door, *slam*. Then the *thump* of Henri's feet up the stairs, two at a time, followed a few seconds later by the slamming of Will's office door. Now he would be installed at her husband's vacant desk, his adopted sanctuary. Valerie clenched her teeth at the thought. "Just going through some papers," is how he'd dismiss her whenever she asked what he was doing. In his lawyer mode, he was taciturn.

No doubts—Henri had aimed his sights at Abby. Dark visions of Abby flying away with Henri gripped her. What rich irony that would be. She couldn't keep the girl at birth but had to give her away. Even with Abby here in her house, she still couldn't hold on to her. But she'd rather possess her daughter in this fragile relationship than not at all. She'd always be here for Abby, waiting to help.

A cloud of ambiguity hovered over Henri. He was divorced. And he was—she sought the kindest word—"volatile." He did possess a kind of magnetism. She chuckled. She'd fallen for that type herself, hook, line, and sinker. Someone with sufficient gumption might think herself fortunate to get Henri for a husband. He was successful at what he did. And life with Henri could never be dull. *But he will not get my daughter.*

Her attitude toward Jim had been tainted by her own experience with men in general. She didn't trust them, except for Will. Having previously expressed prejudice against Jim, she was unqualified to voice her misgivings about Henri. She'd squandered whatever influence she had with Abby by denigrating Jim and only succeeded in driving the girl into his arms. But Jim's prospects were unsure. Were he to be killed, no telling what might happen with Abby. Perhaps it was rash of them to get engaged. Still, Abby couldn't keep herself on ice indefinitely.

Valerie leaned against the windowsill, fighting back tears. Ever since William moved downstairs, due to his failing health, she felt cut off from everything. If he died ... no doubt he was already adjusting his financial affairs, hence all that to-ing and fro-ing by Henri. But Will never discussed these issues with her, and she couldn't broach them now. He'd urged her never to worry about such things, that she would always be looked after. He was quite capable in those areas and she trusted him implicitly. Still, matters were developing in unexpected ways and a future in the hands of Henri appalled her. *You tell me not to be anxious, Lord. I will leave this in your hands too.*

She caught a faint, breathy whistle from outside. She popped her head through the window. Will looked up. "Hello, old girl. Let's sit on the porch. It's cooler there. We can play a game of Monopoly." He chuckled. "Or do the crossword puzzle."

"Looks like we're getting somewhere. Between Mr. Roosevelt and Mr. Churchill, we should win this war." Uncle Will lowered the volume on the radio and pointed to a chair, grinning. "Have a seat, Abby."

For the past five months, reports of the Allies' success in North Africa and their advances through Sicily and southern Italy raised the spirits of the household. Uncle Will seemed to undergo a youthful transformation.

Abby placed the chair alongside his. "What about the Russians?"

"Not sure about that lot." He grunted. "You never know what's up with them. I think when the European war is over, they'll make trouble for us."

Aunt Val stood in the doorway, hands on her hips. "And when will it be over, General?"

"It can't take much longer. All the assets are on our side. Production of materiel—tanks, planes, ships, trucks, small arms—by us, Canada, the British. Intelligence assets. And don't forget oil. Germany will eventually run out," he said, pausing to catch his breath. "We won't."

His tone turned grave. "We've got right on our side. Oh, I'm not saying we're God's favorites or anything like that. I shouldn't think this war is an unalloyed credit to any of us. But we didn't start it and—" He burst into a coughing fit and reached for a glass of water. "Sorry, Abby, I must go to bed," he said, leaving with Valerie at his side.

Alone, Abby turned up the radio. A cacophony of whistles and burps streamed out as she rotated its glowing, cheery dial before selecting dance music. Swaying in place, she tapped her foot and drummed her fingertips against the top and visualized herself under a star-studded sky—her head nestled on Jim's shoulder and his strong arm around her waist—as they moved across the ice on their skates. How distant Christmastime, two long years ago, seemed when they'd first fallen in love and all was right with the world.

Would Jim's memory of their time together be powerful enough to bind him to her? His horizons had broadened. His experiences could cause him to put things into perspective, modify his priorities. Perhaps Jim was having doubts about her.

Then the music stopped, and the broadcaster broke into the program, "General Eisenhower publicly announces the surrender of Italy to the Allies."

She turned off the radio and bowed her head. *Please let this war be over soon.*

As the weeks and months passed, Abby began to feel hopelessly out of touch with Jim. She couldn't hide from her heart the heaviness inside. Nor—to her own private shame—the recurring doubts.

His next letter, postmarked Sicily, did not reach her until the end of September.

Her reaction to these military epistles was now a blend of pleasure and anxiety. She was desperate to know he was well, but fearful of the revelation that his affections had altered and that perhaps they should reconsider their decision to marry.

Aug. 10, '43

Sweetheart,

I hope you got my last letter before I left Tunisia. Yours have been coming to me in clumps. We left there for [censored] earlier this month with a landing at [censored] near [censored]. Be on the lookout for a package from me. I know you'll love wearing what's inside. On my birthday, the boys treated me to a small party. The wine is plentiful, and I have a glass occasionally. My father was a drunk, so I know the danger of going overboard. But a little helps to numb my senses to the ongoing tragedy.

It's my job to look out for mines. I put up the [censored] wherever I see them by [censored]. I've been doing a lot of [censored]. Lots of heavy fighting to drive out the enemy. My best buddy was wounded by shrapnel but is recovering.

Searching for mines. Abby winced at the images his words conjured. She knew a little about the danger in that work. Her father had told her about the UXB teams in London who defused the bombs that landed and refused to go off. Hardly a week went by without one of the squad being blown to smithereens.

Abby resumed reading, hoping for more recent news. Where was he, and what was he doing now? He could be in another country for all she knew.

The landscape is mountainous and rugged, and there are many vineyards here. The farmers travel on mules to town over bad roads. Fish is here in abundance. Nearby is another old town with a medieval-looking castle and courtyard and other historical buildings. It's charming to look at.

The locals are friendly and cheer us as their liberators. They've suffered bombing, occupation, and slaughter—their homes and churches destroyed. We will have victory here also. America doesn't know what misery is. I heard about the rubber workers and coal miners going on strike. How is Uncle Will's old factory managing with the steelworkers' strike? What's going on? Why can't they be content with a little less pay? I'm bitter about it.

Abby set the letter face down on the desk. Bad enough to think that Jim might get blown up any minute—*he might be dead now*—but she couldn't bear to discover that he had changed toward her. The need to know was too strong. She had to be sure. She read on, her hand trembling.

And is it right for a General to strike a soldier who is shell-shocked and accuse him of cowering from battle? And not much of an apology from him, either, even after being ordered to do so. It's a disgrace to the brave wounded. Those who are mentally damaged have wounds as great as the physically injured. My buddy had a crack-up too. I feel sick about the whole business but must press on to the end. How I do miss you.

Always and ever, Jim

Always and ever. There it was. Abby finished the letter with relief. But even as she gleaned this assurance, she could not ignore the profound changes that his experience at war seemed to have worked in him. He sounded angry and disappointed with humanity. Would he become disappointed with her?

She wasn't very good with all this ambiguity. Here she was, holding one end of the string and Jim the other. But it wasn't much of a string and could break at any time. *Maybe we should have married before he left.* The uncertainties that nagged away in the back of her mind now broke through, and she dropped to her knees. *Dear God, please renew my hope and help me to be more trustful.*

CHAPTER TWENTY-TWO

December 1943

"Heart attack," read the doctor's report. These past six weeks had been shrouded in loneliness for her aunt. Neither could Abby reconcile herself to the loss of her uncle. The atmosphere in the house resembled a tomb since the afternoon of November fifteenth.

That morning had been bright and clear, and by noon was jacket-warm. After lunch, Uncle Will wanted to go for a short walk, alone. "You never know, I may not get another chance," he'd told them. When he didn't return by four o'clock, Abby and her aunt searched the grounds. They found him in the Adirondack chair by the pond, slumped over.

At Uncle Will's funeral, three hundred mourners had paid their respects, including many workers from the factory. They all said how good he was to them and how they would miss him. How very much she'd miss him.

Today, standing by Aunt Val's side at the cemetery, Abby took some consolation from a growing closeness to her. They'd have to stick together to get through all this. She glanced over at her aunt, head bowed before the glistening granite headstone. "Dearly Beloved Husband of Valerie" was chiseled in three-inch-high letters. Abby placed a wreath on his grave, biting her lip to hold back the tears.

Aunt Val looked up, eyes dimmed with sorrow. "I think I'm ready now, dear." Then she reached for Abby's hand. "Let's go home."

She put an arm around her aunt's shoulder, and they trudged along the narrow path toward their car. How devastated she'd be if Jim were taken from her. Abby trembled in the cold wind and quickened her pace in an effort to keep them both warm. But why hadn't he replied to her telegram about Uncle Will? Was he safe? Abby's heart pricked at her selfish thoughts.

She must concentrate on making life easier for her aunt instead of being sorry for herself.

"Here we are," she said in a cheerful tone, opening the door.

She drove past acres of mausoleums and gravestones before reaching the exit and highway. Aunt Val leaned over and touched her arm. "Henri said there are a lot of papers to go through. William let things go during his illness."

This morning in his office, Henri had been his usual efficient self when he read out the will. He'd taken pains to dampen any enthusiasm about an early resolution. "It could take some time. It's complicated. There's the probate, due to the size of the estate, and the special provisions." He emphasized, "special provisions."

"I do wish I could've been more helpful to William."

"Don't blame yourself. You know he loved being in the thick of things," Abby said, anxious for the estate to be settled soon for her aunt's benefit.

Aunt Val nodded. "A bit too possessive of things, perhaps." She smiled. "Still, he had a head for it." She heaved a sigh. "I hope Henri can sort things out."

"Until I'm told otherwise, I will pay our bills from the school account Uncle set up for me. I told Henri the funds are low. Still, this is not good form." Henri's decision today to suspend the school until further notice came as a blow. Didn't he understand the mothers depended on her? Where would their children go?

Abby passed through the high gates of the estate onto the gravel drive then walked to the passenger side to let her aunt out. "I'll be in soon."

She squeezed the vehicle through the garage doors then shut off the motor. The wind had picked up and rain pelted against the corrugated roof, cascading onto the driveway. Resting her head against the steering wheel, she closed her eyes. *Where are you, Lord, in all of this?*

In addition to concerns for Aunt Val and the school, she now had the estate to watch over. She had yet to adjust to these new prospects. Had Uncle Will made the best choice in appointing her as administrator?

Abby buried her face in the woolen scarf Jim sent, yearning to hear his footstep outside her door, see it swing open, have him walk toward her and hold her in his arms. The flesh-and-blood Jim. Today she wore his charm bracelet on her wrist and a leather belt he'd sent from Italy around her waist. Still, the sum of all these gifts were not Jim.

She placed photographs of him around her room to catch a glimpse from every angle, tilting a mirror on her bureau to see him in his service uniform while she stood at the bathroom sink. This ritual intensified Jim's presence, brought him close, made him appear real. But this was the historical Jim. From every photograph, there looked out a man who no longer existed.

Even before she'd received his most recent letter dated weeks before, he'd departed the scene in which he composed it. His pictures, his letters— all symbols, expressions of where he had been, what he had done, who he was. She'd exchange all of her precious icons for one hour with him.

Henri's imminent presence mocked her attachments. She'd caught his thinly veiled sarcasms, uttered when his guard was down. His jibes at the fighting men overseas. The insinuations as to the futility of their cause. More than once she chided him on that score. She knew Henri resented her idea of Jim and was determined to demean and take that from her.

That Henri pursued her, she had no doubt. Until he took her to a posh restaurant for her birthday last October, she hadn't seen him for two months. After her uncle's death, she'd reassessed her friendship with him.

Abby crossed to the window and looked out. Rivulets of rain bubbled over stones and carried the flotsam of twigs and leaves along the driveway. Had she encouraged him? If by being vulnerable, unskilled in relations with men, perhaps. Besides no one could ever love Henri as much as he loved himself. Henri occupied the beginning and end of his own universe.

She would never let Jim down. *Dear God, please give him this assurance.*

In the evening, Abby and her aunt listened to the radio in a brave imitation of the old routine. Before long Aunt Val lapsed into morose silence, and Abby picked up a book. When Auntie wanted to go to bed, Abby left the room for her own.

The hall clock struck eleven. In the gloom on the landing, a yellow lamplight filtered beneath the door to her uncle's office. From inside came the sound of drawers being opened and closed in swift succession. Abby inched the door open. There, silhouetted against the lamp, his back to her, a figure rummaged in the filing cabinet.

"Henri." What was he doing here at this hour?

He swung around and pressed himself against the open drawer before slamming it shut. "You took me by surprise." He forced a laugh. "I get so engrossed when I'm working."

Abby stepped into the room. "I thought you'd left ages ago."

"Forgot something. Had to come back."

"I see. Can I help you?"

He lurched toward the desk and snatched up his jacket and vest from the back of the chair. "No, no. I'm just winding up." He glanced at his watch. "My, is that the time? Did I waken you?"

"I've been in my aunt's room."

"That's good," he said, relief apparent in his voice. Henri put on his hat and walked to the door. "I'll be off."

"Will you be here tomorrow?"

"I don't think so. Goodnight."

She set the book she was carrying on the desk and leaned across to switch off the standing lamp. Why was he here in the first place and why hadn't she been informed beforehand?

The next morning, remembering she'd left her book in the office, Abby went to retrieve it.

Cardboard boxes, stuffed to overflowing with paperwork, lined the walls. Henri certainly had been busy last night. Abby sat in the same chair she'd occupied during her meetings with Uncle Will. Those were happy days. Seeing the top drawer open, she bent forward to shut it.

There, amid the jumble of paper clips and pencils lay a bundle of photographs, face up, bound with a thick elastic band. A large, foreign-looking coin rested on top. Younger versions of her aunt and uncle smiled up at her. Abby thumbed through the stack, overjoyed. *My parents and me ... and Amelia ... there's Peter.* She'd show the pictures to her aunt and return the coin to her uncle's collection later. Abby placed them in the pocket of her dressing gown. Returning to her room, book in hand, she set her new-found treasures on the dresser.

The following morning, Henri showed up, dragging Edythe by the arm. "I've got urgent work upstairs," he said, shoving the girl at Abby. "I'll leave her with you."

She bristled at his presumption—bursting in like this without notice and then demanding a favor. He was using Edythe to coerce her. "W-W-Well, I—"

Henri raced for the stairs. "Shouldn't be long," he called out over his shoulder.

Edythe pulled off her gloves, handing them to Abby. "I'm hungry."

"Let's see what's in the kitchen," Abby said, helping the child with her leggings.

Half-an-hour later, Henri poked his head inside the door. "More urgent business to look after." He cleared his throat. "Perhaps you'll take care of Edythe until I get back?" He left without waiting for a reply.

Abby whisked Edythe upstairs to her room and picked up her knitting. The bone and ivory needles clicked in accompaniment to the child's chatter.

"I want to be like you when I grow up."

Abby put aside the sweater and laughed. "I'm flattered, but I don't know why."

"Because you're fun to be with."

"I like being with you as well."

"And I want to go to England too."

"Oh, you do?" Abby pulled at the navy-blue yarn and began another row. "I don't know when I shall be going home again. Not with this war on." Then she held out the half-finished garment. "This is for my sweetheart." She pointed at a stack of gloves and socks in olive drab on the dresser. "And those are for the Red Cross. In their military pattern."

"Auntie Abby?" Edythe looked up from her coloring book. "Are you getting married?"

"Yes. But Jim, my husband-to-be, is at war."

Edythe frowned. "Can't he come here to marry you and then go back?"

"I wish it were that easy." Abby sighed. "Jim has a job to do, and he can't come back until it's finished." But why hadn't he written? It'd been six weeks and nothing. Were her letters getting through?

Edythe waved a red crayon. "I'm getting married too."

"Oh, you are. Who to?"

Edythe twirled around the room, touching whatever caught her fancy. "I'm thinking about it." She lingered at the dressing table, studied herself in the mirror, then worked at her hair with Abby's brush. She stopped mid-stroke and pointed at a photograph on the dresser. "Who's that?"

Abby went over and lifted the stack of pictures she'd found in her uncle's desk two days ago. "Let's see. That's my brother Peter, that's your great Uncle Will, and this is your great Aunt Val, taken a long time ago." Then holding up the photograph beneath, "These are my parents in England," she said. "Come, sit beside me and we'll look at them."

A coin dropped from the middle of the pile and hit the floorboards, spinning to a halt under the bed. Edythe fell to her knees. "Let me, let me get it!" She thrust her shoulders under the bed, squirming with delight, then emerged with the piece in hand. Edythe studied it, her lips in silent motion. Like a spring, she shot up and pulled on Abby's arm. "Look, look!" She read out the inscription. "'EIN EINIG DEUTSCH SOLDATENTUM'. That's German. I know," she said, a big grin across her features. Then she handed the piece to Abby. "Daddy's got one just like it."

Henri's House, one week later

"Can Auntie Abby come to see us here sometime, Daddy? Oh, please, can she?" Edythe stood at the kitchen door, waving a hair bow. "See, she gave me this."

"Look at you, sweetheart. Come, give me a kiss and let's make you beautiful." Henri combed out her long, black hair and fastened the bow in place. He hadn't seen her this excited in a long time.

Claudia had agreed to let Edythe stay with him for the whole week. Under the terms of the separation agreement, he was allowed to have his daughter only one weekend a month, but Claudia was once again in Canada and this exception suited her convenience.

"Do you want toast or corn flakes? Or I can boil water for eggs."

"Just toast and milk, thank you." Edythe danced around the table. "Can she, Daddy?"

He'd not talked with Abby since he dropped Edythe off at the big house. Abby said nothing on that occasion about the late-night incident in Uncle Will's office, when she caught him going through the files. She'd probably forgotten. In any case, he couldn't worry about that now. Spilt milk and all that.

"We'll see her when we go over to visit Auntie Val again." Henri set his dishes in the sink.

"She's nice," Edythe said, spluttering a mouthful of milk. Wiping a hand across her lips, she banged the empty glass on the table and skipped away.

Henri let the hot water run over the dishes, then set them on the draining board, all the while thinking about Abby. The woman was rather naïve, a fact that would work to his advantage. He'd already decided to make her his wife. One way or another he would have Abby, because she would have Jolie Fontaine. He laughed aloud. All's fair in love and war— the expression he'd repeated to himself that day in December when he arrived at Jolie Fontaine the same time as the postman and offered to carry a stack of letters into the house, all addressed to Abby from Jim.

CHAPTER TWENTY-THREE

There'd been no word from Jim in weeks. Abby tried to picture him in the V-neck sweater she'd sent. How was he coping in the cold, gray English winter? Was he well? She heard the gossip around the house about GIs unfaithful to their sweethearts back home. Might Jim have reconsidered their future together? Though she fought to push such a possibility from her mind, still it nagged at her.

Then one morning in mid-January, Anna ran up the stairs shouting her name and waving a blue envelope above her head. "This just arrived. Guess who?" she said, her eyes wide.

"Jim!" Abby snatched for the treasure, but Anna stepped aside, dangling it over the railing, daring her to take it.

Abby laughed. "You give that to me, now!"

Shutting her door, she dropped onto the bed. Afraid her initial thrill would not be justified, she held her breath before slitting open the flap with her fingernail.

She peered into the envelope, turning it over several times, her heart pounding. Suppose this was his goodbye note after all this time? Did he still ...

With a shaky hand, she drew out a single sheet of paper written on both sides.

Jan. 4, '44, England

Dearest One. I'm so sorry that you haven't received anything from me.

Today I got your letter written before Christmas, but it seems that not all mine got through. I hope they turn up eventually.

One contained a poem I composed for you. It wasn't very good, but I tried to put all that I feel for you into the words. I'll recite it when I see you.

She fell backwards on the bed and let happy tears flow. *Thank you, Lord, and forgive me for doubting.*

My poor girl. I know how you must've felt when your uncle died. I was crushed by such sad news. I so wanted to be there to comfort you. I didn't know about his heart condition. He always seemed to be so sturdy. He gave me my start at Jolie Fontaine, and I'll always be grateful for that. He was a real Christian gentleman. I'll always be thankful that it was he who brought us together. He'll live on in our memory for that, won't he?

I hope your aunt will soon be past the hardest part of her grief. Give her my condolences. Having you there will be an enormous help to her. I don't know what she'd do without you if you weren't. I don't know what I'd do without you. Sometimes when I think I'm losing my mind, I think of you and want to hurry to your arms and hold you. You are my sanity. As far as I'm concerned, your leaving England for America is the best thing you ever did. I hope you feel the same way, darling.

It's cold here, but not like the tough winters back home. We celebrated Christmas on base with turkey and everything. We pulled the famous crackers! I'd like to think this was my last Christmas away from you, but I dare not hope for that. I think this war's got a long time to run. I hear news of the fighting in the Pacific, and it seems that the whole planet is at war.

I hope you and my mother can spend some time together. I got a letter from her yesterday.

Always and increasingly yours, Jim xxx

She folded his letter, a dead weight lifted from her mind. Whether it was the crushing of her fears or the confirmation of her belief in Jim, she didn't know. She had Jim and she was his.

The next morning, Abby watched for the postman. "Thank you for my letter yesterday," she said, flicking through the stack he handed her.

He touched his cap. "Good news from a far country?"

She smiled. "From my fiancé. The first time I've heard from him in ages." She furrowed her brow. "Says he wrote, but I never received anything. I suppose his letters could've been lost."

"That's odd," he said, stroking his chin. "I delivered a batch for you shortly before Christmas." He folded his arms and nodded. "A packet for Mrs. Bluette—I remember that, because she mentioned it the next day—and a separate clump for you, tied with string." He tilted his head toward her and winked. "I thought more love-notes for Abby. A gentleman was coming up the driveway, said his name was Frey, and offered to take the post in. I gave everything to him."

Tonight, she'd confront him. He wouldn't get away with it. After some resistance over the telephone, Henri agreed to meet with her.

A car door slammed below the office window, and Abby peered out into the dark night. Henri strode toward the entrance. It's fight or flight. Wedging herself into the desk, she gripped the edges tight. All the better to meet the onslaught head on. She glanced at the clock on the opposite wall. Eight-twenty. As ever, Henri had arrived ahead of time.

She heard his heavy tread on the stairs, followed by his muffled stride along the hallway that led to where she sat, waiting. Then the *rat-tat-tat* of his big fleshy hand against the doorframe. She stiffened. "Come in."

The door creaked open, settling half-way on its hinges. Henri's six-feet two bulk filled the aperture, his outline accentuated by the wall lights from the landing. Shutting the door behind him, he lumbered toward her. Balancing on the corner of her desk, he groped in a side pocket for his cigarettes and offered one to her.

She flashed him a withering glance. "You know I don't smoke."

Henri's eyes drilled into her. "So, what's this all about?" Henri said, his lips curved.

He knew why she wanted to see him. She'd learned long ago that Henri's genius alerted him when things weren't going his way. That's when he would change his tack from suave to sneer and back again. And it gave him the advantage over her.

"The theft of my private mail for a start," Abby fired back, gripping the side of her desk tighter. "You s-s-stole Jim's letters to me." She narrowed her eyes. "That's a crime."

Abby's shot hit home. Henri colored. "Ah, the letters." He got up and ambled over to the window and stared out. "I've been curious as to why you and your Jim didn't marry before he left."

Abby glared at his back and watched him like a cat, preparing for his next move. *None of your business.*

Henri turned toward her, smiling. "You must know by now that I'm attracted to you."

Her stony silence amplified the short distance between them. She blamed herself for being in this predicament.

"We've had some nice times together." Henri jammed his hands into his pockets. "But fact is, I want to spend a lot more time with you."

Abby sat stock still, her expression masking the turmoil within. She had allowed herself to be pulled along at the whim of this man.

Henri returned to her desk and rested his hands on it, palms down. He leaned in and fastened his eyes on hers. "Do I stand a chance with you? Just say the word and I'll try my best to give you all you want and make you happy."

Abby fixed her gaze on the floor. "How unbelievably presumptuous you are."

Henri pressed on, oblivious to her outburst. "You know, of course, that your lover boy is in danger every day," he said, hissing the words like a snake circling its quarry. "He might never come back." He tapped on the desktop with a well-manicured finger. "You have confronted that possibility? And if he does return, he might only be half a man."

Abby looked up in time to catch a glimpse of his taunting smile. She tensed, struggling to remain in her chair. Jim would always be twice the man Henri was.

"What kind of a life can he give you?" Henri droned on. "No money—" He tallied the negatives on his upraised fingers. "No prospects unless you consider gardener a profession." He sneered. "Besides, I happen to know that your beau's vagrant father is in prison." Straightening, he smiled at her in self-satisfaction. "Tut, tut," he clucked, raising one eyebrow in mock horror, "the very prim and proper Abby Stapleton engaged to the son of a convict."

"You're a vicious creature, Henri Frey." She rose to her feet, fists balled at her side, fighting the urge to strike him. "How dare you s-s-say such things." She hurled her words at him. "Jim loves me, I love him, and we will be married."

Henri's jaw slackened and he took a step back, as if reeling from the unexpected onslaught.

"I feel sorry for you, Henri Frey. You're a s-s-sick man." Abby threw back her shoulders. "I don't ever want to see or talk to you again."

"All right, girl. I'll go, but mark my words, you'll see things in a different light before long." His tone dripped with rancor, all compassion wrung out. The veins on his neck bulged. Swinging around, he tramped toward the exit. "You'll come begging to me on your knees," he called over his shoulder, waving the back of his hand. At the door he halted and turned to face her, jabbing a finger at the floor. "On your knees," he said, his eyes fiery slits, as though aiming for better effect.

"How dare you—" The slamming of the door cut her short. She slumped back in the chair, Henri's threat lingering in the space he vacated.

She didn't hate Henri. His life was so vacuous, empty of everything but his own ambitions, like the rest of his shallow, prattling class. How could she love such a man? But why on earth did he want her? The will! In a shattering instant she'd answered her own question. It's all to do with the will. A chill ran up her spine as the revelation sunk home. She did not doubt that Henri's blow would fall. But when and how heavy would it be?

CHAPTER TWENTY-FOUR

London
February 1944

Jim vaulted up the escalator two steps at a time and plunged into the busy street, blinking in the sunlight. The rain that marked his descent into the Tube an hour-and-a-half earlier had stopped. Only the grubby hulks of the barrage balloons spoiled the aspect of a cloudless sky. He scanned for his bearings, then struck off at a brisk trot in the direction of Kensington, exhilarated. It'd take ten minutes to reach the Stapleton home.

Two days ago, he'd received a reply from Abby's father to his letter. Yes, he'd be welcome to visit and stay with them. Jim could scarcely believe his luck. He instantly swapped with a buddy for this forty-eight-hour pass that began at 0700.

Caught up in the pace of the morning rush, Jim navigated between the crowds on the pavement. He dived into the street to the honking rebukes of the hackney cabs. As he bumped along, Jim nurtured some anxiety about his reception. "Hello, Jim Wright, peasant," he joked to himself. For encouragement he fell back on his image of Abby. If she loved him, perhaps her parents would too.

When the park came into sight, he dashed the last hundred yards to the line of Georgian houses on the far side. The homes in this stretch were double pillars, set back behind a low retaining wall that ran the entire length of the street.

"One-five-nine," he repeated, glancing at the paper in his hand. "Ah! Brass knocker in the shape of a lion's face, fan-shaped window above the entrance." He rapped on the door, rocking back and forth on the balls of his feet.

A butler appeared in the doorway. "You must be Mr. Wright." He smiled. "I'm Chadwick."

In the vestibule, Chadwick hung Jim's cap on the brass stand by the mirror and set his duffel bag on a wooden chest. "I'll announce your arrival." Then he tramped off down the hall.

In a furtive movement, Jim stole a glance at his reflection and ran a clammy palm across his scalp. Abby had stood before this same mirror.

Phillip Stapleton approached, smiling. "So glad to see you," he said, pumping Jim's hand. "We've looked forward to this meeting."

"It's a real pleasure for me, sir. I can hardly believe I'm here."

Ellen appeared at her husband's side, her hands clasped in front of her. "So. We meet at last." Her smile faded, and she gave him a curt nod.

"Glad to meet you, ma'am." He rummaged through his bag and extended a box. "From the commissary, I'm afraid."

"American chocolates. How nice. Shall we go into the parlor?" She led the way along the corridor.

Phillip placed a guiding hand on Jim's shoulder. "Yes, come in and take the weight off your feet."

Ellen whirled around to face them. "Doesn't look like he has much weight to take off."

"I'm sorry I'm a bit late." Jim cleared his throat. "There was a bomb scare on the line from the station at Salisbury. We got held up for over an hour."

"Don't apologize. Par for the course, I'm afraid," Phillip said.

Jim whistled through his teeth when they entered the parlor. He'd held Abby's description of the room in his head, and this scene matched perfectly. Phillip motioned him to the armchair, while he and his wife took the sofa opposite. The butler set a tray of tea and pastries on the low table between them and poured three cups.

"Chadwick, please take his things up to Abby's old room." Ellen turned to Jim. "Abby knows you're here?"

"I wrote to her about the possibility. I've had nothing from her for weeks."

Phillip nodded. "We tried to ring her last week. It's not easy at the best of times, but right now it's well-nigh impossible."

"I do hope she's happy," Ellen said. "We get the occasional letter, but I'm not sure she always tells us what's going on."

"Oh, I think that's your imagination, dear," Phillip countered.

"I don't think so. I sense she's a troubled girl."

"Well, things are hard for her since her uncle died." Jim leaned forward. "And my condolences to you both. And she's worried for her aunt." He frowned. "The war. It seems to go on and on—"

Ellen's eyes widened. "It's hard for all of us."

Jim clanked his cup down. "But the rest of us are here in the thick of the action." Jim unbuttoned his jacket and tossed it across the back of his seat. "What I mean is, there's a rush of adrenaline that comes with that." With both hands he snapped his fingers together, *clickety-click.* "There's movement, vitality. It's destructive—God knows it is. I've seen it overseas and in London. But it's tangible, if you know what I mean."

Ellen frowned and shook her head. "Now then, I think my daughter's just where she ought to be."

"But she feels she's been left behind, out of the action," Jim responded, beating a tattoo on the coffee table. "She gets your letters and mine, but it's old hat by the time it reaches her." He draped his arm across the back of his seat and grinned. "Abby's a girl with energy," he said, swinging his fist through the air, like a plane in flight. "She tingles with it and she longs to do something useful." Catching Phillip's rapt gaze, he blushed and faltered.

"Right you are. That's the Abby we know." Phillip chuckled. "One determined young lady. Is that not so, Ellen?"

"We were sorry she left under a cloud. But we stand by our decision." A smile crept over Ellen's face. "I think it will work out for the best."

"Our Peter is in the RAF," Phillip said. "He's got a girl who lives in Kent, but he only gets to see her once every couple of months."

"Will I get to meet Abby's brother?"

"Afraid not. We don't know when Peter will show up. And Amelia, our daughter, is in Yorkshire with her children." Phillip reached for a framed picture, handing it to Jim. "That's Valerie with Abby, Amelia, and Peter, taken many years ago at Jolie Fontaine."

Jim studied the photograph. "Amazing. Abby bears such a close resemblance to her Aunt Val in this. You do see it too?" he said, passing the picture to Ellen.

She looked at it, shrugged her shoulders, and turned to her husband. "Well then. Ask Chadwick to show our trooper to his room so he can relax before we eat."

"Thank you, sir. I would like to unpack my bag and wash up."

Phillip reached for a tasseled bell pull, then tugged on it. "By the way, let's drop the *sir* and *ma'am*. I'm Phillip and my wife is Ellen." He chuckled. "If we're going to get to know one another, we may as well start there, don't you agree?"

Ellen motioned for Jim to take a seat at the dining room table. "Probably not what you're accustomed to."

Jim looked over the food and smiled. "It's my first home-cooked meal in ages."

Phillip laughed. "Tuck in, soldier."

"Rabbit pot roast, parsnips, some greens, and steamed apple for dessert," Ellen said. "The ingredients are dictated by our meager rations, but I think you'll find it goes down all right."

Jim helped himself to the piping hot dishes. "Soldiers have big appetites, and I'm no exception."

After the meal, Jim and Phillip sat in the living room by the bay window. Phillip gestured in the direction of the street. "A wonderful place to watch people go by. You know, the latest joke is that if a couple of women stop for a chat, they're likely to start a queue. The others will think there are extra rations available and fall in behind."

Jim laughed along with Phillip.

"I don't know how long people will put up with this. My wife and I are well fixed, and we haven't been bombed out—yet. Ellen works at the local aid station and sees parents gone in some cases. We've had kids here before the evacuations started. It's heartbreaking to hear their stories. These high explosives do a terrific amount of damage." Phillip settled back in his chair. "It must have been a difficult time for all of you in North Africa. That business at the Kasserine Pass was tragic. But perhaps you'd rather not talk about it."

"I don't mind." Jim lowered his head. "Occasionally, I do have nightmares though." He rubbed the back of his neck. "One member of our platoon was evacuated on compassionate grounds. His mind couldn't take it any more."

"I'm up on the intelligence, given the work I'm in. Still I can't talk too much about it," Phillip said. "We're up against a formidable enemy." He steepled his hands. "But with America's heft in the fight, I don't see how we can lose. Of course, there's still the Pacific and Asia. Our 'Forgotten Fourteenth' in Burma, for example. But London will survive." He smiled. "She's been here for two thousand years, and we'll weather Hitler until we dispatch him and his thugs."

Jim sat on the edge of the bed and removed his boots and socks, glad to be alone in Abby's room. By the dusk light from a window, he surveyed the furnishings. Apart from an old sewing machine and a few cardboard boxes—probably relocated from elsewhere in the house—he guessed the room was pretty much as when she'd left.

Wandering over to the low dresser, Jim picked up a framed photograph of Phillip and Ellen standing with Aunt Val and Uncle Will in front of the lake at Jolie Fontaine. He studied the picture as though taking in a premonition. Odd how events circle back on themselves. He would've explored his musings further, but tiredness beat him. He drew the blackout curtains and returned to the bed.

He stretched out fully clothed, clasped his hands behind his head and yawned. He'd taken to Abby's father right away, but her mother .... Well, he wasn't so sure about her. Or, rather, he guessed she was unsure of him. Jim frowned. He'd volunteered some details on his background, except the business with his father, and although polite, she'd demonstrated little interest. He stared up at the wallpapered ceiling. Throughout the meal he'd been conscious of her silent, probing observation as though she questioned his right to be here. Was it his imagination?

"It's seven, sir. You asked me to wake you."

Jim peered at the clock and groaned. "Thank you, Chadwick, I'm awake."

"Breakfast is at eight, sir."

Jim rolled to the edge of the bed and sat there, trying to orient himself to his surroundings. He stumbled to the window and opened the heavy curtains, flinching at the harsh light. Judging by the puffs of frosty breath from pedestrians below, it was cold outside. After washing and shaving, he dressed, putting on the sweater Abby had knitted for him.

Downstairs, the aroma of food in the dining room dispersed the fog of sleep from his brain. He raised the cover from each tureen on the sideboard and sniffed, selecting scrambled eggs and two slices of buttered toast, then stood at the table, waiting. Chadwick did say eight.

"Slept well, I trust?"

He turned to see Phillip and Ellen standing in the doorway.

"Thank you, sir ... Phillip."

Ellen laughed. "'Sir Phillip'. I like that," she said, helping herself to the dishes. "I think my husband should be knighted. But those ministry types—"

"Steady on, dear." Phillip put his plate down. "You know we've discussed that before."

Ellen pushed back her shoulders. "I'm sorry, Phil, but if it hadn't been for you-know-who you'd be higher up today."

"Sit down, my lad. We don't stand on ceremony." He looked at Jim, as if in apology. "My wife thinks I'm the bee's knees—outstanding," he added. "But not everybody does."

He pulled out a chair for Ellen, then addressed her in a mock whisper. "I'll tell you what, when the war's over, I'll raise the matter again and see what happens."

"And if nothing does?"

Phillip caught Jim's eye and winked. "We'll emigrate. How about that?"

"Ha! To where? Australia? Some remote colonial outpost?"

"How about America?" Phillip laughed. "We'll live with Abby and Jim."

"Tosh!"

Jim smiled. Abby had told him this exclamation was an adopted favorite of her mother's.

"This war's especially hard on the women." Phillip reached over and patted Ellen's hand. "They do most of the worrying and are hit hardest by the rigors of life on the home front. This business of total war is a devilish thing." He wiped a serviette across his mouth. "A man goes overseas, gets shot at, survives and comes home, only to find that his wife or parents have been killed by a free-falling bomb in his own house."

"All I know is that if it were up to us, as Eleanor Roosevelt puts it, we women would find other ways of solving our problems rather than blowing one another up," Ellen said, her American accent reasserting itself.

Jim was about to comment on the similarities between the English and American halves of Abby's world—similarities that went deeper than the language—when Ellen's eyes locked on his. "Just what are your prospects for after the war, young man?"

Her words hit Jim like an arctic blast, and he reeled. "I'm not sure I understand, Mrs. Stapleton."

"It's quite simple. How will you provide for my daughter?" She fired the question like a practiced gunner.

From the corner of his eye, he saw Phillip reach for his wife's hand. "Ellen, can't we have this conversation at another time?"

She pooh-poohed her husband's intrusion. "Well, from what Abby tells me, you're from a poor background and have no notable credentials to speak of." She leaned toward him. "In short, what do we know about you that would particularly encourage us to commend our daughter to your lifelong care?" she said, slowly and confidently.

Jim refolded his napkin, gritting his teeth. Abby had related some of his dismal history in letters to her parents, but nothing she'd revealed to her mother justified an attack like this. His heart thumped like a jackhammer. He lacked the resources to counter such an onslaught. Why was she doing this? *Oh, God, what a mistake I made in coming here.*

Temples pounding and almost giddy with rage, Jim envisioned himself soaring to full height, hurling his napkin at her, shouting at the top of his voice, demanding an apology, insisting that he would marry Abby, no matter what she said—

But he did none of these things. Facing her straight on, he stared her down. "I love your daughter—number one. I know it's not enough in itself, but it's a good start. In fact, it's the only place to start from." He pushed his plate to one side and rested his elbows on the table. He raised his palms toward her and spread his trembling fingers. "The only guarantees I have to show you are these. I am very good with these: I can fix things, make things, and bring beautiful things from the ground—number two."

Ellen met his gaze, unflinching.

"I believe in Abby. She inspires me to be better than I am—number three," Jim said, perspiration running down his cheek. "I'm no great warrior, Mrs. Stapleton. Or a great brain, come to that. And I'd rather not be fighting in this crazy war. But in the end, I must simply fight for what I can understand—for Abby and, if we have them, the future of our children. If I can do something to help save all the other Abbys and Jims and their children too, well, all to the good."

Phillip grabbed Jim's arm and grinned. "Well said, my boy. Well said."

Ellen looked at her husband and shifted in her seat.

Jim took a deep breath and lowered his voice. "My mind's not big enough to comprehend all that. All I know is that your daughter is the best thing that ever happened to me. I've never been so happy in all my life as I am when I'm with her. She's brought me hope and a new assurance that God is over all and will bring us through." Jim came to an abrupt stop. He dropped his hands to the table and studied his pulsating veins. Though on the verge of tears, he would not solicit Ellen's sympathy with a show of tawdry emotion. He'd said his piece. *Hang the consequences.*

CHAPTER TWENTY-FIVE

Henri's Office, West Chester
Late March 1944

Henri parted the wooden slats of the blind and peered through. Gas lamps in the street below flickered and flared up one by one, their ragged points of light striding to the intersection three hundred yards away. He swirled the drink in his glass. At the traffic signal, cars idled, waiting to turn, their exhaust plumes billowing white in the frosty night air. Along one entire block on the opposite side of the street stretched the colonnaded front of the bank which held the accounts of Henri Frey, Esquire, Attorney-at-Law. A banker's bank, the kind of place that made you feel important. He turned away from the window and scanned the documents and blueprints spread out on his desk. He couldn't believe his luck. If ever his stars aligned, it was now.

When the old firm that had handled the business of William Bluette's estate dissolved five years previously, he'd got the account. A stroke of good fortune, especially in light of his own family's peculiar estrangement. Uncle Will treated him cordially, but Henri always felt alienated, unforgiven for the sins of his father. Probably why he was never granted full fiduciary control of the assets. Still, he possessed fingertip knowledge of the credits and debits, expenses and liabilities of the estate. He recalled the expression his uncle used in reference to the grounds—they held "capabilities of improvement."

He reached for a slim, gold-plated case and studied the cigarettes snugged in behind the white elastic band—the symmetry of them a metaphor for his life. Except for Abby—that ungrateful woman had rebuffed him two months ago in her office. Made him feel like dirt. He snapped the case shut and tapped it against his chin.

Leaning back in his swivel chair, he studied the patterns on the ceiling. His late father wouldn't have stood for guff from a woman. Swift back-of-the-hand retaliation, that was his philosophy. Henri winced. As a boy he'd been on the receiving end of it himself a number of times. He shook his head. An image of his mother, cowering by the front door, lips bleeding, came to mind. She'd crossed his father—said something he didn't like. She never did so again. Seems she disappeared soon after that. "Gone back to the old country," his father explained over the newspaper one morning, adding, "and good riddance." Henri rubbed the knuckles of his right hand. No, drunken thuggery wasn't his style. He'd get what he wanted by different means. His jaw tightened. His weapon of choice was the law. All neat and respectable.

Only one love claimed his heart. He was awkward around women. They were unfathomable, their emotions changeable. But the *law*. This was key to everything Henri ever wanted. Or needed. Its form and dimensions, the beauty and elegance of its logic, its supreme dependability. The honed argument, weighed and polished, held in reserve until the right moment, then plunged into the opponent. This was an addiction he was proud to confess.

And now for that Stapleton woman. Abby would've been the perfect wife. But now she was in his way. Stirred up the clumsy boy in him. He hated her for that, and he would make her pay. If he couldn't win her by consent, he would resort to other means. Conquest, submission, ownership. All perfectly legal. Almost.

Slipping the case into his side pocket, he returned to the task at hand. These detailed maps of Jolie Fontaine told an eloquent story. Of acres and frontage and cubic feet of lumber. And dollars and cents. The buildings— the main house, carriage house, and assorted structures—were easily worth three-quarters of a million. With the land, the figure rose to over twice that amount. Say, two million, conservative.

Henri tallied the numbers in his head. Not that he needed to. He'd worked them over numerous times, with the same result. When this war was over, hordes of men would return home to marry, start families. They'd need houses. And there were the others, the financial types for whom this war had turned out to be a godsend. They'd be looking to invest. Sold off in parcels, the estate might fetch five or six times its current valuation.

Henri exhaled, giddy with the prospects.

Thanks to financial incompetence in high circles, there were many down-and-outers now. He'd protected his own investments with foresight and solid planning. This socialistic mumbo-jumbo that Roosevelt had foisted on the country was a mere stop-gap, a ruse to keep the feeble-minded from revolting. The worm would turn. When it did, he'd be ready to take advantage of the situation.

Henri cataloged his legal victories with precision. Color-coded file folders in the just-right subcategory, cross-referenced, meticulously ordered. He often retrieved these case histories and studied them as a veteran general might rehearse military campaigns. Henri exulted in these reviews as a spectator, separate from the action, blameless of any dire consequences. He had become a wealthy man. A few creative adjustments here and there for well-to-do clients and the occasional padded bill worked wonders. And the opportunity which now presented itself was too good to pass up.

Henri tipped his head back, drained the last of his drink and glanced at his wristwatch. Quarter past eight. He looked over at the bank, where a light still burned in a second-floor office. He slid out the drawer of a cabinet, extracted a brown folder under "S" and fingered through the papers to the one he wanted, then angled it toward the lamp to verify its contents. Perfect.

He returned the folder to its place. The letter he creased in half and slipped into his pocket. He patted his jacket in smug congratulation. Crossing the room, he heaved on his overcoat, snatched his Homburg from the rack, and descended the stairs to the street.

Five minutes later, he made himself comfortable behind locked doors in the well-upholstered office of Conrad Eggers, assistant manager of Farmers Bank.

"Nice to see you, Henri. It's been a while."

Henri puffed at his cigarette like a man at ease with himself. "I need help with a certain matter which requires some finesse. Access to certain resources. You understand?"

"As a friend?" Conrad said.

"As one member to another," Henri replied.

WHEN VALLEYS BLOOM AGAIN

Henri's Office
Two Weeks Later

"Your niece is a fraud," Henri said. To support the bald assertion, he once again directed Aunt Val's attention to the documents and checks fanned out across his desk. "She used friendship to manipulate Uncle Will for her own gain and that of her paramour and to your loss."

Valerie stared at the floor, shaking her head in disbelief. "No, I'm not having any of this."

"Or you'd rather not?" Henri charged on. "You know how generous Uncle was." He cleared his throat. "She took advantage of his illness to raid the funds."

On the reading of her husband's will in December, the full extent of his intentions were made known to her for the first time. Yes, she was surprised. Not that she objected, in principle, to the general plan. She knew of William's desire to do something for the community. She shared it. He was ever the philanthropist, and she supported him in his endeavors. She would be well looked after, her needs and wants provided for. *Just like William.*

But she also pondered how things might have turned out otherwise. She had always expected to inherit everything. And true—the arrangements were not revised until Abby came along.

Henri stared at her, unwavering. "I think we should take immediate action on this matter."

"I don't know, Henri. Your claim's so outlandish. Abby diverted monies from the school to her private account? I can't believe it." She leaned forward. "Could you perhaps have misunderstood something? Could these papers"—she waved at them as if to make them disappear—"admit of another explanation?"

Henri shook his head. "I can find no other."

"What do you propose to do about it?" Valerie straightened in her chair. "I won't condone any publicity."

Henri spread his fingers across the desk and studied his nails. "I could get a legal action going. On the other hand, I ... we could get the thing taken care of without any publicity whatsoever. No one knows about this version of the will except the three of us. So, let's try a few judicious threats."

"You mean get her to sign a statement of some sort, a confession, revoking any interest in the will?"

"That's about the size of it. Frighten her. Of course, she may not cooperate. That sort usually never do."

Henri's emphasis on "that sort" did not escape Valerie's notice. "And that would invalidate the will? We'd go back to the first one?"

"Yes."

"Perhaps you're a little harsh, Henri? After all, she's just a girl. Might she have come under the influence of another?"

Henri tensed. "Who do you have in mind?"

"You know, that soldier fellow, James."

"Oh, I see what you mean. In that case, he needs to be taken out of the picture." He chuckled. "And if we can get this questionable will voided, that should take care of him."

"Is there something you're not telling me, Henri?"

He fidgeted and rummaged in the top drawer. "I think I've covered everything for now. I'll certainly keep you informed at every step of the way."

"Do I need to make a statement?"

"You will need to show that your interests have been damaged as a result of the revised will." Henri leaned back in his chair. "That your latter inheritance will be less than the former, had the old will stood." He tilted his head toward her. "Is that not so?"

"I suppose that's true. But I could hardly argue that I would be impoverished. You know that the amount I am to—"

"It isn't that. It's a technical point, a legality. Would you want to let her get away with this just because she didn't do as much damage to you as she might have done?"

"Not when you put it like that. Still—"

"All you need do is acknowledge that I've laid out the facts before you, consistent with my responsibility as the Executor appointed by your late husband. I think you'll agree they are convincing."

Valerie stood. "I should be going." She wished she'd never come.

Henri walked around the desk and helped her with her coat. "I'll try to sort it all out for you. Leave everything to me." He kissed her cheek. "I'm sorry things have turned out this way."

"Don't come down with me. I can manage."

"It would be best to keep this quiet for now. I'll stay away from the house." He half-smiled. "Could create some legal problems later on, if you know what I mean? Abby might get suspicious. If you need to see me, come here."

Valerie's automobile waited at the curb. At the traffic light, the driver made a turn onto the road leading to Jolie Fontaine. She reached for the leather door strap and rested her forehead on the window. The scenery rushed from city clutter to flat open fields fenced in with wire netting on weathered gray posts.

In the distance, rain clouds hovered above the outline of the undulating hills of Chester County. A bolt of lightning raced through the gap, illuminating the scene. Valerie could barely discern the slanted brown roofs of unfinished houses, testimony to a boom gone bust. She doubted they would ever be occupied, grateful herself for the security of the estate.

At the faint rumble of thunder, the driver picked up speed. Valerie unbuttoned her coat and rested her head against the seat. She'd never taken an active interest in the affairs of Jolie Fontaine. William told her about the general provisions after they married. On his death, she would own the house and all his personal assets. Simple. She'd left things at that and gave the matter little thought. He took care of the household bills and accorded her a generous monthly allowance. If she needed more, funds were made available. She found no fault with the arrangement. After all, the man was rightful head of the home, and he should provide for his family.

Abby—the only secret she ever kept from Will—is family. Valerie always intended, on her husband's death, to relay his generosity through a bequest to Abby. At least then William would have a tangible role in the welfare of the girl to whom she gave birth and whose enforced anonymity she had long detested. She would even be content with this posthumous adjustment of affairs, were it not for this new wrinkle Henri had proposed.

Val mused over the complications that had emerged from her past transgressions. She'd hoped against hope she could one day tell William that Abby was her daughter, and he'd love her as his own. As mother, father, and daughter, they'd form the family she longed to have. But years passed and the circumstances of life dictated otherwise. Valerie sighed. Inch by inch, the dream slipped out of sight. Then through an unexpected turn of events, Abby was here on their doorstep and admitted into William's affections. She'd become like a daughter to him—a rightful heir.

The seat pressed against her as the car turned into the driveway. Could Abby have possibly scorned the hospitality offered her? Could Henri be right? He himself had been friendly with her until recently. What happened there? Yes, Jim Wright was penniless, and the new arrangement of the will would certainly be a nice thing for him. But was he really the malign influence?

She resisted the urge to make a snap judgment there and then. Inside the house, she went through the envelopes in the letter rack, three for her and two addressed to Abby.

Abby picked up her mail, made a cup of tea, and curled up in a chair before turning to Jim's first letter in the customary V-mail format. It began without fanfare.

Mar. 5, '44

Our liberties are to be restricted until further notice and we'll be confined to barracks after duty hours beginning next week. We're going onto [censored] but have not been told why. So many things I can't mention to you here. USO show here again yesterday with an American-Canadian band. They were pretty good.

You'll be glad to know that since I returned to England, I try not to miss worship services in the nearby village. The church is up a steep hill and overlooks the bay. Very picturesque. If I can't get out, I go to chapel on the base.

"Thank you, Lord," Abby breathed, conscious of an answered prayer.

So that you will understand when you get this, we've been told some of our mail from this end will be held up indefinitely. (I got three letters from you today!) But I'll keep writing to you just in case. I'm putting a lot of my thoughts in my journal, so if the censor has to cut something, at least you'll get to see the flavor of things on my return to you. [Censored]

As always, Jim

Abby re-read the morsel from Jim's truncated letter—the first in weeks. She drained her teacup and gazed at the leaves in the bottom, scoffing at the notion of predicting the future from such a random aggregation. Still, the diversion nudged her mind toward a bleak prospect—her lifeline with Jim was to be severed by some bureaucratic decree. And there was Henri. Jim remained enthroned in her affections, but when she conjured up his face, Henri's overlaid it.

She cringed. The wounds from her confrontation with him still hurt. At least he hadn't been in touch since that night in her office. Still, he lurked in the recesses of her mind. Vindictive. A devil waiting to pounce. *Lord, I want to believe that this, too, is working to my good, but it's hard to see right now.*

CHAPTER TWENTY-SIX

Jolie Fontaine,
April 1944

"That arrived early this morning by courier." Aunt Val gestured toward a large brown envelope beside Abby's place setting. "I had to sign for it."

"MISS ABIGAIL STAPLETON, C/O JOLIE FONTAINE" in heavy, black type. The return address showed a post office box number. Abby sat at the table, then slit the flap open with a knife, releasing a chemical odor from inside. She withdrew three, glossy, letter-sized sheets of paper. Why had her aunt chosen this method to present a piece of her correspondence instead of placing it in the hallway stand?

"Is it bad news?" her aunt said.

Abby shrugged her shoulders. "I don't know." She turned the sheets over in her hands before placing them back in the envelope. "I'll look it over after breakfast."

In her room, Abby laid the papers on the bed, side by side, to study them. They appeared to be reproductions. One showed the image of a canceled check for nine hundred dollars. Another one, a receipt for the corresponding sum. The third, a letter authorizing a transfer of funds in the amount of twelve hundred dollars. Her signature appeared at the bottom. *What was this all about?*

The telephone in her room rang, and she answered.

"Ah, it's you, Abby," Henri purred. "Just the woman I'm looking for."

Her heart began to race. "Wh-what do you want?"

"What-do-I-want?" Henri spoke slow and deliberate, as if mocking her. "That's a large question." He chuckled. "One on which your fate hinges."

"G-G-get to the point, Henri."

"Perhaps you'd like to sit while I expand on the answer."

"I don't need to."

"Okay. You got my little surprise?"

"Surprise?"

"Oh, come on. I know you did. The envelope. The Special D."

Her gaze swept across the room to her bed. "Those papers are from you?"

"Curious?"

"Henri, what's all this about?"

"Those papers can send you to prison."

Abby sat on the stool beside the telephone and clutched the receiver, her throat tight.

"Did you hear me?" Henri hissed. "I said those—"

"Wh-what are you talking about?"

"Put simply, they prove you used your position at Jolie Fontaine to enrich yourself. That you coerced the late lamented William Bluette to alter his will in your favor. 'Undue influence' in legal parlance."

Abby tightened a trembling hold on the receiver. "How dare you accuse me of such a thing."

"It's all plausible—happens all the time." Henri's voice resumed its oily confidence. "And this soldier of yours—what if he conspired with you to get something for the two of you? Like a cozy berth on the estate after the war? Eh?"

She closed her eyes. "That's absurd. You know it is."

"I have here in my hand"—Henri seemed to be waving it at her—"an envelope addressed to one 'James Wright, in care of US Forces at Blandford Army Base, England.' What does it contain? Let me see. An anonymous letter stating that Abby Stapleton and Henri Frey were seen together on several occasions and that they are lovers." He laughed. "You'll be interested to know I got his address from those letters I purloined."

Abby froze in place, unable to slam the phone down. His thunderbolt confirmed her opinion that he possessed a cruel streak a mile wide. She'd seen his moods and suspected something nasty lurked under the polished facade.

"Of course, you could deny everything, but no one will believe you. You don't have the right connections. Regardless, the damage will have been done."

Curse you Henri Frey, she mouthed to herself.

"But there is a solution." Henri paused, as if to heighten the tension. "Can't you guess what it is? No? All right, I'll tell you. I will keep all this to myself on one condition—that you agree to marry me."

"Wh-Wh-What?" she said, a chill running up her spine. "Don't be so utterly stupid."

"It won't be so bad," Henri's voice snapped back. "As for your bucolic boyfriend—well, he wouldn't be the first to discover his girl played him false. Sitting under the apple tree with someone else and all that." He gave a sinister cackle.

She jumped to her feet and screamed into the mouthpiece. "You're stark raving mad to even think I would—"

"If I don't get the decision I want by, let's say, May 20, those papers go to the Office of Wills and Probate, with a note attached. The letter to James Wright goes in the mailbox," Henri said, unruffled. "And destroying the documents won't do you any good. I've got copies in several places. And if you breathe a word about any of this, I'll not only carry out my threat but deny this conversation ever took place."

The blood in her temple boomed in the earpiece. "Leave us alone."

"Remember, the twentieth." Henri's voice clicked off.

She glared at the accusing documents on the bed, unable to comprehend the horror of the situation. *Gone. Everything gone.* Destroyed by that detestable man. And her own gullible stupidity.

Stumbling to the bathroom sink, she turned on the tap and splashed cold water over her face. Catching sight of herself in the mirror, she recoiled from the pale and haggard face which stared back. She wrenched open the door of the medicine cupboard and took down a bottle of tablets, unscrewed the top, filled a glass with water, then perched on the edge of her bed. Tipping the pills into her mouth, she drained the glass. In an angry sweep of her arm, she scattered the papers into the air. Dropping her head onto a pillow, she closed her eyes. *God help me.*

The Same Day, A Barracks in England

Jim craned his neck through the window of the Quonset hut. A stream of covered army trucks swung through the main gates, a few feet separating each one as the convoy passed his section. They hung low on their springs, weighed down by extra-heavy loads. The drivers shifted into low gear in anticipation of the incline up to a two-lane road that led to the south coast. Their motors labored in unison, then spun up as the vehicles crested the hill and disappeared over the top.

Pulling his head back inside, Jim flopped onto the bunk. His days in England were numbered. All signs pointed to a big operation at hand—training stepped up, all leave canceled, military police swarming over the base. And tomorrow all mail service was to be halted.

The barracks held forty men, but at the moment Jim was alone. He looked at the clock on the far wall. The gang would soon return from the mess. Jim swung his legs over the lumpy pallet and hunched over what served as a writing desk. He'd make one last attempt to finish a letter to Abby. Who knows when she'll get it anyway?

"—to the beach, due to the—" He crossed it out. He couldn't say that.

Jim tapped the pen nib against his teeth. Abby might not recognize him as the same man who left her two years before. Sometimes, he hardly recognized himself. A veteran of North Africa and Sicily, he'd become inured to most hardship and a bit callous. He had watched men die around him—some died in his arms—and his idealism had taken a beating. He longed for this war to be over and done with so he could go back to Abby and his gardens and live at peace with the world.

When he'd found the time, he diverted his anguish to the entries in his diary. When all this was over, he would let Abby read them. Were he to be killed, the little volume would be sent to her. He hoped she wouldn't judge him harshly. His reading hadn't been wide, but he was aware of the literary generation of men who perished in the blood-soaked trenches of the Great War. He longed to capture his own experiences on paper and fancied that he'd made some creditable entries in his journal. He couldn't write about those experiences in a letter. Can't let the nice folks back home know how bad this is. He'd become cynical too.

Unable to find anything to say, he put his pen down and jogged around the inside of the hut. If they'd married before he left, it would have tied Abby securely to him. Was she still waiting for him? Perhaps another man had "muscled in on his territory"? He couldn't help but smile at the borrowed expression, the one his bunkmate had used. George knew firsthand all about that. His girl had written to him, wished him well, then politely informed him she'd fallen for someone else.

He returned to the unfinished letter on the upturned crate, reproaching himself for his selfish thought. Anyone would think he didn't trust Abby. What on earth was she doing anyway? He hadn't heard from her for weeks. Any attempt to weave a chronology from the intermittent correspondence, proved unsatisfactory. It was a patchwork business. Newer letters would arrive before older ones, and he couldn't always tell which of his she was replying to. He often forgot which ones he'd sent. He kept a log, but on the move this proved difficult. On occasion, ships and planes carrying letters never got through, and whole batches were lost when crews were sunk or shot down. He shuddered.

A commotion at the back door diverted his ruminations as his buddies filed in. "Still at those sweetie-pie letters?" George said. "It's amazing you've got any fingers left." Then, a few minutes of communal hilarity as one man pulled his sleeve down over his hand, bent double, and strutted and clucked around the room, two stubby fingers poking out. Jim laughed along. He couldn't begrudge them their fun. They were a dependable gang and had been through a lot, most of them fighting through the same hard campaigns with him.

One was a fellow Christian. And only with Mike did Jim share confidences. They prayed and studied the Bible together and tried to make sense of their common experiences. He had a girl back home too.

"When Frances and me marry, it's gonna be in that big church in St. Louis, the one with all the stained glass and spires and stuff," Mike said one day. "All her Italian relatives and mine. And I want you there, Jimmy boy, with your Abby."

Mike wasn't much of a writer, so he'd dictate his thoughts to Jim, who'd improvise something suitable. He referred to Jim as his Cyrano, "minus the long snout." In praying for Mike's safe passage through this bloody war and a return to his sweetheart, Jim hoped to ensure his own happy ending.

After lights out, Jim lay on top of the covers, wide awake. He completed his letter to Abby in his head, hoping he would remember his words in the morning. The crisp sound of the bugler playing "Taps" floated over the roofs of the huddled buildings. How could any sound be so pure and clean in this soiled world? Listening to the steady breathing of his bunkmate above, his eyes grew heavy. On the cusp of slumber, Jim willed his brain to dream of Abby, but her image faded.

The Same Day, Jolie Fontaine

Boom, boom. The sound thundered through Abby's head like a river cannon in a pea soup fog. Then from out of the mist, Jim ran toward her, arms outstretched. How she longed to run into those arms. But someone was shaking her. She heard a voice close up. "Abby." Struggling to open her eyes, Aunt Val's face came into focus.

"Are you all right?" Her aunt stroked Abby's brow, frowning. "I thought you'd gone out, but when you didn't return, I came to your door. I banged for a long time," she said, taking Abby's hand. "When you didn't answer, I let myself in with a spare key."

Abby propped herself up on the pillow and licked her parched lips. Her aunt's narrative tumbled from her so fast that she barely caught the drift.

"I know how you must be feeling, dear," her aunt said, tears welling in her eyes.

Abby swung her legs over the side of the bed and attempted to stand, wincing from the pain in her head.

"I was so afraid that you'd tried to—"

"To what ... hurt myself?" Abby said, shuddering.

Aunt Val began to sob. "Was it awful of me to think that way?"

"I couldn't do that."

Aunt Val wiped her eyes, glanced at the papers scattered over the floor and scowled. "Henri's doing, I'll wager." She picked them up. "I can guess what this is about," she said, jabbing at the pages in her hand.

"Henri telephoned and th-threatened to blackmail me if I didn't m-marry him. And to tell Jim a pack of lies about me. I was down at the bottom of a pit and had a throbbing headache." She stroked her aunt's arm and managed a smile. "I lay awake for the longest time and thought about Jim and you, and Uncle and the house, and all my blessings. I knew that things would work out all right."

"I'm aware of Henri's accusations. I don't believe any of what he says about your plotting to get the estate." She put an arm around Abby's shoulder. "You're too honest to be guilty of such a monstrous thing." Her eyes narrowed. "Henri wants the house. I think I've always suspected that." She stood to her full height and placed her hands on her hips. "He won't get it, and he certainly won't get you." She pushed back her shoulders. "You and I will take care of this together."

CHAPTER TWENTY-SEVEN

"This photograph was taken on our trip to New England." Aunt Val smiled. "William got so excited with the fish he caught that he almost fell out of the boat. He used to say I'd hooked him too."

Abby hadn't seen her aunt this happy in months. "Let's put them in your album soon." She set the last photograph atop the stack and secured it with a rubber band. "Oh, I almost forgot." Abby reached into her skirt pocket. "I found this with the photos in Uncle's desk. "I thought I'd return it to his collection." She passed the foreign-looking coin to her aunt.

Valerie squinted at the piece through her spectacles. "Pretty, with all that gilt-finish." She rubbed her thumb against it. "But this isn't a coin, dear. More like a medallion. Your uncle bought something similar years ago. Not this pattern, of course. He used to hang his watch from it." She held the piece up and pointed to a slit in the top. "A ribbon or strap goes through here and the other end attaches to a buttonhole on a man's coat or vest. Like so," she said, pressing it against her chest. "A watch fob, I think. He lost his ages ago." She dropped it into Abby's palm.

"Perhaps he got this to replace the one he lost?"

"I shouldn't think so. German, you say?" Valerie shook her head. "No, I should say not. You know how your uncle felt about that." She laughed. "Perhaps he found this watch fob on his rounds and dropped it in the drawer with his other clutter. How else could it have got there?"

Abby turned the piece over several times, deep in thought. "I need to drive into West Chester."

"Must you go today?"

"Something's come up." She sprang to her feet. "I should leave right away."

Heart pounding, Abby edged the car into a tight spot behind Woolworth's, hurried past Henri's office, and crossed to High Street, afraid she would bump into him. She jostled along with the lunchtime crowd for two blocks to the address and name she'd written down, "Branson's the Jewelers."

The chimes from the shopkeeper's bell above the door announced her entry into the old-fashioned store. Clocks of all shapes and sizes lined the shelves. Abby crossed threadbare carpet over an uneven wood floor. As she approached the high counter at the rear of the premises, an elderly man with a shock of white hair emerged from behind a curtain and smiled. "Good day, Miss."

Abby set her handbag on the counter. Removing her white gloves, she reached into her purse, took out a white handkerchief, and unfolded it. The medallion clinked onto the glass top and spun around, settling face up. "Can you tell me anything about this?" She smiled.

The jeweler slid it into his palm and flipped down the magnifying glass attached to his glasses. One eye shut, he looked up at her, frowning. "From where did you get this, may I ask?"

"I found it. It's a watch fob, isn't it?"

"Yah, that's right." He read the inscription out loud: "EIN EINIG DEUTSCH SOLDATENTUM".

"I was told it's German."

"Yah, it is."

She frowned. "Do you know what it means?"

"I do. I am German. It's an exhortation to German unity, *Soldatentum*—how best to say in English?—unity in the values of the soldier, courage, valor. It refers to a sort of military fraternity. You understand?"

"Where does it come from?"

The old man removed his glasses. "You say you found this, young lady?"

"Yes."

"Nobody gave it to you?"

The question took her aback. "No." *Why was he asking her this?*

"This belongs or rather belonged"—he emphasized the past tense with a grin—"to someone with a connection to the German army. Or possibly he sold it or gave it to someone with an interest in such things. Someone in a German club or Bund."

"B-bund?"

"Excuse me. B-u-n-d. Such as the German-American Bund."

"What is that?" she said, her curiosity piqued.

"The Bund was—is—a German military veterans' group. They are all over the world. Even here." He rapped at the counter. "President Roosevelt made them illegal a couple of years ago. So, if someone has one of these it is sensible to not wear it. You understand? That's why we change our names now. I come to this country after the Great War, and I was obliged to change my name."

"To Branson?"

"Yah, that's what it says now." He pointed to the name etched in gold scrollwork letters on the plate glass window. "But my surname was Bernhardt. No good for here, not when I come." He shook his head rapidly. "Still, I'm glad I did that. I love this country as my own." He reached over and squeezed Abby's hand. "Excuse me young lady, but I hate what that madman Hitler is doing to my old country. I will jump up and down with joy when he is dead." He handed the medallion back to her.

"Did you come to the United States alone?" She wrapped the piece in her handkerchief and dropped it in her bag.

"My wife and son came too. The rest of my family are in Germany." He cocked his head to one side and grinned. "Have you got a sweetheart? In the military, perhaps?"

"He's in the army, and I worry about him."

"Have faith, young lady. He will come back to you."

She raised her head and met his gaze. "Thank you, sir. I shouldn't take more of your time. You have been most helpful."

"You are very welcome, my dear." The jeweler rested his clasped hands against the counter and smiled at her. "When your young soldier comes home, you will want to get married." He winked. "You bring him here, and I will make you each a nice wedding ring."

As Abby reached the door, he called out, "Remember, we will win," he said, his fists raised.

Walking back to the car, Abby mulled over what she'd been told. The exchange with the jeweler gave shape to the mystery surrounding Henri. Why hadn't she seen the signs earlier? Goose bumps ran up her arms. There were too many coincidences—the trips to South America, Henri's reticence when she quizzed him about them, his off-the-cuff jibes about the Allies. And the medallion. His all right. Probably dropped from his pocket the night she found him going through the filing cabinets. By the time Abby reached the parking lot, she arrived at the inescapable conclusion—*Henri is a traitor*. Something had to be done and soon. But who would believe her? She had no connections. Hadn't Henri told her so?

CHAPTER TWENTY-EIGHT

Downtown West Chester

Abby turned her tires into the curb against a steep incline and pulled hard on the handbrake. This was their only recourse. They had no other choice.

"This must be it," her aunt said, consulting the slip of paper on which was written, "State Street, No. 161. Top floor. Ask for a Mr. Tripp." Her aunt frowned. "It does look a bit seedy. I hope we're doing the right thing."

Abby leaned over and glanced at the note. "This is the address I was given over the telephone."

They ducked into a cobblestoned alley, and Abby located a heavy gray steel door tucked in next to a fire escape. A small square plate above a round doorbell read, "Ring and Come Up". Abby cracked open the door and peeked in. A steep flight of bare wood steps led to a landing illuminated by a single light fixture hanging from the high raftered ceiling.

Abby led the way, glancing up at the peeling wallpaper. "Mind your step, Aunt." What were they getting into?

On the landing, they were met by a secretary. "Agent Tripp will be with you shortly," she said, leading them into a sparsely furnished anteroom before shutting the door behind her.

Abby inched it open and peered out. Three paneled doors ranged along one side of a narrow corridor. Silence. Then one of them swung open. A man of medium height, dressed in dark trousers and wearing a long-sleeved shirt, strode toward her, his hand extended. "Robert Tripp. Pleased to meet you. Come into my office," he said, smiling.

He bolted his door, then turned around and motioned toward two upright chairs. "Ladies, please. Sorry it looks so plain here. We just rent the top floor of this building." He sat at his desk and took out a notepad and pencil. "You won't mind if I jot down a few things?"

Abby leaned forward. "Mr. Tripp, what we tell you could ruin the reputation of someone who might, possibly, be innocent, and—"

"You don't want to falsely accuse anyone." Tripp pivoted back in his chair. "I understand your concern. But these are precarious and uncertain times. It's the job of the Federal Bureau of Investigation to make them less so." He leaned toward her. "I assume that your suspicions have risen to a level sufficient to bring you to me?"

She nodded. "Yes."

"So, you must be convinced you have something important to tell me?"

"Will it go any further than this office?"

"I can't guarantee that. But if I think it has no merit, I'll tell you so and no action will be taken on it." He wrote on his notepad, then looked up. "You are?"

"Abby Stapleton. And this is my aunt, Mrs. Valerie Bluette," she said, taking her aunt's hand.

"Widow of William Bluette?"

Aunt Val raised her eyebrows. "How do you know that?"

"I have reason to know it. But I'll come to that presently." He opened a side drawer and consulted a small black notebook. "Your addresses, please."

"We both live at Jolie Fontaine," Valerie said. "A country estate on the outskirts of town."

"Now, Miss Stapleton—it is 'Miss'?"

"It is."

"Miss Stapleton, you told my secretary on the phone that you wanted to report possible espionage. Is that correct?"

"Yes."

"Someone you know personally?"

She sighed. "Yes."

Agent Tripp placed his thumbs under his suspenders. "So, you have evidence that someone of your acquaintance—perhaps also your aunt's—is working against the United States for a foreign government?"

Reaching into her purse, Abby passed him the medallion. "I found this. I think it belongs to the person in question."

Tripp studied the piece. "I've seen one of these before. You know what it is?"

"A watch fob belonging to someone in a German military fraternity. I had a jeweler look at it."

He smiled. "Perhaps we should employ you." He dropped the medallion onto the desk blotter.

"I take it, Mrs. Bluette, Abby has shared her suspicions with you?"

"And I believe them," she said, gripping Abby's hand.

"Miss Stapleton, you wish to give me the name of this person?"

Abby looked away, hesitant.

"Let me help you," he said, breaking the silence. "It is a man?"

"Yes."

"All right. Let me identify him for you. It is Henrik Freytag—also known as Henri Frey." He tapped a pencil against his knuckles. "Said individual is a prosperous attorney-at-law, with offices on Main Street. Ex-wife, Claudia, a French national. One child, a daughter, Edythe." He leaned back in his seat. "And he drives a 1941 Cadillac. I think you'll find those raw essentials are correct."

Abby's mouth dropped open. "But how do you know all this?"

He folded his arms across his chest. "We've been watching him and his associates for some months. We believe they are engaged in spying. They collect intelligence of use to our enemies—in this case, Germany. Henrik Freytag is one of the most active members of this group." He tapped at the medallion. "As far as we can tell, he's been at it since early 1940, but we've only been on to him for the past eighteen months."

Abby shifted in her seat. "What sort of information?"

"Economic, military, production figures—"

"Manufacturing? That sort of thing?" Abby said.

"Correct." He looked over at Valerie. "The sort of manufacturing that your late husband's factory is engaged in, Mrs. Bluette."

"So that's why my name is familiar to you," she said.

"Precisely. We happen to know that Freytag—let's call him 'Frey'—traveled to various production sites on the Atlantic seaboard, including your husband's old plant, to garner information. He'd gain access by bribery or on a pretense, perhaps with the claim of legitimate legal business, and then glean as much as he could. British intelligence informs us he's visited Argentina via Brazil on at least two occasions in the past three years."

"I caught him going through my uncle's office drawers after midnight." Abby furrowed her brow. "He seemed intent on looking for something, and he behaved oddly when I approached him. Do you think that—"

"That he was trawling for details on the plant? Possibly. Production volumes, materials purchased, shipped, et cetera."

"Henri was legal counsel for my husband," Valerie added. "William retired from oversight of the plant in 1938, but he kept some factory records in his office at the house."

"That's useful to know." Tripp jotted in his pad. "Anything Frey picked up that way would be out of date. Still, it might have yielded useful comparative data."

"What would he have done with all this?" Valerie said.

"Most likely gave it to someone in the organization. Pass it through a few hands and onto a contact overseas, say, a post office box in a neutral country. From there it would be collected by a foreign agent."

Abby's eyes widened. "He removed documents?"

"Depends. Sometimes that's too risky. In that case, he could take photographs."

"Photographs?"

"Yes. With a very small camera. The pictures are then shrunk down and committed to microfilm. You probably surprised him at it, Miss Stapleton."

"What happens now?"

"I must warn you both that anything we have discussed in this office may not—may not," he repeated—"be revealed to anyone. We expect Frey to contact someone of interest to us in the near future, and then we'll go in and get the whole passel of 'em. However, we won't be able to move against him for several weeks. I strongly advise—Miss Stapleton, there's something else?"

"This," Abby said, passing to him the documents with which Henri threatened her.

Tripp switched on the desk lamp and angled them toward the light. Then he sniffed the papers. "How are these relevant to this case?" he said, setting the documents down.

"Henri is blackmailing me with those."

Tripp arched his eyebrows. "Tell me more."

At the end of her narrative, Tripp shook his head. "I've seen some things in my time, but—" He threw his pencil on the desk. "At least one of these is a forgery. The others may or may not be forgeries, but from what you tell me, they most likely have an innocent explanation as far as they pertain to you, Miss Stapleton."

"I know they have," Valerie said, twisting a handkerchief between her fingers.

The agent pointed to several areas on the documents. "These are all high-resolution photographs. This confirms the organization has the equipment to not only shoot but also develop the pictures. They're getting the funds from somewhere, but we haven't tracked that to the source yet." He turned to Abby. "Thank you. This is quality work and good evidence too. It was stupid for Frey to use their resources in a private vendetta against you." He chuckled. "He's played right into our hands." He furrowed his brow. "But you didn't intend to show these to me?"

Abby met his gaze and shook her head. "I didn't know what to do."

"And yet you brought them here?" Tripp paused. "You could not consent to marry the man, yet you dread the thought of losing your fiancé if Henri sends that letter? And by giving me the medallion, you forfeit the means to retaliate against the villain. I understand your dilemma. I commend your integrity." He rose from his seat. "Excuse me while I confer with my colleague."

Valerie reached over and took Abby's hand. "Chin up."

Tripp returned a few minutes later. "When Henri calls and you tell him you will not marry him, he will probably follow through on his threat. He's that kind of man. But don't worry. When those documents get to the Court of Probate they will disappear, never to be seen again."

Abby straightened. "What about the letter to Jim?"

"You'll give me his address, camp number, and so on. We'll see to it the missive is intercepted. Your young man will never see that nonsense. But the medallion and these documents must remain with us. I'll give you a receipt for them." He smiled. "Have you any other concerns?"

Abby drew a deep breath. "What will happen with Edythe?"

"I can tell you she will be looked after. We'll see to that." His voice was calm, but emphatic. "By the way, Henri's former wife, Claudia, has already complained to us about him. She's got her own suspicions."

Tripp rose and escorted them to the door, ending the interview. "I can't say how indebted we are for your help. It's patriots like you, with sharp eyes and ears—and sharp brains, I might add—that will get this war won and all the Henrik Freytags and their paymasters in prison."

Out on the street, Abby swung the car around and rolled to a stop at the bottom of the hill. Aunt Val pointed toward a building with Doric columns spanning the length of the avenue. "That's the Farmers Bank. William kept his accounts there."

CHAPTER TWENTY-NINE

Normandy, France
June 6, 1944

At 0730 on D-Day, Corporal James Wright burst from the navy transport. Top-heavy from the gear in his pack, he crashed head first into seven feet of icy cold water, two hundred yards offshore. In the high swells, his thrashing pushed him further down. His eyes smarted from the acrid mixture of sea salt and diesel fuel that gushed from ruptured fuel tanks. After groping in an eternity of terror, Jim's helmet broke surface, and he felt sand beneath his boots. On the beach, he dropped onto his belly, ripped off the life jacket, and rushed forward.

In the cacophony about him, one trooper after another fell dead under the cannonade from the German revetments on the hills above. Shells from the Allied destroyers lying offshore whistled and slashed through the canopy of smoke and flame, exploding in concert, knocking him flat. Nearby, a buddy from his squad writhed in pain, tangled in the jagged metal of a half-destroyed tank trap. As Jim got closer to him, the soldier raised two fingers and motioned for a cigarette. *Dear Lord, have mercy.* Jim didn't carry any. It would have made no difference. There was nowhere to put it.

Resuming a crouched run, Jim headed for the crest of a hill. *Oh God, don't let me die.* He pushed up the endless hill, dodging like a manic dancer. As flares burst overhead, lighting up the sloping terrain, Jim reached the barbed wire at the top. He pressed his body against the soft ground, making himself small. Prying up the wire with the snout of his rifle, he tried to slide under, but the barbs snagged his jacket, and he panicked. Months of training ought to have prepared him for this. After a few frantic gyrations, he freed himself and hurtled on through the incessant hail of fire. Others raced alongside him, a surging, shouting, lunatic mass intent on suicide.

He scurried through a low hedge and lay still, panting. The outline of a small building rose out of the battle smoke. He made for it, skittering across the field, bobbing and weaving to make himself an elusive target. On reaching the half-demolished structure, he dived over a mound of rubble. The roof was open to the sky, affording scant refuge. Jim flattened against a fragment of the outer wall, its old bricks held firm by ancient mortar, the handiwork of a long-dead farmer for whom these skies had threatened only rain. As the whine of ordnance from the Allied ships grew louder, the *thud, thud, thud* of German artillery responded in an endless barrage.

Here in the thick of it, Jim had no yardstick to measure success or failure. *A thousand shall fall at thy side, and ten thousand at thy right hand; but it shall not come nigh thee.* As a lad, this Bible verse had been impressed on him by his mother. He'd never really understood. What danger faced a young boy? *Was this a promise that he, Jim Wright, would be kept safe?* He could not believe this, and yet, somehow, he did take comfort from these words, willing himself to accept that somewhere in the vast unknowable web of the universe such protection did exist. That there was, after all, a higher purpose, something that could make sense of this vulgar conflict that threatened him and the people he loved.

From his vantage point, he saw American tanks a hundred yards off, lying on their sides, their underbellies exposed in an attempt to crash through the tough tangle of hedgerows. Some of the vehicles were on fire, their turrets wedged into the ground at crazy angles, like large helpless beasts. Against the backdrop of ghastly yellow flames, he spotted a cupola burst open and the driver scramble out, his suit ablaze. Even at this distance, Jim heard his screams of agony.

Horrified, Jim bolted toward him as an enemy plane flashed overhead, strafing the ground before him. Jim dropped flat, his heart drumming in his chest. Then throwing caution aside, he sprinted the remaining distance, sliding to a screeching halt in a shower of dirt and stones. He set his rifle down, slipped off his shoulder pack and removed his webbed belt. He tore off his jacket and threw it over the man, beating it with the palms of his hands to suffocate the flames. *God, please help me.*

Jim extinguished the blaze. Was the man alive or dead? With his fingers he felt for a pulse at the neck. "Weak, but working," he said to himself, repeating the mantra they'd taught him. He retrieved his pack and gun and heaved them back onto his shoulders. He half-carried, half-dragged the soldier away from the wreckage and toward a nearby ditch, then instantly regretted his decision. The long furrow was too shallow to protect either of them from the howitzers ahead. Jim heard moans coming from the shadows. As his eyes adjusted, he recognized his comrades, some with limbs shattered by the wicked fragments of exploding butterflies sprayed by the German pilots.

To the rear, a fusillade erupted from a row of houses, their roofs bursting into pockets of phosphorous flame, as Spitfires and Mustangs banked overhead. From somewhere ahead, an officer yelled, "get out of there men, abandon your positions." Jim watched as helmets popped up along the trench, and the able bodied began to scramble out, heading for surer ground. Jim hesitated. Looking at the injured men, many twisting in pain. Without a medical kit or morphine, he could do nothing to help. Exposed as they were, they didn't stand a chance.

The German guns on the roofs were strafing the area, their aim improving every second. With a prayer on his lips and the taste of blood in his mouth, Jim clambered out, pulling his wounded charge along with him. He would at least try to save him. Bending low, he headed for a stand of trees forty yards off. He glanced back as a shell landed on the spot he'd just quit. Jim groaned, as a wave of sorrow washed over him.

Jolie Fontaine,
June 24

The jangling of the telephone awakened Abby, its raucous sound prowling up the steps and echoing from the high ceiling in the foyer. Urgent. Demanding. Someone lifted the extension downstairs, choking off the clamor.

She jumped out of bed and ran barefoot to her sitting room door, pressing an ear against it. Straining to hear the murmured conversation below, she caught the somber shift of tone in her aunt's voice. Silence. Then the *click* of the handset being returned to its cradle, followed by slow footsteps up the stairs and a *tap-tap* on the door. Her heart dropped like a stone.

"Are you awake, dear?" Aunt Val's hoarse voice penetrated the solid door.

Abby turned the handle with a trembling hand and shrank back. Aunt Val stood outside in her dressing gown, her thin form accentuated by the dull yellow lights from the landing. "What is it, Aunt?"

"That was Jim's mother." She placed her arm around Abby's waist and led her to a nearby chair.

CHAPTER THIRTY

Fourth of July 1944

"Tell her I'm go ... going away. She wo ... won't see Henri Frey for a long, long time."

He swayed in response to the flailing of his heavy arms. "But I wanna see her before I go."

"You're drunk, Henri." Val threw up her hands. "Leave Abby alone. Do you understand?" She walked off then turned around. "Your daughter will stay here tonight."

Henri looked out across the wide lawn and swatted the mosquitoes that bugled in his ears. Somewhere in the fog of inebriation, he contemplated going into the house to fetch Abby but doubted he could negotiate the stairs. Even as he abandoned the idea, his fuzzy logic blamed her. *She's too afraid to face me.*

Henri lurched toward the swimming pool—drunk or not, his situation was hopeless. He would never have Abby or Jolie Fontaine. Still, he'd got his revenge. He leaned against the makeshift fence that surrounded the pool.

"Daddy, is that you?" Edythe raced toward him. "Ooooooh, I'm soooo hot."

He scooped her up. "You see all that nice, cool water?" He gestured at the pool, slopping his drink on his suit. "And you see us two, here, hot and miserable?" He set her down. "Well, how's about you ... how's about you and me going for a swim? One last time."

"But, Daddy, there's a fence. We ought not to go in." She puckered her face and pulled back. "Anyway, your breath smells."

"Who sa ... says we can't go in?" Henri cupped his hand to Edythe's ear and whispered, "I don't see why we can't climb over."

She clapped her hand across his mouth. "No, please don't."

"Nonsense. No one will ever know."

Henri dropped his glass on the cement deck, the shards dispersing in all directions. He laughed. Then lifting his daughter above his head, he lowered her on the other side of the barrier and went over after her.

"We haven't any swimming clothes."

Henri slapped his forehead. "I hadn't thought of that." Then he removed his jacket and tie. "This is Daddy's swimming suit." He jumped in at the deep end and came up, splashing and laughing.

Edythe squealed. "Don't do that. It frightens me."

"I'm sorry. I won't do it again—but only if you'll come in with me."

Edythe stamped her foot. "This is my good dress." Then she ran over to the pump house and switched on the radio. She paraded around the pool to the music of a military band, "broadcasting from coast to coast" with a patriotic medley, while her father trod water, periodically squirting a stream of water from his cheeks in her direction.

When he heard the news bulletin come on, he paddled to the side of the pool. "Blah-blah-blah," he muttered to himself. "D-Day. Allied hopes high ... *huh!*" After a few attempts, he pulled himself out and waddled over to the radio. "False hopes is what I say." He yanked out the wire, tottered to a wicker armchair under the corner eaves, and flopped into it.

"Look, Daddy, look." Edythe sat on the lip of the pool, socks off, splashing her legs up and down.

Her father looked over at her. "Clever gurrl ...." Then he leaned back and shut his eyes.

"Stay out of his way, dear. If you leave Henri alone, he will go away." Abby considered her aunt's advice and this strategy unlikely to deter Henri under any circumstances, sober or drunk. She grit her teeth, seething. She'd see him—on her own terms.

When she last heard from Henri two months ago, he'd pressed her to respond to his ultimatum. When she rebuffed him, no doubt he carried out his intentions against her. Still, no repercussions appeared to follow. So, she continued to trust in the assurances given by Agent Tripp.

But Phyllis's telephone call ten days ago shattered whatever peace of mind she might've salvaged from a brightening situation. Jim's mother had received the telegram delivered by a Western Union messenger. Abby wasn't on the list to be notified—only family. That was the army way. Even in her own grief, Abby cried for Jim's mother.

Henri's reappearance this evening only mocked her shattered hopes for love and happiness. Somewhere out there he waited for her, bombastic as ever, insensitive to the terror he'd inflicted on her.

Abby went out the back of the house to avoid guests who'd stayed after the Independence Day festivities. Music and laughter floated out from the merrymakers inside. Jim had always enjoyed holiday celebrations. She pushed those thoughts away. Tonight's nasty business demanded hardness from her.

The path Abby took ran by a quiet grove she'd discovered when she first arrived. Severed from one geography, she'd made a pact with another, and into this sanctuary she'd imported her fears and aspirations. Here she would think about the island home left behind—about her family and pray for them the same wide, unthreatening sky that sheltered her.

And then Jim came into her life. Those were lovely, happy days. His love illuminated all her dark corners, and she had blossomed. She would have gladly traded her family name for his—she'd tried it on for size many times. The name Abby Wright had a forlorn sound now, like the invocation of a character from fiction, a never-could-be.

As she drew near the little arbor, other memories crowded in. Uncle Will and his predictable daily transit through this quiet scene. Simon sitting with her on the park bench in Kensington and playing the piano at their recital. He and Jim might've been good friends, swapping war stories, telling jokes and pulling pranks.

She dropped onto a bench, yearning for Jim to be sitting beside her as before and holding her close. But he was gone, relinquished to the common, higher cause. The darkness of the night mirrored the blackness in her soul. Sitting here all alone and afraid, gone was the will to believe she could ever win against the pursuer that singled her out. She buried her hands in her face. *God has forgotten me.*

When she looked up again, the moon shone through a gap in the clouds. The outline of the flat-roofed pump house and the fence that encircled the pool were visible. But where was Henri?

Mounting the steps to the deck, she leaned against the fence and stared into the water. The breeze coaxed ripples from the surface and moonlight reflected in a ghastly glow. Then from the deep end, a movement attracted her attention. Something stirred at the bottom of the pool.

Someone.

Galvanized, she bounded the rail and ran to the edge. Looking down, she gasped in horror. Kicking off her shoes, she rocketed to the bottom. Eyes stinging, she thrashed around until her hands caught a piece of clothing, a hand, an arm, a child. *Edythe!* She grabbed the girl by the shoulders, placed her knee in the small of Edythe's back and propelled herself straight up. After what seemed like a lifetime, she broke surface with the limp body.

With one arm, Abby hoisted herself onto the cement rim of the pool and pulled the child up with the other. "Help! Hurry!" Abby called out. No response. "Breathe! Breathe! Oh, God, make her breathe." How long was she down there?

What had Jim said? "You must restore breathing. Every second counts. Don't bother to loosen or remove clothes." She willed herself to work fast. She placed the girl on her abdomen, one arm extended overhead, and the other arm bent at the elbow, her face resting on her hand. Then Abby positioned herself to one side. Dropping to one knee, she placed her palms over the lower part of Edythe's back, one on each side. *She's so small.*

She forced herself to remember what else he'd said. Abby gently shifted the weight of her body forward onto her hands to increase pressure against Edythe's chest and expel any water from her lungs. She raised her body rhythmically, hands firm on the girl's back, and maintained a forward and backward action, every four seconds, fifteen times a minute. *Oh God, help me, please.* She kept count in her head. *Don't-break-the-rhythm ... down-up, down-up.* "Could be many minutes before they breathe independently," she remembered Jim had told her. How long had it been already?

It seemed like an eternity before Edythe's body jerked. Once. Twice. Then she coughed.

From under the eaves came a moan. Henri staggered to his feet.

The Same Day, France

Dreamlike, Jim hovered between upper and nether space. He lay there, disconnected from time, place, and self, and forced his eyes open. Daylight filtered through the canvas sides of a tent, stabbing his eyeballs. He tried to sit up, but his head hurt and his lower body ached to beat the band.

Boxes of various sizes stamped with a bright red cross and heaped in untidy fashion, lined one corner of the room. A tall, white metal cupboard, piled high with bandages, stood in the opposite corner. He fell back on the cot, catching the familiar sound of truck motors revving in the distance, their gearboxes clanking, and muffled voices barking instructions. Where was everyone?

His only memory was of taking shelter in a forester's hut during a battle. Two men from his platoon were hunkered down with him, waiting for the barrage to cease. On the hill overlooking their position, they'd encountered a German battery in a grove of trees. He could still hear the *thud ... thud ... thud* as shells sought their range and feel the pressure waves that engorged the tiny space in which he was crouched, compressing his chest, driving out his breath with a double gut punch. The nauseating, blood-taste sensation as myriad sharp, heavy blows beat about his back and shoulders. And the searing pain in his legs, as though they were being sliced into a thousand pieces. He remembered screaming, his motions slowing, then nothing.

Again, he tried to sit up and do an examination of himself, prodding the thick bandage on his left arm. He touched his heavily wrapped head and groped around his upper body. His clumsy investigation served only to increase his anxiety. He dared not look down at his legs, afraid of what he might—or might not—find. What would the pain be like when the anesthetic wore off?

How he longed to see Abby, recalling those tranquil months by her side, the cloudless blue of a summer sky, the fragrances in the conservatory, the damp coolness of the lush spring grass. His heart melted. Perhaps he was shut off from that world forever.

The flap of the tent rippled open. Through his mental fog, a woman in uniform peered in his direction, as though deciding whether to advance.

"Jimmy?" She moved across the floor. "Jimmy?" the voice repeated, closer this time.

Impossible! He stared at her in disbelief.

She dropped down on her knees beside his bed. "It's me, Carol." Then she pressed her face into his neck and wept.

"Sis? Wh-what are you doing here? he said, his voice thin, as if it belonged to someone else. "What am I doing here?"

"You were rescued, big brother." She lifted her head, tears ran down her cheeks. "Medicos from one of the rear detachments found you in a bombed-out hut. There were two other guys with you. Unfortunately, they didn't make it," she said, sorrow in her eyes. "One was sprawled on top of you. His body must've saved you when the roof caved in. You'd been there for days." She paused, then stroked his shoulder. "They thought you was a goner." She bit her lower lip. "The ambulance men rushed you to a field station, and then they brought you here unconscious."

He frowned. "Here?"

"An evacuation hospital. You're in Normandy. *The* Normandy. Remember?" Carol rapped her knuckles lightly against his temple. "Your tags was found days before you were. Most likely blown off."

"Were Mom and Abby told?"

"About you being likely dead in action? Mom got a telegram. The Army only yesterday found out who you are, if that makes sense." She shrugged. "Anyway, some bright spark made the connection between us and told me. I, *ahem*, work the wireless at the WAC's HQ." Carol breathed on her fingernails, polishing them on her lapel. "Big shot sister—with lousy bitten-off nails," she said, pulling a face. "I'm still on duty, but they said I could come see you. So, here I am."

She flopped into the chair by his bed and lit a cigarette. "So, how do you feel?"

It was impossible to describe in words. He clenched his jaw. Was he feeling anything at all? "Like I'm in a nightmare." He forced a smile. "How do I look?"

"You've been banged up pretty bad," Carol replied, picking a fleck of cigarette paper off her top lip. "They say you're lucky to be alive. You've got what everyone calls a 'million-dollar' wound."

"A what?" Jim caught his sister's fleeting glance toward the foot of the bed. His heart began to race. "What are you telling me, Sis?"

"Not to worry, Jimmy. Everything'll be all right." She sat back and flashed a smile, hope shining in her eyes. "They'll take care of you and ship you back to England. Then home. At least the war's over for you."

Jim shut his eyes, pressing his head into the pillow. Would the nightmare be over soon?

The entrance of the tent flapped open and two officers appeared, stethoscopes around their necks. Carol glanced over at them and stiffened. One of them pointed at her, raised two fingers to his lips, and shook his head in reprimand.

Carol sprang to her feet, stubbed out the cigarette on the sole of her boot, and rammed the butt into a side pocket. "I think they'd like me to take a powder. But I'll be back as soon as I can." She squeezed his hand. "I'll write to Mom—and your Abby. Chin up, big brother. It's a miracle you've come back to life." Carol bent down and kissed his cheek. "It's the swellest holiday I've ever had."

"Holiday?"

"Today's the Fourth of July."

CHAPTER THIRTY-ONE

Jolie Fontaine
July 22, 1944

"Jim's mother has been in seventh heaven since getting the news he is safe and sound. And a hero too," Abby said, closing her suitcase.

"You'll have a lot to tell Jim when you get to that hospital." Abby smiled at her aunt's knack for understatement. Within seven days of Edythe's rescue from the pool, the FBI arrested Henri as he attempted to board a flight to Panama, en route to Argentina. His daughter was with him. Seven of Henri's associates were picked up in Pennsylvania and upper New York state.

"And when do you expect to arrive in England?"

Abby took a seat next to her in the foyer. "My train gets into New York about five o'clock. I'll stay in a hotel tonight and board the ship in the morning. Mr. Tripp said the voyage could take a week if the convoy has to divert to avoid U-boats."

"Oh my, what a thought. I hope you won't go through that again." Picking up a newspaper, her aunt pointed to the front page. "Henri and that bank official are in this morning's *Gazette*. Here let me read a portion. 'An elaborate network of espionage ... Henri Frey ... embezzled clients' funds to pay for the group's spying activities.'" She stopped reading and looked at Abby. "Will's own nephew. At least ten years for him. Possibly hanging for the ringleaders."

"Agent Tripp didn't catch the big fish he'd hoped for, but was satisfied with the outcome," Abby said. "He told me on the telephone that the Bureau's operation struck 'a precise and significant blow' at German espionage activities along the East Coast."

Aunt Val tossed the newspaper onto a table. "And what about Edythe? If you hadn't been there—well, it doesn't warrant thinking about."

"And if you hadn't come looking for her and got her to the hospital."

Her aunt grasped her arm. "Still, that child owes her life to you, dear."

"I called the Children's Aid Society this morning. Edythe's put on weight but is having trouble settling down, especially at night. Her mother visited only once since her daughter was put into care." Abby reached into her handbag. "Claudia did reply to my letter. She's planning to move permanently to Montreal. This letter came this morning," she said, placing the envelope in her aunt's hand.

Valerie scanned the letter and handed it back. "Claudia doesn't say whether she expects to take Edythe to live with her. I hate to think of the girl being handed over to strangers after all she's been through." She furrowed her brow. "But what more can you do? Edythe needs a proper home with a loving father and—" She diverted her gaze to the floor.

"As Claudia's implicated in Henri's actions, there's the question about her immigration status. I don't know what'll happen. Abby shook her head and sighed. "She appears indifferent about her own daughter. I can't understand how a mother can be that way."

Aunt Val went to the mantelpiece, picked up and pressed a white envelope into Abby's hand. Scrawled across the front was "Private and Confidential." She placed an arm around Abby's shoulder. "This is for my sister," she said, her voice quivering. "She will want to talk with you after she reads what I wrote."

Abby put the envelope in a compartment inside her handbag. She kissed her aunt. "I'll give your letter to Mother." There was something else troubling her aunt.

Anna appeared in the doorway. "Excuse me. The cab is here. The driver will take your cases."

Abby took her aunt's arm and together they walked to the taxi.

"God speed, dear. I'll be praying for your safety." She stroked Abby's cheek, love shining in her eyes. "It's a miracle the way everything's turned out. Jim will be all right when he sees you. And so will you."

London, Saturday, July 29

I can't believe I'm here. Streams of passengers flowed around Abby, scrambling on and off trains, a scene at once so familiar and yet so strange. Locomotives belched and hissed in syncopation, plumes of white steam converging beneath the grimy glass roof of the cavernous shed. She positioned herself under the big clock and waited for her father. White-tufted pigeons strutted around her feet, foraging for scraps. A newspaper boy paraded up and down the concourse, his shoulders sagging under the weight of a brown canvas bag. She let out the breath she held, realizing how much she'd missed these sights and sounds.

A family carrying blankets ascended steps from the underground station where they'd sheltered overnight from a raid. She moved out of their way and set her cases down, facing the direction her father might be coming. Would he be cross with her? He'd wanted her in a safe place, but she had to consider Jim's needs. She walked back and forth, thinking about him in the hospital and his not knowing about her. If only she could catch a train west and go to him. But she'd promised her parents to spend time with them first.

Then out of the chaos, she spotted him. How different he appeared wearing eyeglasses, and he'd lost weight. "Father!" She ran toward him and he met her onrush, throwing his arms about her, his embrace full and strong.

"Five years. You'll never know how much your mother and I have missed you."

"I've missed you too," she said, stepping back. His suit looked rumpled, as if he'd slept in it.

He laid a bouquet of yellow roses in her arms. She kissed his cheek. "They're beautiful, Father."

"I've been in the office day and night, but I'm taking this weekend off. Your mother is holding up breakfast for us." He chuckled. "She was ecstatic when she got your telegram." He stooped to pick up her cases. Abby tried to beat him to it, but he insisted. "Not so frail as I may look."

Abby linked with her father's arm—his poise and confidence were the same. They walked to the taxi rank and clambered into the nearest one. He gave the address and the cabby set his meter.

Abby turned to face her father. "I hope you're not upset about my decision to come back?"

"You are a grown woman. You must do what you think best. Incidentally, I wrote to the army hospital and cleared your visit for next week. Jim had surgery, and he's in the recovery ward. He hasn't been told you're coming." He patted her hand. "And no, before you ask, I couldn't get details on his surgery."

Abby gazed out the window. "I suppose I'll know soon enough." She looked down at the flowers in her lap and brightened. "I love him no matter what."

"And I can see why. Your mother and I were impressed by your young man."

Big Ben struck eight as the cab started for Kensington. The Thames lay under a putrid yellow fog. The old historic landmarks remained, but damage to adjacent buildings made them look isolated, as though dropped by some giant hand, willy-nilly, out of time and place. Piles of rubble sprouted at every corner. The vehicle circled Parliament Square, revealing bombed-out patches around the Houses of Parliament. The pictures in *Life* did not tell the half of it. Abby gasped, blinking against a blur of tears. The England of her memories had evaporated.

"A bit of a shock, isn't it? I never get used to it myself."

Everywhere, the view presented a jumble of yawning holes, shattered windows, and blocked-off streets awaiting repair. Outside a church, fragments of leaded, colored glass lay strewn along the pavement. An elderly couple, brooms in hand, worked on cleaning up the mess. The driver threaded his way through a maze of cobblestone streets, passing a rag-and-bone merchant with his horse and cart—a sight that never ceased to enchant her. She turned her head to stare at the spectacle through the back window.

The cabby glanced at her in his rearview mirror. "I'm sorry for having to go the long way 'round, what with the damage and all."

They emerged into a wide avenue swarming with double-decker buses and taxis and waited for the traffic light to change. Then a siren wailed. The crowd on the sidewalks scattered, diving for refuge in shelters, doorways and alleys. Car horns blared. Abby stared straight ahead, frozen in her seat. A terrific explosion shook buildings all around, showers of masonry descended onto the street. Their cab rocked on its springs. Abby clapped her hands to her head. *Lord, help us.* A pressure wave hit.

"Get down!" her father shouted, pushing her onto the floor. Everything went quiet.

After a few minutes they returned to their seat. "V-1 rocket-bombs," her father said, looking through the rear window. "They've got fins on the side and a jet motor on top and make the most awful whining sound. You couldn't hear it then, over the siren, but if you had, you wouldn't forget it. Then the whining stops, and you hold your breath until it lands."

The "all clear" sounded. Abby marveled at the speed with which the scene changed. Pedestrians and drivers continued as if nothing had happened. The Union Jack fluttered from several windows in the adjacent structures and people leaned out to gaze at the activity below. Bus drivers alighted from their vehicles, craning their necks to assess the chance of passage. A police constable, his helmet plastered with dust, directed traffic past the rubble. Firemen played their hoses on the damaged buildings, as flames erupted from split gas mains.

"Curse those doodlebugs," the driver muttered as the cab picked up speed.

"Now you see how it is." Her father pulled her close. "I suppose we're accustomed to this—as much as one can get used to such a thing. But having you here, well, you understand how your mother and I worry about it." He hesitated. "Still, you've done the right thing to come." He smiled. "You have an obligation to Jim."

Abby's gaze took in the old neighborhood as they moved toward home. The familiar large, open square came into sight. No bomb damage visible here. Then their street. "What's become of all the spiked railings from the garden wall?" she said, coming face to face with the stark reality that things would never be the same.

"Sawed off and carried away to be used by the armaments factories."

She pointed to a house bearing the sign, British Red Cross. "How long have they been here?"

"Requisitioned almost four years. They maintain offices and flats for their workers. A very busy place, I might add. Your mother volunteers, arranging shelter for those who have lost everything."

The taxi pulled up to a white Georgian with a large bay window, yellow and salmon begonias bloomed in a box outside. Her mother stood in the entryway, smiling and waving.

CHAPTER THIRTY-TWO

Abby rushed out of the taxi, up the steps, and into her mother's outstretched arms, taking in the scent of lavender she wore. "How I've missed you," she said, kissing her cheek.

"I've missed you too, my dear. So much."

Her father mounted the steps and joined them. "One of those infernal rockets almost hit us on the way here."

Her mother's eyes widened, and she pulled Abby closer. "You must have been quite terrified."

She nodded. "I worry about you all the time here in London."

Abby followed her parents into the parlor where so long ago their last struggle occurred, grateful that her love for Jim and his for her had also enhanced her appreciation and love for them.

She twirled around, then fell back onto the settee. Her favorite needlepoint cushions still adorned it. "It's so wonderful to be back." Her gaze darted around the room. The furnishings were exactly as she remembered. From under the seat, a cat emerged and rubbed against her legs. "Gulliver!" Abby scooped him up and stroked his coat. "Still here, still the same."

Her father pulled back the drapes—three-inch wide strips of brown sticky paper covered the large window from corner to corner in a crisscross pattern. "Unattractive, but necessary in the event of a bomb blast. Wouldn't want anyone hurt by shards of flying, broken glass."

Her mother sat beside her. "The pictures you sent don't do you justice. And your hair is a brighter red." She touched her own light brown hair. "And mine is heading in another direction entirely."

In addition to being grayer, Abby noted the furrows in her mother's forehead and the dark circles under her eyes. Since she'd left, her mother had done more than five years of aging.

"We were so glad to have Jim here. We liked him very much." Her mother lowered her head. "I'm afraid I gave him a hard time. He told you?"

"I heard nothing about this from Jim. The mail was erratic and then dried up completely." She furrowed her brow. "And then I got the call from his mother that he was missing in action, presumed dead."

"How awful that must have been." Her mother reached over and stroked Abby's hand. "I'm sure he will be all right now that you're here."

"Ah, Miss Abby. I heard your voice." A beaming Chadwick advanced toward her. "Marvelous you're back. Breakfast is served."

"Wonderful to see you, Chadwick."

Her father pulled his slippers out from under his chair. "I'm peckish, and you must be too."

"In your honor, my dear." Her mother gestured with her fork at Abby's plate. "The real thing. Not those sausages that pop like fireworks that we are asked to use. I imagine you're eating better in the States?"

"It would seem that way, although restrictions are in place," she said, biting into a toasted crumpet. "It's been ages since I had one of these."

"Sweets are at a premium. We've had to limit our sugar to one spoonful per day since the rationing started." Her mother sighed.

Abby tucked into the fried eggs and sausages. "That's unfortunate. But I suppose it's that or nothing at all."

"I didn't put any sugar in your cup. You never had a sweet tooth." As her mother poured the tea, Abby noticed how thin and rough her hands had become.

"I'm sorry you'll miss Peter." Her father set down his cup. "Amelia wanted to be here, but John won't let her risk the journey."

"I can understand that. Are these flying bombs worse than the incendiaries?"

"The psychological damage they inflict is probably worse than the destruction on the ground." He pushed away from the table. "But we have devised new ways to track them as they're coming in. The coastal batteries shoot them down, or the air force sends up a fighter or two to nudge them off course. Like so," he said, spreading his arms. "Most of the bombs fall on Kent, and a number of villages have been demolished. Since D-Day, I think Hitler knows his days are numbered." He stared out the window and nodded slowly. "I do believe the threat of invasion has passed."

His remarks didn't assuage her fears. Still, she wouldn't press the matter, wanting this visit with her parents to be a bulwark against the realities outside. "I'd like to visit the Academy before I leave," Abby said. Then seeing her mother crestfallen, she added, "but I won't stay long, I promise. It'll be good to see the old place again." What would Simon be doing if things had been different?

"We received your letter last week about this Henri business. Her mother raised her eyebrows. "Absolutely ghastly!"

Abby nodded and set her cup down. Was Edythe eating and sleeping better? What was to become of her? *Please keep her safe, Lord.*

"You did right to keep that business from Jim," her father said. "He didn't need that worry on top of everything else." He rose. "All right, since we're finished here, let's decamp to the parlor. Abby will bring us up to date on Valerie and that remarkable estate across the pond."

Royal Academy of Music
Monday, July 31, 1944

Abby gasped. Plywood panels covered the openings where windows used to be. "How recently did this happen?"

"A doodlebug took out about two hundred and fifty of them in February," the taxi driver said.

Out on the sidewalk, Abby looked up at what remained of the reddish-brown facade she remembered. Shrapnel holes pockmarked one entire side and sandbags stacked several feet high ran across the front. She fought the urge to cry and attempted to recapture her old feelings about the place. They wouldn't come.

Climbing the steps, she went inside. A secretary escorted her to the office of Dr. Jones, the new administrator.

"You came at a good time," he said, shaking her hand. "Next week we close for the summer." He rubbed the back of his neck. "Our enrollment is well down as most of our male students are away fighting."

"If it wouldn't be too much trouble, I'd like to see my old classroom."

"By all means. There's a teacher still here." He pulled a watch from his waistcoat and peered at it. "Good timing. I think he's rehearsing about now."

Dr. Jones walked her to the elevator. "I think you'll find your way. Best of luck."

"Thank you."

Stepping out into the hallway, Abby caught the refrain of an aria. The music resounded bright and clear through the network of high, deserted corridors and beckoned her on.

She took the passageway that angled off the main corridor down to one of the recital halls. She'd been this way many times. The music swelled as she approached the door at the end of the passage. Pushing the door open a little, she looked in. A row of folding metal chairs lined the back wall, and she took the nearest one. A pianist was in full flight, concealed from her view by the upraised lid of a grand piano.

She looked around the once-familiar room. The hall was longer than wide, paneled half way up in dark oak. Daylight struggled through the grimy transom windows set high in the wall. Large blotches of damp disfigured the ornate plaster ceiling. In one corner, a jumble of blackened and water-soaked manuscript pages rested on a mound of glass-flecked debris, a broom propped beside it. How grim it all looked. The excursion stirred bittersweet memories of times spent here and her losses and gains, all mixed up with the uncertainties that lay ahead. *Lord, I need courage.*

The power of the music welled up inside her, sparking tears. The piece ended with a thunderous chord that filled the hall and sent a chill up her spine. Abby lingered by the door, waiting to thank the pianist for the private concert. He stood, his back to her. He slipped into a coat, stuffed a sheaf of papers under his arm, then transferred a cane to his free hand. Head down, the man limped forward. Then within a few feet of her, he looked up, a brown patch across one eye.

She froze. "Dear Lord! Simon? C-c-can it be you?" she choked out.

He frowned. "That's my name."

She braced herself against the door. "Simon. It's me. Abby."

"Abby. Abby Stapleton?" He cleared his throat. "But ... I thought you were still in America."

"And I thought you were—" Abby closed the space between them and threw her arms around his neck, tears welling up.

"Missing. No, I'm here," Simon assured her in his inimitable way, patting around his body. "It's me," he said, a silly grin on his face.

"The same old Simon." Abby laughed, giddy at the turn of events. "My brother wrote that you were missing in action in North Africa." She hung onto his arm. "I just can't believe it. Why didn't you let me know?"

"But I still don't get it," Simon said, frowning. "You're supposed to be where it's safe, in the States." He grinned. "There's a cafe across the square. We can have a cuppa and talk."

While they eased themselves over their mutual shock with several pots of tea, Abby described a little of her new life. Then she shook her head. "But why didn't you write?"

Simon leaned forward on his cane. "It was at least a year before I could even talk about what I'd been through. I spent three months in a field hospital, then several more in one clinic and convalescent home after another." He tapped the eye patch. "Thought I'd go completely blind. They saved the sight in one eye, and it's pretty good now. Nothing to be done for the other. So, yes, I came back—sort of."

Abby studied the intent expression on his face. "I'm truly sorry, dear friend. I've thought about you so many times."

"Same here. But I shouldn't be too glum. My music helped to pulled me through, and I landed a position at the Academy." A smile spread across his face. "And there's my wonderful wife, Leah. She's nursed me through all of this from the time I was her patient in the hospital."

Abby's heart did a flip flop. "Simon, you're married! How wonderful."

He pointed to the ring on her finger. "I see you've found someone too," he said, searching her eyes.

Over the next few minutes, Abby recapped the significant events since their last time together. She ended with her engagement to Jim and his tour in the army. "We had planned to get married after the war."

Simon diverted his gaze to the floor, tracing a pattern on the tiles with his cane. "Someone was bound to snatch you up."

"Jim was wounded on Normandy. He's receiving care at a hospital in Newton Abbot."

"So that's the reason for your being here, then?"

"I leave for Devon on Friday."

He rose from his seat. "I should get back, as I have a student coming."

Out on the street, Abby slipped her arm into his and together they walked to the Academy. "I never thanked you properly for the music you wrote for me. I've been singing the piece."

"That's all the thanks I need." He grinned. "I'm sorry we couldn't spend more time together." He halted at the bottom step and signaled for her taxi. "Before I went to war, I was poor and Jewish. Now I'm poor and Jewish and an invalid." He looked heavenward. "With a loving wife." Then he kissed her cheek. "This Jim is a lucky fellow, like me."

CHAPTER THIRTY-THREE

Paddington Railway Station, London
Friday, August 4, 1944

Abby waited on the platform for the incoming passengers to get off the train bound for the west coast. A wounded soldier led by an army companion descended the steps. How would she react when she saw Jim tomorrow? She recalled Simon's parting words, "Your soldier will need you now more than ever."

"Looks as if it will leave in time for me to see you off and still get home for my cricket match on the wireless," her father said, gesturing toward the locomotive puffing and hissing like a restless beast.

"I'm so glad you saw Simon at the Academy," her mother said. "I'm sorry I wasn't more accepting of him."

Abby put an arm around her shoulder. "All forgotten, Mother."

Time to board. The coaches had separate compartments and no communicating corridor. Abby and her father located a half-empty compartment. He heaved her suitcase and coat onto the overhead rack and stepped back onto the platform. Abby put the window down and leaned out.

"Cheerio," her father called out. "Broad shoulders."

Her mother reached up. "I hate to let you go," she said, clinging to Abby's hand. Her lower lip trembled, and a tear slid down her cheek. "Things are so uncertain these days." The conductor blew a whistle and doors banged shut down the length of the train.

"Don't worry, Mother. I'll be back as soon as I can." Abby squeezed her hand. "Thank you for all you've done for me." The train jerked forward, and Abby lost her balance, dropping onto the seat. She jumped up, beckoning through the open window and shouted, "Here, here. Aunt Val asked me to give you this. I forgot."

Quickening her pace to keep up, her mother snatched the envelope from Abby's hand. "Thank you, dear."

"Look after yourself," her father shouted in a hoarse voice, attempting to keep up with her mother and the train.

Abby blew kisses and waved to them, standing with their arms around each other. Her eyes blurred as their forms receded and disappeared into the shadows of the busy railway station. She'd spend more time with them when she returned.

She closed the window and sat back, facing the engine, a concession to her queasy stomach. The polished wood interior of the coach presented a stark contrast to the faded upholstery. She pressed into the hard seat. How did other passengers cope with this discomfort for hours at a stretch?

The carriage flitted through seas of rolling hills and fields of grain, past sheep cropping grass beside dry-stone walls. Whitewashed cottages clad in roofs of thatch and slate *whooshed* into view and vanished in a blur. Ancient hedgerows snaked alongside the tracks, animated by the motion of the train as it hurtled forward, taking her to Jim.

A man in a bowler hat sat opposite, immersed in the pages of the *Times*. A woman accompanied by a little girl huddled in the corner—both appeared ill-nourished and distressed. Was this child being evacuated from London? How frightening for them. The colorful poster on the opposite wall—depicting children at play with buckets and spades on the golden sands of the Devon coast—belonged to another era. Would this girl be treated to a day out at the seaside?

The *clickety-clack* of the rails transported her back to happy weekend holidays with her family, before the cares of public office pressed on her father. Her mother was different then, with a sense of fun and adventure, less concerned with "status." Perhaps when she returned, Amelia and Peter could come to London, and they all could go to the seaside again as in the old days. She vowed to never lose her appreciation of simple, ordinary life.

Approaching the first stop, her traveling companions collected their belongings and poised on the edge of their seat. The platform came alongside, and the conductor opened the door from the outside. As the child passed her, Abby touch her hair and whispered, "God bless you."

They stepped off and walked away and out of sight. She too knew how it felt to be uprooted.

Alone in the compartment, she opened a window and leaned out. Her hair blew in the onrushing wind as they picked up speed. The smell of hot engine cinders mingled with the fresh earthy scents that wafted in from the pastures. She waved to groups of Land Girls driving tractors or raking in the fields. Telephone poles whisked by within a few feet of her. As a child, her father had tried to teach her how to count them to estimate the rate of speed. But she'd forgotten how.

Being absent from her parents had modulated her feelings in ways difficult to define. *Where is home?* She no longer pined for England as much as before. Was she somehow being disloyal and ungrateful to this long-suffering land and her family? The attachments formed in America—her beloved Uncle Will, Aunt Val, friends, and other faces now familiar in her world—these had become home. But most of all Jim—the one she loved more than life itself—had changed her in profound ways. She wanted to go back to America, to care for him there.

The steady rhythm of the clicking rails evoked a fancied refrain from childhood. But a refrain much altered to a woman with a mature and steadfast purpose. Silently, she sang, *I'm go-ing home, I'm go-ing home.*

The train pulled into Torquay at seven in the evening. Abby waited for her ride from the railway station to the Cock and Bull Inn. On the wall opposite her, a sign exhorted all citizens to "Be Alert." The drive to the hotel traversed a palm-dotted beachfront and then branched off into a semi-rural landscape. She removed her sweater and inhaled the warm evening air.

As the taxi rounded a bend, a tidy village of whitewashed cottages appeared. Pink, purple, and blue flowers cascaded over the window boxes of each home. On one corner stood a cluster of makeshift structures, festooned with bunting and Union Jacks. "What's this?" she said.

"The village festival and well-dressing contest takes place next week. A feast for the eyes, ain't it, Miss?"

"Can we stop?"

The driver rolled up to the curb. "It's an ancient custom the churches adopted." He pointed to a large panel adorned with flowers. "There's a well behind that and another one up that hill near the Cock and Bull Inn. The idea is to give thanks for water, the gift of life." He looked up at the sky. "And especially in times such as this." He turned around and smiled. "Tell you what. You could look 'round here and then walk to the Inn. I'll take your things and leave 'em at the desk."

She got out and crossed the road. An upright board similar to a wide door formed the central part of the structure and portrayed a Biblical scene that contained thousands of flower petals. She read the words spelled out in petals across the arch, making a mental note of the text. "They shall beat their swords into plowshares, and their spears into pruninghooks—Micah 4: 3."

Abby made her way up the steep hill, pausing half way at a gray stone church. From here, she could see a fringe of sand and the broad ocean stretching south. The sun glinted off the water, and a breeze wafted up the salt air. Taking a deep breath, she pictured herself down at the beach in her childish knee-length bathing costume, tossing scraps of bread to seagulls, and licking an ice cream cone.

A handwritten sign at the entrance to St. Mark's announced choir practice was under way. She went inside. Light from the tall stained-glass window at the far end flashed against the electric-blue robes of the choir, huddled like a painting before the altar.

Abby slipped into a rear pew under the balcony and leaned back. A man mounted the steps to the organ. He hunched over the instrument, pulled out several stops, then raised his arms and bore down on the keyboard. Deep-throated notes swelled up to the rafters that criss-crossed the ceiling and boomeranged down, striding up the aisle toward her, ebbing and flowing like the wash of the sea. A glimpse of heaven.

Then a door burst open and banged against the stone wall. "Air raid alert! Down to the cellar," someone shouted.

As though the procedure were a part of their rehearsal, the choir filed out. Abby followed down flights of winding steps to a cavern excavated beneath the church, shivering in the damp cold. A few provisions and bottles of water lined the rough shelves above the earth floor. Before long a shrill buzz from overhead drifted into their hearing. She cocked her ears, trembling with fear.

The group began to murmur. "It's a flying bomb."

When the buzzing stopped, Abby braced herself for the impact, terrified she might be lost to Jim in this subterranean crypt, a few miles from his arms. Then a dull *thud*, followed by a shock wave that rippled beneath her feet, folding the soft ground like a washboard. Above them the building shook and fragments of plaster showered down. The shelves around the room unloaded their contents in a jumble of broken glass. A shard struck Abby and blood trickled down her leg.

Silence.

CHAPTER THIRTY-FOUR

The all-clear sounded. "Let's see. What were we doing before we were so rudely interrupted?" the organist said. Everyone laughed. Still shaking, Abby trudged back up the stairs behind the group.

At the top, a tall man approached her, his hand outstretched. "Gordon Cooper. The vicar here. Everyone calls me Cooper." He smiled and shook her hand. "I'm terribly sorry for the crude welcome. Can I show you some less explosive hospitality at the cottage?"

Taking to the vicar right away, she followed after him. Cooper dodged through a side door and set off at a half-run across a lawn with a V-shaped goldfish pond.

He halted at the door of a slate-roof bungalow, gesturing for her to go in. "Have a seat while I put the kettle on for a cuppa and get something for that," he said, pointing to her leg.

Abby dropped onto the couch out of breath.

A few minutes later, he returned and handed her a wet cloth and a bottle of iodine. "While you take care of that cut, I'll pour the tea."

"Thank you. Was anyone seriously hurt?" she said, trying to quell the fright in her voice.

"We'll know soon enough when the civil defense warden telephones me. Coastal protection is better than before. Still, last year several children were killed when a bomb landed near St. Mary's Church."

Abby searched the vicar's face and detected a sadness in his eyes, as if he were struggling with a private grief.

"And before that, German pilots dropped their lethal loads along the harbor and on a village school."

She flinched at the scene his words evoked. "So much destruction and misery."

"It can't end too soon. We're longing for the day when the valleys bloom again."

Abby nodded in agreement.

He smiled. "You're American."

"I was born there. Father is British. Mother is American."

"By the name of?"

"Abby."

Cooper leaned back in his seat. "Abby ... Stapleton?"

She straightened. "Why, yes." She didn't remember telling him her name. Perhaps the raid played a trick with her memory.

"You've just arrived from London?"

Abby recounted events leading up to her arrival in Torquay.

He winked. "So, you've come to see how this Jim of yours is getting along?"

"He's at Newton Abbot."

"The military hospital on the bay. I know it."

"They won't let me in to see him until tomorrow. I'm staying at the Cock and Bull."

Cooper poured her another cup of tea. "He knows you're coming, does he?"

"No. And I don't know how he feels about me." She swallowed down the lump in her throat, uncertain how to proceed. "I don't think I'm prepared—"

"For the worst."

Abby's eyes darted around the room.

"You love him very much." Cooper leaned forward and took her hands in his. "I can see that you do. You wouldn't have come over three thousand miles through Jerry-infested waters if you didn't. And you intend to marry him."

"It's all I can think about these days."

The vicar guffawed and slapped his knee. "His words exactly."

"I don't understand."

A smile swept across his face. "Corporal James Wright said the same thing when I talked with him a few days ago."

Abby's jaw dropped in astonishment. "You know Jim?"

"Certainly do." Cooper clapped his hands like an excited child. "I often visit the hospital. Your Jim and I have enjoyed many conversations together." He laughed out loud. "It didn't take long to put two and two together, once you told me your side of the story."

Abby sighed with relief. Her worst dread had been removed—Jim hadn't fallen out of love with her. How could she have doubted him?

"He's had the stuffing knocked out of him, mind you," he said, his voice cracking.

Perched on the edge of her seat, she wanted to ask about the extent of Jim's injuries but couldn't bring herself to do it. No matter. She would take Jim without reservation, no matter what.

He cleared his throat before speaking. "He's anxious about you. He doesn't know how you feel about him." Cooper leaned back and gazed into her eyes. "Imagine our meeting up this way."

The telephone rang, and he left the room to answer.

"That was Roger, our warden and a member of my parish. He said the railway station was hit, but there's not much damage. The rocket made a big hole, and there's a lot of loose stuff lying around, but our boys will clear that up in no time." A smile crept across his face. "No one hurt, thank the Lord."

"This was my second attack since arriving." Abby took a deep breath. "Last week I was caught in a raid on London."

"It's a good job you got out," Cooper said. "The latest BBC bulletin reported another rocket landed there today."

US Army Hospital, Newton Abbot, Devon
That Same Evening, 7:00 p.m.

Jim rolled his wheelchair onto the flagstone terrace. He removed the blanket from his knees and basked in the warmth of the sun on his face. Following his evacuation from Normandy three weeks before, he'd been admitted to this nineteenth-century Victorian villa that served as an army hospital.

He worked his chair toward a sequestered nook on the parapet and gazed at the broad sea, sparkling beneath a pastel-blue sky. A thousand thoughts crowded his brain. This had to be the longest month of his life. Carol got it right. He was out of the war but at what cost? Should he be grateful or sad? Sure, they'd give him a medal for saving that soldier from

213

the tank. But after all, he'd only done his duty. And he'd been scared stiff at that. On the continent, his comrades were still hammering away. He got word today of another buddy killed a week ago—the third soldier in the past month. Jim pinched the bridge of his nose to stanch the oncoming tears.

From his spot situated high over the estuary, the coastal town of Torquay with its long, sandy beaches, coves, and crystal-clear water seemed so close. In vicarious fashion, he toyed with scenes of life outside the confines of the hospital, such as riding trains to and from the terminus. He'd learned the arrival and departure schedule by heart. Tonight, a breeze blew in the right direction, and the whistle from a passenger train pulling into Torquay station could be clearly heard. Jim looked at his watch. Right on time.

As a lad, he would lie awake at night, listening for the outbound freight trains as they hooted and clanked from a nearby shunting yard to faraway places. He envisioned his father nestled amid the lumber and cold steel on a flat car, making an escape from his humdrum world of responsibility.

Recently, he'd begun to feel sorry for him. Perhaps his dad's experiences as a soldier in the Great War had warped his mind, like some Jim knew—men from his own brigade—who'd been sick-listed out, went home, and wasted away from too much booze and too little compassion. He'd like to help these men somehow. But how could he with this handicap?

As if out of nowhere, a dot appeared on the horizon, growing larger by the second. Jim sat erect, his ear angled in its direction. Then the telltale buzz as the dot got closer and closed in, resolving into the ominous shape of a V-1 rocket, the high tail emitting a trail of dark smoke. Jim winced. The rocket seemed to be heading straight at him.

He gasped as a Spitfire flashed into view and flew alongside the enemy craft. The pilot matched his speed to that of the intruder, then slipped the tip of his right wing under the leading fin of the missile. He banked his plane to the left and the rocket veered off at a tangent from its original course, falling in altitude toward the southeast, over Torquay. Pursued by the Spitfire, the rocket passed overhead, so low Jim could read the markings on its fuselage. He narrowed his eyes and shook a fist at it.

The throng on the terrace raced to the wall on the other side, looking in the direction of the rocket's flight. Someone wheeled him to the railing. A few minutes later came a muffled *boom*. Jim tried to picture the mad scramble taking place on the ground in Torquay. *Let no one be harmed, Lord.* He consoled himself with the assurance Abby was safe in America.

The onlookers dispersed. Jim remained. He hadn't received a letter from Abby since his return to England. He'd put off writing to her. Tomorrow for sure he'd let her know where he was being sent to in the States. She was his best, his only hope.

Pumping his arms against the large spoked wheels, he spun his chair around and went back inside. Jim tried to push his doubts aside, but they were there beneath the surface of his skin.

Saturday, August 5

The next day Jim stood at the window, leaning on his crutches as he watched the pedestrians on the rain-soaked street below. They spilled over the cramped sidewalks and crossed back and forth, snagging traffic. He'd give anything to be down there with them. To be on his feet. To walk like the man he used to be.

He rubbed his left leg. Or what remained of it above the knee.

"You'll get used to it." That's what the doctor said when he was measured for an artificial contrivance. He didn't want to get used to it.

He clenched his fist, his uncertainties resurfaced. "She wouldn't want me now," he muttered, as he had yesterday and the day before. This wouldn't do. He had to get a grip. He'd always pictured himself running to her when he got home, sweeping her up in his arms and twirling her around. Now looking down at his trouser leg tucked under a stump, "no hope of that," he said out loud. And although he hated the thought, Jim persuaded himself it wouldn't be a bad idea for Abby to find someone else.

"Good morning, James."

He swung around. "Reverend Cooper?"

Cooper held out his hand. "How are you today?"

Jim shrugged. "Miserable. I just want to get home."

"Have the doctors said when that will be?"

"They said I'll be shipping out in three weeks."

"I think you may want to alter your plans," the Reverend said, shifting his feet.

Jim took a moment to absorb his words. "I'm not going home?"

A smile crept across Cooper's face. "Perhaps not so soon."

Jim tightened his grip on the crutches. "I don't understand why you were asked to tell me this." His brows shot up. "What's all this about?"

"Something important has come up, my boy. But I'll let someone else tell you." He started to go, then turned back, placing a hand on Jim's shoulder. "Just remember that courageous men and women sometimes lose their way, but prayer can help one find the right path again. And sometimes a miracle or two."

Jim stood frozen in place before the large window, shaking his head.

Two nurses entered, wheeled out a couple of soldiers engaged in a game of checkers, and motioned for others to leave. The place was empty except for him.

Jim punched the open palm of his left hand. More bad news. He pressed his forehead against the windowpane, sweat from his brow imprinting itself on the glass.

A light rapping on the doorframe, and he spun around, belligerent and prepared to give anyone an argument.

"Hello, darling."

He caught his breath, dumbfounded. His sweetheart walked toward him as though unsure of herself. He dropped a crutch and laid a hand on the wall to steady himself. "I can't believe it."

Abby stopped a few feet away from him, her lower lip trembling. "Oh, Jim!"

He searched her eyes. "You're supposed to be—" His voice cracked as he held out his hand, attempting to take it all in. Then he lurched forward and fell into her waiting arms. "Abby, my love. It's you. It's really you," he said, stroking her hair.

The Cock and Bull Inn

What a glorious day. The grandfather clock in the dining room struck nine. Enough time for a leisurely stroll around the village before catching the bus to the hospital. She'd pick up a bunch of flowers from the shop at the bottom of the hill and take them to Jim.

Lingering over breakfast at a corner table, Abby relived the events of yesterday, over the moon. She'd talked herself out. Jim, too. Laughing and crying together. When he looked exhausted, she left, promising to return after his therapy session this morning. She couldn't remember being so carefree. Her trip home to England had turned out far better than she dared hope for.

The manager of the inn stood at her side. "Miss Stapleton." He bent toward her, extending a round silver tray. "This telegram just arrived at the front desk for you."

When he'd gone, Abby slit open the envelope with her knife. "My dear Sis," it began. As she read on, her eyes pricked with tears and her lower lip twitched. Stunned beyond words, she sobbed, wishing the earth to swallow her whole.

CHAPTER THIRTY-FIVE

London, Two Days Later

When Abby alighted from the train, Amelia and Peter rushed to her side. She threw her arms around them, and they stood on the platform clinging to each other.

Abby buried her face in her sister's hair. "I was there ... with them ... for six glorious days," she wailed. "Everything was j-j-just as it sh-sh-should be. Perfect. Oh, God. Maybe if I'd not gone to s-s-see them—"

Peter pulled away. "Sis, don't talk like that. That's absurd."

The street that ran by their parents' shattered home was closed to traffic. They got out of their taxi and walked the rest of the way, holding hands. The icy knot in Abby's stomach grew larger as they approached the site of the conflagration. She drew in a breath, attempting to brace herself for the shock. But this! Pressing a trembling hand to her head, she shut her eyes to block out the horror. *Why, why? Dear Lord, I just don't understand.*

The rocket had landed dead center, obliterating the front and rear and one whole side of their home. The gable end abutting the Red Cross building where her mother volunteered stood intact. She could recognize little else. The upper floors of the house had piled on top of one another, like a set of dominoes, compressing a lifetime's contents into a twelve-foot-high mound of ash-covered debris and smashed rafters. Peter had said the people from civil defense found three bodies burned beyond recognition.

Wisps of black smoke curled up from the still-smoldering timbers. The smell of death wafted into her nostrils. Abby gagged and buried her face in her hands. She mentally calculated that her parents were killed the same day she'd left them for Torquay.

A knot of gawkers, hands in their pockets, loitered by the safety barrier in front of what used to be her blessed home, chatting with one another like day-trippers on an excursion. Abby shook her head, astonished. What attracted these people to this grisly scene? A police constable clambered over the mess to tack a large metal notice onto the remaining wall. In six-inch, bold, black letters it proclaimed, "LOOTING is punishable by the death penalty or life imprisonment." Appalled, she looked away in disbelief. What was left to steal?

Amelia pulled her closer. "If it's any consolation, I talked with Mother on the telephone after they returned from seeing you off at the railway station. She told me it was blissful having you there. She'd made things right with you—that you two had patched up your differences," she said, smoothing Abby's hair. "And Father, well, he was always the same. You always knew where you stood with Dad."

"I know Mom and Dad always had my best interest at heart," Abby said, holding back a sob.

Amelia nodded. "It's a difficult job being a parent. I only found out how much when I had my own children."

Her brother stood hunched forward, opening and clenching his fists, in his eyes the determination of revenge. What was he thinking? She'd never been able to fathom Peter's emotions—the gap of years between them prevented that. As a pilot, he saw war close up, and she guessed that for him it was do or die, conquer or submit. She couldn't blame him.

But she could no longer hate. The Lord had brought her too far for that. Abby bit her lip to stop the flow of tears. She must try to reconcile the loss confronting her in this hideous heap of rubble with her new responsibilities to Jim. He needed her more than ever. *Lord, help me to be strong for him.*

Army Hospital Chapel, August 18

Reverend Cooper sat back in his seat. "Mr. Churchill regarded the army's rescue at Dunkirk a miracle. But it wasn't for my son," he said, his eyes dimmed in sorrow. "After I lost my boy on the beach there, I struggled with my own faith." He fixed his gaze on Abby. "I'm sorry for the death of your parents." His voice broke. "I know what you're going through."

Abby brushed away a tear and lowered her head. This explained the pain she'd seen in his eyes when they first met—he's been living with the loss of his son while bearing the grief of others.

Then he took Abby's hand and pressed it into Jim's. "Don't regret the way God has led you so far. Never forget he rules over the ways of men. He is sovereign, and there's a purpose to the whole thing." He smiled. "It's just that we don't see it yet. We can't see it, because we ourselves are too close to the ground."

Cooper's words sparked a chord within her. She leaned into Jim's shoulder, recalling scenes from the past five years like a speeded-up dream. Her uncle, the school, Jim, and deliverance from the malicious Henri. And there was Aunt Val, who loved her like a daughter. She met the vicar's eyes and smiled. "Thank you for the reminder," she said, cheered by his words and her reflections.

He slapped his knees and removed a notebook from his coat pocket. "And so to the wedding plans."

"We'd like the twenty-sixth, if possible." Jim grinned. "I should be well along with my rehabilitation by then."

"At eleven o'clock," Abby added.

The vicar flipped to a page and ran his finger down it. "The church is available that Saturday." He licked the pencil point and scribbled in their wedding for that day.

"My sister is the matron of honor. My brother will be best man." She sat forward. "And my friend, Simon, says he'd like to play the organ."

Cooper slipped the notebook into his pocket and rose. "It's a blessing to see two people come together like this." He took their hands in his. "All through the war and across an ocean, the Lord nurtured the love that had woven you together, bringing you both to this point in time." As he spoke, sunlight streamed through the stained-glass windows, bathing the chapel in a warm amber light. "God's providence leading you through the valley, whether the road was smooth or rough or the day bright or cloudy."

Abby straightened her shoulders. She didn't know how all the pieces fit, or where the journey would end, but she had the assurance God was leading.

St. Mark's Church

"Marriage is like a garden and requires patient care if it is to prosper." Reverend Cooper stood with Jim at a flower-bedecked altar, watching last-minute guests file in. He swung a fatherly arm around Jim's shoulder. "And I don't need to tell you that you've got a treasure in Abby."

Jim smiled, his heart full to overflowing with happiness. "How well I know that."

"Had you considered that she is an argument for the existence of a loving God?"

Jim cocked his head. "No, I hadn't."

"I'm sure she has her faults, but I don't imagine that they offset her virtues. You agree?"

"Yes."

"Well, the way I see it, there is plenty of evidence in this world for the goodness and love of God. The trouble is man has a perverse tendency to total all the cons in one column and ignore the pros in the other."

"I've been guilty of that," Jim said, recalling his melancholy during the worst months of the war.

"Don't make that mistake in your marriage. The love between a godly woman and a godly man is unique," Cooper said, leaning into Jim's ear. "It's a paradox sometimes but stick with it. Out of all the collisions, you'll come to see the power of God's forgiving love in your relationship because of, and in spite of, your failings and hers." Turning toward the pulpit, the vicar shook Jim's hand and whispered in his ear, "Tend your garden well, lad."

As Simon played the wedding march, Jim fixed his eyes on Abby—advancing down the aisle toward him in an ivory lace gown with a white tulle veil. *Gorgeous.* She'd soon be his. He'd always love and care for her, no matter what.

Amelia followed, wearing a white organdy dress with a blue floral print. Jim winked at Carol, the maid of honor. His sister looked proud and dignified in her WAC uniform. Then Peter left Abby's side and slid in beside Jim, holding the ring.

For his homily, the vicar drew on the first book of Corinthians, chapter thirteen, ending with "love bears all things, believes all things, hopes all things, endures all things." Abby and Jim exchanged vows.

Under a cloudless summer sky before the parish church, guests tossed confetti as Jim's army buddies in dress uniform heckled him.

When the wedding party moved into place for a picture, everyone stopped talking. Abby tugged on Jim's sleeve and leaned in. "Peter insisted we have a proper photographer."

Jim tightened his hold around her waist. "Are you ready for the perfect picture?" he called out. "All right, watch the birdie."

During the reception, Jim studied Abby's flushed, excited face. He pulled her close, taking in the scent of the lilies of the valley fragrance she wore. He kissed her again. "Are you happy?"

She extended her hand and gazed at the wedding band on her finger. "A dream come true."

Later, they cut their wedding cake—one baked and decorated by Amelia—with real icing.

Southampton Dock, August 30, 1944

Abby stood at the railing of the naval ship sailing to America, Jim's hand in hers. She stared into the blue water as a rush of ocean breeze ruffled her hair. Seagulls squawked around the deck, diving in to grab the crumbs offered to them. Wherever Jim was, that would be her home. She bowed her head and closed her eyes, profoundly grateful and unworthy of all God's blessings.

Jim wrapped his arm tight around her waist and whispered in her ear, "How does the name Mrs. Wright sound to you?"

She looked up and smiled. "Perfect."

He kissed her as soldiers standing nearby whistled and stamped their feet in delight. Then his gaze swept across the wide sea. "It seems like an eternity since I was home."

A memory pricked her, and Abby fought back tears. She would forever remember her mother racing to keep up with her train on their final day together. She'd have to ask her aunt what was in that letter, now that she couldn't ask her mother. "It'll be good to see Aunt Val again," she said.

"Carol says Mom and Sis have planned something special for us."

"It's five years to the day that I left London and sailed to New York." She heaved a sigh. "I was such a pathetic girl then. Now here I am. Wife and mother-to-be."

"With a husband and father-to-be." He laughed. "No one can deny we're off to a flying start."

Abby reclined against his chest. "Oh, I'm so glad you're happy with the decision we've made. God answered that prayer too."

"I hope I can keep up with her." Jim reached down and tapped his leg, clucking his tongue to mimic the hollow sound. "From what you tell me she's a lively thing."

"Papa Jim." Abby laughed. "Just as soon as we settle in, we'll bring Edythe home."

Jim squeezed her tighter. "We'll love her as our own."

"And there'll be others," she added in haste. "Boys too. I can see them now, running around the grounds, following in their father's footsteps."

"Their father's very muddy boot steps," Jim countered, rubbing his nose against hers.

She followed the ship's frothy white wake fanning from the stern to the receding shores of England, propelled forward by an inexpressible longing for a new life with Jim. The question mark over Amelia's and Peter's security there remained a blight on her own assurance. The war might go on and on. She would entrust them to God's care, yearning for the day when valleys bloom again.

Abby gazed toward the horizon, resolving then and there to plant a garden in memory of her parents. A sunny spot by the window where she could watch their children play and see the bright flowers grow. The future would be good as she allowed God to direct her path.

THE END

ABOUT THE AUTHOR

PAT JEANNE DAVIS has published essays, short stories, and articles online and in print. She has a keen interest in mid-twentieth century American and British history, particularly the period of World War II. Pat's father-in-law served in the British Eighth Army during the war. She lives in Philadelphia, PA, with her British-born husband, John. They have two grown sons. She enjoys flower gardening, genealogy research, and traveling with her husband—they recently returned from a trip to England. Pat may be contacted at patjeannedavis.com.

Made in the USA
Middletown, DE
25 October 2022

13391017R00136